One Smooth Stone

One Smooth Stone

MARCIA LEE LAYCOCK

One Smooth Stone

Copyright ©2007 Marcia Lee Laycock
All rights reserved
Printed in Canada (2)
International Standard Book Number: 978-1-894860-34-5

Published by:
Castle Quay Books
1-1295 Wharf Street, Pickering, Ontario, L1W 1A2
Tel: (416) 573-3249   Fax (416) 981-7922
E-mail: info@castlequaybooks.com
www.castlequaybooks.com

Copy editing by Janet Dimond
Cover design by John Cowie, eyetoeye, design
Printed at Essence Publishing, Belleville, Ontario

Scripture quotations, unless otherwise indicated, are from the New
King James Version of the Bible. Thomas Nelson Publishers
©1984, 1982, 1980, 1979 and New International Version of the
Bible, copyright ©1973, 1978, 1984 by the International Bible
Society. Used by permission of Zondervan Publishers.

Library and Archives Canada Cataloguing in Publication

Laycock, Marcia Lee, 1951- One smooth stone / Marcia Lee
Laycock. -- Rev. ed.

ISBN 978-1-894860-34-5

I. Title.

PS8623.A944O64 2007   C813'.6   C2007-904625-8

CASTLE QUAY BOOKS

Chapter One

Alex Donnelly was alone. That's how he wanted it. He told himself that's how he liked it. That was a lie.

He twisted the throttle on the boat motor to the off position, leaned back, pulled his floppy-brimmed river hat off his head, and turned his face toward the sun. The silted water hissed against the bottom and sides of the boat. A breeze tussled his thick black hair. He heard a hawk whistle from a high cliff and squinted to watch it plummet from its perch.

Closing his eyes, he slumped low. He'd let the current take him home. He had all day and there wasn't anyone waiting for him, except his dogs. At least they'd welcome him, if only in anticipation of food.

The hawk whistled again and Alex opened his eyes, letting them fill with the sweeping green hills and wide brown Yukon River. As the boat caught and circled in a whirlpool he dipped his hand into the cold flow. Two minutes, he'd been told. If he fell in—or jumped—it would take two minutes for this river to kill him. He knew it was true because it had almost happened. He'd been looking for the cabin where he now lived, had beached at the mouth of the wrong creek, and decided to wade to the other side to search for a trail. Halfway across he realized he was in trouble. It was deeper than he'd thought and his legs were giving out. Then the bottom dropped off completely and he'd had to swim. He barely made it to the shore in time and when he got there he couldn't stand. His legs were useless for several minutes, even though the sun was high and hot that day. He remembered he'd shivered for two days.

His eyes caught the gray shifting of mist in the rift of a small valley far ahead as thick clouds spilled their burden of moisture down toward

7

the river. He could smell it as the wind brought the fragrance of poplar toward him. The trees on the banks seemed to turn their leaves toward it. He pulled his hat back on and shrugged into an old slicker. As the rain came toward him he started the motor and steered the boat closer to shore. He knew a wind could come up strong enough to keep him at a standstill. He snorted as he thought about that. It was the story of his life right now. Standing still. But at least he wasn't running anymore. *How long would **that** last?*

Just before the rain hit him a sudden shifting of light curved over the hills in a faint rainbow. *God's promise.* Funny how he always thought that when he saw a rainbow. Someone somewhere must've said it to him. He pulled his hat down and cut the motor again, to listen, as the first softness of rain touched him. Everything around him seemed to whisper. He breathed deeply and almost smiled. Out here a person could almost want to believe in God and promises. *Almost.*

August 19, 2003–Vancouver, British Columbia

Inspector Stan Sorensen slumped into the driver's seat of his unmarked car. *Another case closed.* It was a good feeling, but as his eyes absently scanned the neighborhood he knew it wouldn't last. There was always another case, always more people who'd been hurt, more creeps to chase down. He sighed. There was a time he'd thrived on it, but retirement was going to feel so good. He flipped open his notebook, wrote down one more detail, then reached for the ignition. His hand froze as his eyes rested on a small house across the street. Much like all the others, it had seen better days. His eyes narrowed as the memory surfaced. A young girl's face with dark eyes that held such longing it hurt him to even remember. He sat up straight. That case had never been closed. He reached for his notebook again and made another note. *I hate loose ends.*

August 20, 2003, twenty miles downstream from Dawson City on the Yukon River

Alex heard the boat, but couldn't see it. He took his binoculars down from a nail on the wall and walked to the bank. Making sure he was screened by the low-slung branches of a spruce tree, he scanned upriver. He caught the long outboard, skimming with the current about a mile down. Adjusting the focus, he peered at the two people crouched in the back. He knew the one with his hand on the motor—the son of the town mechanic. Alex couldn't remember his name. Probably hired himself out to the man in the suit.

The suit was hunched into himself, a large leather briefcase clutched in his arms, his knees drawn up, head down. His tie escaped now and then, flapping in the wind with sudden urgency until he caught it and tucked it in again. The sight of a man in a suit on the river was so out of context that Alex kept watching until the boat veered and headed directly toward him. He lowered the binoculars and squinted as it beached just below his cabin. Within seconds the men were out of sight, but he knew they were scrambling up the embankment. *They missed the trail.* He considered slipping into the bush and pretending not to be there, but his curiosity got the better of him. He went back into the cabin and waited.

As the two men breached the top of the slope Alex's dogs erupted into high-pitched howls. The suit hesitated, peered around, and seeing the animals were chained, approached the cabin. Alex stepped back from the window and waited for the knock. When he opened the door he took in several things at once: the man looked young, no older than Alex himself, but smaller in stature. He was wiping his face with a handkerchief, but wasn't breathing hard from the climb. His hair was the color of sand and short, spiked at the front, reminding Alex of a small porcupine he'd seen that week. The man's eyes weren't visible behind dark sunglasses, but Alex had the feeling he was being sized up in return.

"Mr. Donnelly? Alexander Donnelly?"

Alex kept one hand on the door latch, shoved the other into his jeans pocket, and willed his heart to stop racing. "Who's asking?"

The man yelled over the barking. "I'm George Bronsky, of Adams, Ferrington, Lithgow and Bolt, attorneys at law, Seattle."

When Alex didn't respond the lawyer slipped off his sunglasses. "You're a hard man to track down, Mr. Donnelly."

The dogs continued their cacophony. Alex just stared. Bronsky stared back. Alex blinked first. He stepped out, turned his head and hollered, "Lie down!" When the barking subsided he turned back to the lawyer. "State your business, Mr. Bronsky."

"I have some good news for you." He glanced past Alex into the interior of the cabin and took a step. "If you'll allow me...."

Alex didn't move. "I said state your business."

Bronsky shifted the briefcase and slipped the glasses into his pocket. His head turned slightly to the young man standing behind him. "I suggest we speak in private."

Alex tilted his head toward the mechanic's son. "Mind waiting in the boat? This won't take long."

The young man shrugged and turned away.

Bronsky cleared his throat again and lifted his chin. "I'm pleased to inform you that you're the recipient of an inheritance, Mr. Donnelly. Quite a substantial inheritance, in fact, and my law firm would very much like to—"

"You've got the wrong guy." Alex turned his back on the man and stepped into the cabin.

Bronsky stepped forward. "You just turned twenty-one, isn't that right?"

Alex glanced back. "So?"

"So this sum has been held in trust until your twenty-first birthday, which—"

"My parents died when I was a baby."

Bronsky nodded. "I know." Digging a sheet out of the briefcase he kept his eyes on Alex. "You were born in Seattle. Your birthday was three weeks ago." He glanced at the paper. "July 30, wasn't it?"

Alex hesitated for another moment, then turned and pushed the door wide. "That much I know," he said. "Watch your head."

Bronsky ducked under the doorframe and entered the dim room. Alex watched him take it in: the rough wood table, one chair, and the small bed in the back corner; the large worn chair by the barrel stove in the other corner; the wall lined with shelves holding his few items of clothing and a number of books. Alex was suddenly aware of the smell—wood smoke with a strong overlay of tobacco, sweat and animal musk.

Bronsky placed the briefcase on the table, flipped it open, and began removing papers. "I'll need to see a birth certificate. Then we'll need your signature to certify that you've been notified. You'll have to come to our offices and sign the rest of the papers, and be sure to bring a bank account number where the funds can be deposited." Alex felt his neck stiffen when Bronsky lifted his head and looked at him. "Uh...you *do* have a bank account?"

"Yeah, I have a bank account." He took a step toward the table. "This inheritance—where'd it come from?"

Bronsky blinked. "Your parents...."

Alex shook his head. "If my parents left me money, why didn't I know about it before now? You sure you've got the right guy?"

"Well," Bronsky read from the paper in his hand, "are you Alexander Gabriel Donnelly, born Alexander Gabriel Perrin, 6:45 a.m., July 30, 1982 at Virginia Mason Hospital, Seattle, Washington? Is that you?"

Alex cocked his head. "I know I was born in Seattle, but—"

"Mother's name Janis Marie Perrin, father's name Thomas Allan Perrin?"

"I never knew their names." Alex's voice was so low Bronsky leaned toward him, holding out the sheet of paper.

Alex took it, stared at it, and scratched his dark beard. "This can't be me." He laid the page on the table.

Bronsky sighed. "Do you have a birth certificate here?"

Alex stared at him for a moment, then shook his head. "No."

Bronsky raised his eyebrows. "You were adopted in 1985?"

"Yeah, when I was three."

"Their names were Christopher and Anna Donnelly?"

Alex nodded. "They died when I was five."

"That fits. Do you have any documents from the adoption?"

"No."

Bronsky pursed his lips. "Child Welfare in Vancouver must still have them. We'll have to verify everything, of course, but...." George smiled. "Congratulations, Mr. Donnelly. I think it's safe to say you're about to inherit one million U.S. dollars."

Alex's head jerked up. "What?"

Bronsky chuckled. "I thought that might get your attention. It appears your biological parents were rather wealthy. I believe the original amount was considerably less, but some good investments were made and interest does accumulate over twenty-one years."

Alex shook his head. A hank of black hair fell into his eyes. He pushed it away. "But that's...that doesn't make any sense."

"No, it doesn't." Bronsky chuckled again and reached into his briefcase. "It makes dollars. Lots of them." He handed Alex another sheet of paper, then pointed to a line on the bottom. "Now, if you'll sign here please I'd like to get back to Dawson as soon as possible."

Alex stared at the paper. He took the pen the lawyer held out, but didn't move to sign it.

Bronsky straightened. "Go ahead and read it for yourself. All it says is that you've been informed."

Alex picked it up and moved toward the window. He read it twice, then signed.

Bronsky handed him a business card. "Here's our office address, our phone number and my extension. Call if you need anything. We'll be glad to help." The lawyer shifted the flap of his briefcase until it closed with the soft click of the magnetic clasp. "Uh, it would be expedient if you could arrange to come to Seattle as soon as possible. We've been looking for you for over six months and we'd really like to close this file."

Alex stared at the card.

"Mr. Donnelly?"

He lifted his head and frowned. "I've never been to Seattle. Been back, I mean."

"We'd be happy to make all the arrangements. How soon can you be ready to leave?"

"I don't know." Alex looked down at the paper again. "Maybe tomorrow."

"Tomorrow?"

Alex shrugged off the surprise in the lawyer's voice. "Maybe."

"Oh. Well, fine, that would be fine. I'll see if I can make the arrangements this afternoon then. I guess that means we could travel together, at least to Whitehorse, if there's a seat on the plane. It leaves at 1:15 so we should meet somewhere, say at 11:00? I'm staying at the Downtown Hotel."

"I'll have to arrange something for my dogs. If I can go, I'll be at the Downtown at 11:00."

"Good. I'll see you then."

Alex heard the boat motor roar as it pulled away from the shore and fought the current upstream. He looked around. For a moment

12

nothing seemed familiar, nothing seemed real. He picked up the papers the lawyer had left, scanned them, then tried to read more carefully. The legalese got in the way. Tossing them down he ran a hand through his tangle of black hair and sighed. The last thing he wanted was to go anywhere near a city, but.... He pulled the papers toward him again and slid a callused finger over the smooth words. *Janis Marie Perrin. Thomas Allan Perrin.*

Slumped in the chair Alex let his mind search into corners he'd closed off long ago. A small boy sitting on a bench, his thin fingers outlining initials carved into the wooden arm. Swinging his legs over the edge, he made sure they didn't bump and make noise as he listened to the voices of strangers coming through the half-open door.

"This one must have a black cloud. Twice in five years! Who'd wanna be number three?" The man's voice sounded tired.

"He's a cute little guy, though." The woman's softer voice was hopeful. "Maybe they'll find somebody willing to take him."

"A five year old? Not very likely." The man sighed. "Well, he's off to Clareshome for now. They can hold him and deal with the paperwork while he goes into the system. I'm swamped. There's some legal stuff here from his biological parents. Perkins. That's the name, right?"

"Something like that. His legal name is Donnelly now. Wonder how many more times it'll change before he grows up?"

And there he was, that small boy being led down a long hallway by the clutching hand of a stranger.

He stood, hunched his shoulders against the memories that slipped like slivers of ice through his veins, and turned away from the table. *That was then. Stay in today, Donnelly. Stay in today.* He took a long-handled axe down from beside the door and went outside. The cold bite of late August air hit him like a slap, but he breathed it in and deliberately turned his thoughts toward preparations for winter. His wood supply was getting low. There wasn't much left to split, but he fell into it with an easy familiar rhythm. It was the kind of work he loved—physical and mindless.

But now his mind wouldn't stop. Questions swirled one upon another like small whirlwinds stirring up everything in their path. And in the midst of them two names glowed like red-hot brands. Two names he'd always wondered about.

He stopped, pulled off his T-shirt, and used it to wipe the sweat from his face and the back of his neck. His hand brushed the scar that ran down his neck from the base of his right ear. He tilted his head as though to hide it and dropped the hand quickly.

Resting the axe against the chopping block Alex left the wood where it lay and went back into the cabin. He stared again at the papers. He was tempted to toss them into the stove. *I don't need this. I don't want it. It's too dangerous to go back. But what if...?*

He picked up the documents. It was then he realized his hands were shaking.

Chapter Two

Gil slipped into the warmth of the house and listened. Nothing. He dropped the key into his pocket, leaned his rifle in a corner, and walked to the kitchen. He poured himself a large glass of orange juice from the fridge and downed it almost in one gulp. Closing his eyes he savored the taste. *Real orange juice.* He started to thank God, stopped and grunted, then gave a nod of his head.

"Okay, I do thank you," he mumbled, "though I suppose that won't help much since I'm stealing it."

He lifted the lid on the long deep freezer and smiled. *The company always did feed us well. But how long will it be before the caretaker arrives?* He lifted out a steak, thawed it in the microwave, and fried it just the way he liked it. He was about to have another glass of orange juice when he heard the dog.

Pulling on his coat Gil stepped outside. The intensity of the dog's bark increased. Gil jogged around the house in time to see the grizzly ambling away, then went over and scratched the dog's head. He turned back to the house and froze. Straining his ears he turned toward the south and listened. The wind was gusting, but every now and then he was sure he heard the sound of a helicopter. He jogged back to the house, stacked the dishes in the sink and left, making sure he locked the door behind him.

Once within the safety of the trees he stopped and listened again. The whap-whap-whap seemed to get louder, then faded away entirely. He thought of that second glass of juice, but decided not to risk it. Settling the rifle in the crook of his arm he headed into the dense bush, the silence growing deep as he walked.

○ ○ ○

George sat on the bed in the hotel room, tugged off his suit coat, and dialed the long distance number. Kenni picked up on the second ring.

"I found him."

Kenni's voice was excited. "In Whitehorse?"

"No. Dawson City. Actually, he lives twenty miles downriver from Dawson in a small cabin. The whole woodsman trip."

"What's he like?"

"Pretty much the way you thought he'd be. Not very friendly. You'll see for yourself. He might be coming down with me tomorrow. The flight gets in about 7:30. Can you book a slot the next morning, just in case?"

"Let me check."

George heard the clicking of a keyboard.

"There's an opening at 9:00. What was his reaction when you told him?"

"He didn't believe it. Thinks we have the wrong guy."

"No doubt. It'd be a shock, considering what his life's been like."

"Well, pray for me. I may be traveling with him for the next thirty-six hours. Oh—I guess we'll need to book a hotel room for him."

"I'll take care of it," Kenni said. "I'll book one for you too."

"You think he needs supervising?"

"It's taken us forever to find him, George. We don't want to risk him bolting when he gets here."

"You think he might?"

"I think it would be good for somebody to be there."

"Okay, I'll babysit for the first night, but that's it."

"Good enough. See you on Friday."

○ ○ ○

Vancouver, 1988

The smell of mold filled the boy's nostrils. He tried to back away from the dark entrance to the stairway, but the fist clutching the collar of his shirt held him above the hole. Dampness crept out and wrapped cold tendrils around his legs as the fist shoved him down. The voice above him cursed.

"Scum like you belongs down here."

A blow to the back of his head sent him sprawling to the concrete below. Grit scoured skin from his hands and elbows as heavy boots thudded behind him. One of them slammed into his side. The sound of a rib cracking made bile rise in his throat. He curled into a tight ball, knowing what was coming as he heard the familiar sound of the belt being yanked from its loops.

He tried not to cry out, but it seemed like the blows would never stop. Already panting with pain he howled when a hand grabbed his arm and wrenched him to his feet, jolting the broken rib. The fist shoved him further into the cellar. He heard the scraping of the small door under the stairs. He started to plead.

"No. Please. Please, don't lock me in there. No. Please. Don't. Please."

Another blow to his head knocked him to the floor again. The boot connected with his thigh as he tried to squirm away. There was nowhere to go but into the hole, into the darkness. The small door slammed and he heard the latch click. His head and body throbbing he pressed his face to the floor and tried to suck clean air through the crack at the bottom, tried to get away from the smell of whatever lay rotting in the darkness.

ᗣ ○ ○

Alex lay on his back, watching the dawn light seep through the small east-facing window. The nightmares had wakened him halfway through the night, and now memories pressed in on him as he lay still. The touch of soft hair on his cheek, the light scent of peaches and dark eyes filled with laughter. They swam before him until he felt like he was floating. Then they changed, changed to small piercing dark eyes, eyes so full of confusion and longing they made him moan. He rolled over and put one hand on the rough floor. What was done can't be changed. He passed his hand across the planks. *That was then. Stay in today. Stay in today.*

Forcing himself to focus on the present he listened to the sighing rush of the river, the soft sound of the wind in the spruce behind the cabin, the rattle of a chain as one of the dogs moved. Familiar sounds, sounds without any guilt or fear attached. He listened for a while longer, and decided maybe he'd let that lawyer fly back to Seattle alone. He couldn't take the risk. He rolled over and stared at the roof.

The familiar surge of apprehension and then anger filled him. *How did they find me? If the lawyers had, the cops might be right behind. Wish it would snow. With snow on the ground I could head out to the trapping cabin. They'd never find me there.* He turned his head toward the table. The papers still lay there. *Should've known better than to feel safe. Should've taken more precautions. Should've changed my name.* But it was the only identity he had. The only thing that was really his, even if it wasn't.

He sighed and stared again at the weathered boards in the roof. *Would the cops in Vancouver have contacted the cops in Seattle? Not likely. They'd have no reason to. Maybe going back **would** be worth the risk.* Images floated through his mind again—those dark eyes pleading, the sound of sirens. He rolled out of bed and scrubbed at his face. *No. Don't let your mind go there. And don't go to Seattle.*

He scratched his beard and thought briefly about shaving. *If I'm going to…no. I'm not going anywhere.* He didn't bother digging out the razor. He had to get ready for winter. No time for chasing ghosts. A sudden urgency hit him as though if he rushed to prepare, winter would come more quickly. And when winter came he'd be harder to find.

By the time he lit the fire and made coffee he'd repeated that *No* to himself several times, but kept coming back to the questions he wanted answered. He stared out the front window and watched the flood of silt-laden water stream by. Eddies and undertows, swirls of gray in the early light. *Will there be answers in Seattle?*

Pulled by the energy of sudden decision, he tugged his pack out from under his bed and tossed in a change of clothes and a few other things. He fed his dogs an extra large portion and made sure their water bowls were full. Tacking the standard "Use what you need, replace what you use" note to the front door he shouldered the light pack, pulled on a battered floppy-brimmed felt hat, and headed for his boat.

○ ○ ○

Alex was sweating by the time he reached the small round-ended trailer sagging into the side of the hill. Sal's huskies let out enough howling to wake the dead, but no one came to the door so he knew she wasn't home. He pulled out a scrap of paper from his pack and wrote a quick note, asking her to check on his dogs. Then he trudged back down the long hill toward the center of town.

The thud of his boots echoed along the boardwalk. The streets were quiet, the sharp gusts of wind stirring up dust devils as they whipped around the false fronts of clapboard buildings, sighing as grit scrubbed at wood and window. He nodded at a girl sweeping the entrance to one of the tourist traps. They'd be closing for the season in a few days. The town was reverting to its previous ownership. The tourists were gone. A pickup truck rumbled slowly by as Alex stepped into the street. He gave the driver a short salute, though he didn't know his name. Everyone was a local now. He stopped in front of the Downtown Hotel, stared at the front entrance and sighed. He glanced down the street. *The streets of Seattle will be nothing like this.*

○ ○ ○

The flight out of Dawson was noisy so neither man made much attempt to talk at first. Alex peered out the window, catching glimpses of the spectacular Yukon scenery through flat-topped clouds. He'd flown over it a few times in small planes and helicopters, canoed its rivers and tramped over some of its mountains, but it never ceased to make him catch his breath. The most beautiful place on earth. A good place to get lost in. A good place to hide.

But now I've been found. His stomach flipped and twisted into sudden panic. *This was a mistake. It's too risky. I'll get off in Whitehorse and tell Bronsky I've changed my mind.* But then the what-ifs filled his head again, and he wondered if at least some facts and figures might be found—facts and figures that might answer the questions he'd asked all his life. *Are my parents really dead? Or did they abandon me? What were they like? Where were they from? Where am I from? Where do I belong?* He let out a sigh that was almost a groan. Letting his mind wander in that direction made him feel adrift with no way to anchor himself. *But now, maybe....* Alex felt his pulse quicken. *Do I really want to know? What if the answers only give me more nightmares? More questions?*

He thought about the money. *One million dollars. What would it be like to go out and buy anything I wanted? Anything at all?* Alex sighed. There wasn't really anything he wanted that badly. A new boat and motor, maybe.

A tap on his arm made him jerk. He turned to see George holding out a package of gum. Alex popped one out and nodded his thanks.

"Beautiful country!" the lawyer yelled.

Alex nodded again.

"Good fishing, I bet!"

"The best." Alex started to turn away.

"I'd like to come back some time!"

Yeah, with an R.V. and all the conveniences of home. The territory flooded with tourists each summer. Alex avoided them as much as possible.

But Bronsky surprised him. He pointed to the rugged landscape below, the wide ribbon of the Yukon River snaking through it. "Any whitewater on that river?"

Alex shook his head. "Not much, but there are others."

"Ever done any whitewater rafting?" Bronsky asked.

Alex shook his head again. "Too much money!" he shouted.

Bronsky grinned at him. "Not anymore!"

Alex shrugged and turned back to the window. His chest felt tight and he shifted in an attempt to relieve it. *Not anymore.* He closed his eyes against images that swirled up like the stench from a rotting carcass. Those were some of the last words his foster father said to him as they waited for the cops to come and take him away. "Time for a dose of reality, kid," he'd said as he held him down. "No more soft touch. Not anymore." He remembered the man's scheming look, remembered how he'd suddenly released his grip. "Or...you could run...."

And those small dark eyes, pleading.

He rubbed at the pain in his temple, then laid his hand over the long scar on his neck.

Soft touch. Right. No more back-handed blows or belts that snapped like a whip. No more nights when he lay rigid, hoping, even praying, that the man's footsteps wouldn't stop at his bedroom door. It was a huge relief to be out of that house, even though it meant living on the streets, eating out of dumpsters, running scared every time a police cruiser drove by.

He opened his eyes and scanned the landscape again. It looked dark, the thick growth of spruce, birch, and poplar flowing over hills, encroaching on mountainsides, and crowding down to the edges of rivers. The memories crowded him too, even here. Alex sighed. *Just when I was getting used to being a hermit and now they're telling me I'm a rich man. Maybe. What if I get all the way to Seattle and find out they've got the wrong guy after all? What if I end up in a jail cell instead? That'd be typical—another one of God's cruel jokes. I've been the brunt of enough of those. Pastor T said that God doesn't play those kinds of games, but I know better.* Experience had taught him better. He glanced sideways at the lawyer. Something about the man kind of reminded him of the pastor who'd tried to help him long ago. He slouched into the seat again. *And how would I get back?* He had enough in the bank to make it through the winter, if he was careful, but that didn't include a plane ticket from Seattle to Whitehorse. It'd be a long way to hitchhike. He began to seriously regret getting on the plane.

They touched down at the airport in Whitehorse and took a taxi into town. On the way Alex voiced his concerns. "What if this is all a mistake? How do I get back?"

Bronsky smiled. "My firm will take care of you. Don't worry."

"I've heard that one before," Alex mumbled.

Bronksy peered at him. "I'm hungry. Know a good place to eat in this town?"

"You like pizza 'n beer?"

"I'll skip the beer, but pizza will work."

They sat across from one another at a small table. The bar was crowded, the music loud. Bronsky pulled his tie off and slipped out of his suit jacket. He stretched and grinned at Alex. "Don't tell my boss. He insists on the professional look, no matter where, no matter what. I think he'd send me to Timbuktu and insist I go in a suit and tie."

Alex noticed the difference the lack of jacket and tie made. The lawyer looked even younger. Younger, and more friendly, though still way too trendy by Yukon standards. Bronsky stared at him for a moment, then extended his hand.

"Why don't we start again, on...uh...more even ground? I'm George."

Alex nodded once and shook hands. "Alex."

George grinned. "It's obvious you value your privacy, Alex." He took a huge bite of pizza and seemed to swallow it whole. "But we have all night and a long flight south ahead of us. Tell me about yourself."

Alex took a long gulp of cold beer. "Not much to tell. You already know I went into the system when I was three, then the Donnellys moved me to Vancouver. When they died in a car crash I was bounced through group homes for a while, then into foster care for the next eight years."

George downed half his glass of soda. "Must've been rough."

Alex peered over the crust of his pizza. "You want horror stories? I could tell a few."

George took another bite and Alex decided to be sociable. "What about you? How long you been a lawyer?"

"Passed the bar two years ago."

"How old are you?" Alex realized he'd blurted the words, but didn't care enough to cover the social blunder.

"I'll be thirty-five in a couple of months."

"You don't...."

"I know. I don't look it. I think that's why Mr. Adams hired me. He uses my baby face to his advantage."

"Does it work?"

George raised his eyes to meet Alex's. "I'm good at what I do."

Alex had a hunch and voiced it. "Your father a lawyer?"

George laughed. "No. He's a pastor. Been preaching in country churches all his life. Still does. Can't figure why I chose to be a big city lawyer." George swallowed. "But I know he's proud of me."

"How?"

"What?"

"That he's proud. How do you know?"

"He keeps telling me."

Alex blinked and took another gulp of his beer. He was studying the sheen on a large piece of pepperoni when George blurted out his own question.

"Are you good at what you do?"

"I've survived up here for five years." Alex knew his tone was too defensive.

George looked around at the bar's clientele. "I guess that does take some kind of...stamina."

Alex snorted. Then gave a rough laugh. "You could call it that."

George grinned back at him. "So what do you do to survive up here?"

Alex shrugged. "Whatever's going. Fish some, when they allow it. Trapping brings in some through the winter. I work construction when I have to. Sometimes the gold mines."

"So I take it you're between jobs right now? That's why you're able to just take off?"

Alex nodded. "Just finished working with a Parks Canada crew, a renovation. Ended just in time to start getting ready for winter." He pushed his empty glass around. "How long will this take, anyway? Freeze-up isn't far off."

George's eyebrows shot up. "You mean you plan on going back out to that cabin, even with the inheritance?"

Alex glanced away. "Hadn't thought about it, but yeah, probably. It's where I live."

"Maybe you'll like Seattle."

"Doubt it."

"A rich man can go anywhere he likes."

"I'm still not convinced you've got the right guy. If my parents were so rich, why didn't they leave a will? Why weren't there relatives to take in a little rich kid? Or at least a guardian or something?"

George shrugged. "Valid questions. Maybe you'll find the answers in Seattle."

"Yeah, maybe."

George was about to respond when a lanky young woman screeched Alex's name from a couple of tables away. Before he could turn around she'd thrown herself into his lap and wrapped her arms around his neck.

"Hey, babe. Where ya bin?"

Alex grinned at the girl, then flashed a glance at George. "Workin', Sal."

Sal twisted around to peer at George. "Who's this?"

George extended his hand across the table. "Name's George Bronsky."

Sal let go of Alex's neck long enough to shake hands. "Sally. Call me Sal. So you guys in town for a good time or what?"

"Just a one-nighter. I left a note on your door. We're leaving tomorrow for Seattle."

"Seattle! What for?"

"Business. Can you check on my dogs? I left the boat at the usual spot."

"Sure. No sweat. When ya comin' back?"

"Quick. Gotta get my wood in." Alex's mouth twisted into a sideways grin. "Wanna help?"

Sal sat up straight and peered into Alex's eyes. "You serious?"

"Sure. I'm tired of cookin' for myself."

Sal tossed her long hair. "Well, I can cook, dude, but you'd be doin' half of it."

Alex dumped her off his lap. "What kind of arrangement is that? A man comes home after a hard day's work and you tell him to cook his own supper? No way."

Sal shook her head, her hands on her hips. "Guess we just wouldn't make it then, Alex. Too bad. You're kinda good lookin', ya know."

Alex smirked. Shaking his head he grinned at George. "The Yukon—where men are men—and the women are too!"

Sal slapped his arm and Alex chuckled. He looked up at her. "What's up tonight?"

"I'm headin' over to Melanie's pretty quick. Heard there's a kegger goin' on. Why dontcha come?"

Alex glanced at George, then winked at her. "Sure. We'll show George here some real Yukon hospitality."

George was shaking his head. "I...uh, I still have to try and arrange your flight. Then I think I'll call it a night."

Alex's smirk widened as he stood up. "Somehow I figured you'd say that."

Chapter Three

Back at the detachment Sorensen drummed his long fingers on the open file in front of him. His large frame rocked back and forth as he leaned back in his chair. He stared at the pimply-faced teenager in the small photo clipped to the first page. *Twenty-one,* Sorensen thought. *This perp would be 21 now. And who knows how many more young girls he'd hurt in the past five years.* The inspector let his chair snap back to vertical. He turned the pages, scanning for details. "Fee, fi, fo, fum," he mumbled. "I smell the blood of criminal scum." He flipped back to the picture, unclipped it, and propped it up on his coffee cup. "They don't call me the Swedish giant for nothing, Alex Donnelly. And it's time I sniffed you out."

○ ○ ○

George knocked on Alex's hotel room door at 7:30 the next morning. When there was no answer he knocked louder. A scantily-clad Sal opened it. He stepped back and looked at the floor.

"Uh, sorry...is Alex up...uh...in?"

"He's in, but he's definitely not up."

George knew Sal was enjoying his embarrassment. "Uh...can you tell him our flight leaves at 10:00? So we should be at the airport in less than an hour."

"Sure." She smirked. "I'll get him dressed."

George felt himself turn a deeper shade of pink and Sal laughed. "We'll meet you in the restaurant."

He nodded and backed away. "Yeah, okay, in a few minutes then."

He bumped into the wall, whirled around, and strode quickly down the hallway.

When they arrived at his table George tried not to show how uncomfortable he felt. When he failed he pretended not to see Alex and Sal exchange amused glances.

Alex slid into the booth. "How's the coffee? Or do you drink milk in the morning?"

Sal giggled and slid in beside him. George ignored them.

She suddenly jumped to her feet again. "Hey, I've gotta go, Alex." She leaned down and kissed him. "So I'll see ya when you get back?"

Alex nodded. "Sure. Practise your culinary skills."

She smirked. "I'll think about it. You take care of yourself, okay?" She turned to George. "Nice to meet you, George."

He nodded, but she turned away before he could say goodbye. He picked up his cup and answered Alex's question.

"The coffee's strong."

"Good." Alex picked up his menu and talked over it. "So you got me on the same plane?"

"Yes. We have a bit of a wait in Vancouver, but we get into Seattle at a decent time tonight. I've booked you a room and made an appointment with Kenni Adams tomorrow morning at 9:00."

"Who?"

"The researcher who worked on your case. You'll meet the others later."

"It took others?"

"Three, actually. One to do the research, one to do the legal work, one to do the legwork. I'm the leg man. As I said the firm is anxious to close the file."

"Why?"

"Stipulations in the contract."

"What?"

"They don't get paid 'til we've delivered the documents and the inheritance into your hands."

"Ah. And how much do they get if I sign the papers?"

"I don't know the exact amount, but you might want to prepare yourself. It did take six months to find you."

"What if these other lawyers—"

"Lawyer. Kenni Adams is just a researcher, not a lawyer."

"What if Kenni Adams isn't so sure I'm the right guy?"

"I think Kenni will be convinced. All the research led to you."

"Oh?"

"The trail took a while to follow, but Kenni says you fit the profile."

"The profile? What profile is that?"

George sensed he was on dangerous ground. "Uh...you can discuss that with Kenni."

Alex's eyes narrowed. "Yeah. I'll do that."

The waitress arrived to take their orders. When she left, Alex lit up a cigarette and squinted through the smoke. George wanted to object, but leaned away and said nothing.

When Alex spoke again his tone was still hostile. "So what happens if I refuse to sign these papers?"

George didn't care that his shock showed. "Why would you do that? You'd be cheating yourself out of a million dollars!"

"Maybe I don't want it."

"If you don't claim it, the government will pocket it all."

"After you and your firm take your cut, of course." Alex was sneering openly now.

George frowned. He'd had enough of this guy's attitude. "So don't go. Stay here. Run back to your cabin and hide in the bush. No one will care."

Alex ground the cigarette into an ashtray. His eyes flashed. "Maybe I'd like it that way."

George opened his mouth to reply, but the waitress came to their table and poured more coffee. He stared at the steaming liquid. When she was gone he cleared his throat. "I apologize." He sighed. "I shouldn't have said...."

Alex waved him off. "Forget it." He stared out the window until the waitress brought their breakfast plates. They ate in a silence that hung heavy in the air.

George finally broke it. "You'd really consider turning down that much money?"

Alex stared at his plate. "That much money draws attention." He looked at George. "It already has."

"Kenni had to find you. It wasn't a matter of invading your privacy."

"I don't like the idea of everybody knowing all about me."

"Welcome to the twenty-first century."

"Big Brother is watching."

"Oh, yeah."

Alex sighed. "You'd think I'd be used to it."

"How so?"

Alex used his teeth to pull another cigarette out of the package. "When I was shifted around in the system they always knew all about me. My file was there before I was. I'd walk into somebody's office and there it'd be, my whole life, flopped open on a desk for anybody to read." He lit the cigarette. "Sometimes I did things just to make it more interesting."

"Bad attention better than no attention?"

Alex shrugged and blew smoke out the side of his mouth. "Something like that."

"Well, this time the attention will all be positive. I have no doubt you'll be treated like royalty once we get to Seattle. My firm takes good care of its clients."

"Especially rich clients?"

"Yeah, I admit they get special treatment, but Mr. Adams runs a good firm. He's a good man, a fair man."

"What about the other guys?"

"Other guys?"

"Didn't you say it was Adams, somebody and somebody? You haven't mentioned the other guys."

George nodded. "Mr. Ferrington is pretty much a silent partner. He's in his late sixties. The others are full partners, but Mr. Adams is the boss."

"Ah. So Adams runs the show."

"Pretty much. Why?"

Alex let the smoke billow between them. "I'd just like to know whose pockets I'll be lining...if I sign the papers."

"Right."

"So how will they prove it's me?"

"Were you ever fingerprinted?"

George noticed how Alex stiffened, then leaned back and hung his arm across the back of the booth, cigarette dangling between his fingers. "You saw my profile. You tell me."

"Twice." George drained his coffee cup. "For break and enter, then robbery."

"My rebellious stage. I was fourteen."

"But you didn't graduate to bigger and better. Why not?"

Alex shrugged as his hand moved to the scar on his neck and his head tilted sideways. "My foster father's belt had a lot to do with it and—you might appreciate this—a pastor."

"Really?"

"Yeah. Pastor T, they called him." Alex's mouth twisted into a sardonic grin. "The second house I broke into belonged to him. He convinced the judge to give me 300 hours of community service in his church. Worked me hard too, but he was a good guy, ya know? Knew how to get a kid to talk. If not for him I probably would've ended up in prison. Maybe even dead." He stared out the window and his voice dropped an octave. "Couple of times I thought Wild Bill was going to kill me."

George decided to push it. "Who's Wild Bill?" When Alex's eyes met his he felt he'd opened the door to a freezer.

"They called him my foster father. I called him other things. The man had a mean temper."

"I thought foster parents weren't allowed to get physical."

Alex snorted. "On paper, maybe." He took a deep draw on the cigarette. "We were always getting knocked around."

"We?"

"Usually five or six lived in the house."

"Didn't anyone ever notice? Neighbors? Teachers?"

"Oh yeah, they noticed."

George saw Alex's face darken as the memory surfaced.

"Like the time in junior high when I had a gym class the morning after Wild Bill had laid into me with his belt. We were doing wrestling moves that morning, you know?"

George nodded and Alex continued.

"My partner knew pretty quick something was wrong. I told him to shut up and fake it, but the coach noticed. Told me to hit the showers, then walked in on me. Stood there for a while, having a good look. Then all he said was, "Looks good on ya, Donnelly.""

Alex shifted and flicked the ash from the end of the cigarette. "Guess I wasn't one of his favorite students."

George dropped his voice a notch. "How long did that go on?"

"'Til...." Alex stopped. His eyes shifted around the room. "'Til I decided not to take it anymore and got outta there." He waved his coffee cup at the waitress. "Wasn't *that* in my file?"

George didn't meet his eyes. "I didn't read the whole thing."

Alex slumped in the seat and massaged his forehead. "Don't get me started on the horror stories."

"Maybe it's good to...to talk about it," George replied.

Alex stared out the window again. George watched his hand clenching and releasing around the coffee cup. When he turned back his words came out in a mumble.

"I don't usually...talk about it. The memories—they can take over sometimes."

The waitress arrived then with their bill. George picked it up quickly. "We'd better get going."

○ ○ ○

Alex had a hard time sitting still in the cab. *Get out*, he kept telling himself. *Get out now*. But he followed George through the airport, through the security checks, and down the sloped ramp to the plane.

Once on board Alex had another question. "Okay, so you have my fingerprints, but what is there to compare them to? I mean they'll tell you I'm Alex Donnelly, the kid who got arrested, but how will they tell you if I'm the Alex Donnelly who should inherit this money?"

George shrugged. "I'll let Kenni sort that one out. I do the legwork, remember?"

"So when we get there your work is done?"

"If you sign the documents, it will be."

Alex was quiet for a while, then twisted in his seat to face the lawyer. "Is there anything else?"

"What do you mean?"

"Any other information you're not telling me. I still don't get how I could inherit a pile of money now, and go through the hell I did for eleven years."

"I honestly don't know anything more, Alex. There is a package waiting for you in our office, but I don't know what's in it."

Alex ran his hand through his hair and slumped back into the seat. "So I have to wait 'til tomorrow."

"Tomorrow at 9:00 a.m."

Alex glanced up at the no smoking sign above him and cursed.

Chapter Four

Gil stepped out into the growing light of early morning. He took a deep breath and sighed. Another winter was closing in on him fast. He'd heard the distant helicopter again yesterday and wondered if it had landed at the mine site. *Will there be a caretaker at the house already?* He'd have to tread softly this time until he found out.

And if there isn't? Will you stick around this time and wait for one? He envisioned running toward the chopper, watching the ground sink beneath him as the machine rose into the air, seeing the town grow on the horizon as they beat their way toward it. There would be so many things he could enjoy again. A normal bed. Running water. Fresh vegetables and fruit. Coffee.

He shook himself and turned back to his cabin. *Not for you. Never again for you. But maybe you can scoff another steak and glass of that orange juice before the new guy arrives.*

○ ○ ○

Steak dinner and huge hotel suite complete with fruit basket and room service. George was right. They'd laid out the red carpet. The only thing missing was the bottle of champagne. He wished it had been included. It might've helped him sleep. But he didn't sleep well at all that night. The bed was too soft, the nightmares too real. He spent most of the night clicking through the drivel on TV. He was tempted to wake George, but waited until 6 a.m. and pounded on his door. Alex smirked when the young lawyer opened it, his hair sticking up at odd places, his eyes half open as he peered at his watch.

33

"It's only 6:00, Alex. The appointment isn't until—"

"Nine. I know. But the restaurant's open. I'm hungry."

George opened the door wide. "Come on in. Give me a minute to shower."

Alex paced as he waited, firing questions through the partly opened bathroom door while George dressed.

"How far is the office from here?"

"Five minutes by cab."

"Can we change the appointment to 8:00?"

"No. Nobody gets there 'til 8:30."

George poked his head out. "Alex, I know you're anxious but—"

"Okay, okay. I'm trying to be patient." He pulled a pack of cigarettes out of his pocket. "Hurry up, will ya?"

He was patting his pockets for his lighter when George said, "This is a no smoking room."

Alex rolled his eyes and slipped the cigarette behind his ear. George's head disappeared and Alex started pacing as he heard the buzz of a razor. When it stopped the door opened wide.

"Uh...would you like to use this?"

Alex rubbed at his coarse beard. He'd intended to let it grow for the winter, but decided he'd like the change. He nodded and took the razor from George's hand. When he emerged from the bathroom a few minutes later he had to admit he felt better.

George grinned. "You clean up pretty good."

"So the girls tell me."

"Uh, there's a barber downstairs, you know, if you'd like a haircut. We have time."

Alex gave his head a quick shake. "The shave'll do. You ready?"

They both dove into the breakfast buffet and an hour later emerged on the busy Seattle street just as the morning rush hour took hold. The noise, the speed at which everything moved, the smell of wet concrete and exhaust fumes–it all made Alex twitch. He felt the muscles between his shoulders tightening.

George glanced at his watch. "We still have lots of time. Want to walk?"

Alex nodded as he reached for the cigarette behind his ear. "Yeah, that might help."

The downtown district was filling with people. They crossed intersections that made him feel like a drone in a beehive. He felt a vague
dizziness as he joined the sway of so many bodies. Looking up a few
times, his eyes followed the straight lines of glass and steel, trying to
catch a patch of open sky and regain perspective. George seemed to
take that as a cue and pointed out some of Seattle's famous buildings.
Alex wasn't much interested, but welcomed the distraction. When they
stopped in front of a large modern building with gleaming blue windows George waved his hand. "This is it," he said. In a few long strides
he was at the door, holding it wide.

Alex stared from the sidewalk. His heart raced, the palms of his
hands felt clammy. He took a long last drag on the cigarette, tossed it
on the sidewalk, glanced at George, then stared again at the open door.
He tried to swallow the dryness in his mouth. When that didn't work
he turned and strode away.

George called his name and jogged after him. Alex sank down on a
bench and put his head in his hands. George stood back for a minute,
then approached.

"You okay?"

"All these years I've wanted to know. Now I'm not so sure. I'd just
like to wipe the past away, the known and the unknown."

"Somebody once said there is no future without a past."

Alex looked up. "Yeah? Wonder what kind of past he had?"

George sat down. "You really want to walk away now when you're
so close to the truth? At least maybe some of it?"

Alex sat silent for a time, then sighed. "Okay. Let's go."

George stayed by his side as they strode through the door of Adams,
Ferrington Lithgow and Bolt.

○ ○ ○

The receptionist waved them past with a smile as George led Alex
toward a door marked with a nameplate engraved in gold: G.A.
Bronsky, Attorney at Law. As the door swung open a young woman
stood up.

Alex stared. She wasn't what he'd call beautiful, but there was
something about her that captivated him instantly. She was dressed in

a trim beige business suit, expensive and tailored to fit. The collar of a light blue silk blouse made a smooth line along her neck. It matched eyes that stared steadily into his. He blinked when he realized she was standing in front of him, her hand extended.

George completed the introduction. "Alex, this is Kenni—uh, Kendra Adams. Kenni, Alex Donnelly."

Alex put his hand in hers.

"Everyone calls me Kenni, Alex. It's good to meet you at last."

Alex wished he'd taken George's advice about the haircut as he watched Kenni return to her chair. George moved quickly behind the desk and waved at another chair angled beside it. Alex settled himself in it, noticing an open file on the desk. George flipped it closed.

Tucking a long strand of honey-colored hair behind her ear Kenni smiled. "How was your flight?"

"Okay," Alex said.

"And the room? It was comfortable, I hope?"

He nodded. "Fine." *Dolt, make an attempt.* He added a quick "Thanks."

Kenni flashed a glance at George. "I know you're probably anxious to know about the inheritance, Alex, but we do have to confirm that you're the Alex Donnelly we're looking for. I'm quite sure you are, but we'll have to verify it."

"How?" *Monosyllabic moron.*

"I'm going to ask you to go to a local police station."

Alex gripped the arms of the chair.

"They'll take a print of your foot," Kenni continued.

"My foot?" Alex knew he was doing a bad job of hiding his tension.

Kenni's smile beamed again. "Yes, I'm afraid so. The only positive identification we have is the footprint of baby Alex. If you and he are one and the same, your footprint will match. It will take a few days for the experts to tell us."

Alex slumped. "I thought it would be today, this morning."

"I'm sorry, no. Since it's Friday we probably won't get the results until Wednesday or Thursday of next week at the earliest. We have to be certain. I'm sure you can understand."

Alex nodded. "Yeah. I guess. So where's this police station?"

"George will take you there. It's not far."

Alex glanced at the file. He turned to Kenni and pointed with his chin. "Does that belong to me?"

Kenni's eyes flicked to the file for a second, then back to him. "Well, not exactly. It's the information I collected as we tried to find you."

"My profile." His eyes flicked to George, then back to Kenni.

Her eyebrows arched slightly. "Yes. Your profile, and other information. Once we determine that you're the right person you'll have access to all of it, if you want to read it."

Alex nodded and turned to George. "Let's go, then. The quicker we get this over with, the better."

George stood. "Okay." He nodded to the woman. "Thanks, Kenni."

As she stood the smile she gave George was warm. "See you tomorrow?"

George nodded. "I'll be there."

Kenni extended her hand toward Alex again. "It really is good to meet you, Alex."

As he took her hand in his again he felt like she could see right through him. *But how could a woman like her know how someone like me would feel?* When their hands lingered he thought she turned a very slight shade of pink. He dropped his eyes.

"Yeah. Uh, thanks," he mumbled and followed George from the room.

In the elevator Alex turned to him. "Why didn't you tell me?"

"What?"

"That Kenni Adams was a woman."

"Oh." George shrugged. "Guess I didn't think it was relevant."

"Relevant? How could a woman like that not be relevant?"

The lawyer smacked the Main button on the wall of the elevator. "She's my boss' daughter. Not to mention about fifteen years younger than me. I don't think of her that way."

"Right. So what's going on tomorrow?"

"Tomorrow?"

"Yeah. She said, 'See you tomorrow.' So what's that about, you work Saturdays?"

"Sometimes. But this is a social thing." George looked sideways at him.

Alex smirked. "Yeah, right."

○ ○ ○

Kenni opened the file and noted the date of the meeting. Her hand shook a little as she jotted down a few words. She stared at what she'd written, then at the chair where Alex sat. She'd tried to prepare herself for meeting him, for the way it might stir up old memories, old scars. But she was not prepared for the way the strength of his features seared her mind. The line of his jaw, the wide shoulders that seemed tight with tension. The strong hands. And his eyes. She turned her head away, but the haunted look she'd seen there stayed with her. She knew that look well. She'd seen it often, in a small chipped mirror on the wall in a dingy bedroom.

"Oh God," she whispered. "Help."

○ ○ ○

The time at the police station took only about an hour, but it felt like ten. Alex forced himself to make eye contact with the officer who took the print of his foot. But he couldn't make himself relax. If there had been any communication between the Vancouver police and the Seattle police five years ago, he'd know it pretty quick. He'd know it by the handcuffs they'd slap on him before he could get out the door. He came close to bolting a couple of times. His shoulders dropped with relief when the officer finally told him he could leave.

George had work to catch up on at the office so Alex spent the day wandering the city alone. A fine drizzle painted the concrete streets gray and Alex's mood gloomy. He shivered more than once, reminding himself how much he hated the dampness. He walked for hours, wondering if maybe his parents had strolled these same streets years before. For what must've been the millionth time he tried to visualize what they might've looked like. He stared at his reflection in a shop window and imagined that his father would've been a lot like himself—broad in the shoulder, dark haired, a bit stocky, gray eyes. But his mother...he'd never been able to picture his mother. He had only a vague memory of her voice and long soft hair. Black hair, like his. Or was that the woman who had adopted him? Alex couldn't really be sure.

It was well past dark when he got back to the hotel. There was a note for him at the desk:

Alex,

Babysitting's over. I've gone home for the night. Will call in the morning.

George.

He tossed the note into a garbage can as he headed for the bar. He ordered a steak, chased it with a beer, and followed that one with several more. The familiar numbness was well entrenched by the time he made his way back to his room and fell into a restless sleep.

Chapter Five

Ruby stood with her hands on her huge hips. Her face, like an overblown candy-pink balloon, slowly descended to his. The boy tried to back away, but took only one step before he felt the cold chrome of the kitchen table behind him. She arched her painted eyebrows and pulled her red lips over yellow teeth in a sneer.

"You've been rooting in the trash again, haven't you?"

The stench of her breath made him want to gag. Shaking his head slowly he tried to pull his eyes away from hers. He barely saw the flash of her hand as it smashed across his face.

"I know what was in there, you little pig. I know what you took. Maybe you'd like some more, huh? Maybe we should see what else is in there that you can stuff down your ungrateful throat!"

He cried out as she grabbed him and flipped the lid of the garbage can open. The stench rose into his nostrils. He saw something move—a slithering motion. Two small red eyes swirled in the blackness. His stomach erupted as she forced his head into the can. He was afraid to scream, afraid to open his mouth for fear the creature would leap at him, but he couldn't stop the spew that came out. Ruby held him there until he was dry heaving, then pulled him up, whacked him again, and pushed him toward the stairs to the cellar.

"Get down there. Out of my sight!" she screamed. "Bill will deal with you later."

Then a strange noise intruded. A sound he didn't remember from the other times, a shrieking sound.

Alex woke with a jerk, sending the screaming phone flying from the bedside table. He threw the covers back and scrambled for it, but only a dial tone buzzed in his ear. He replaced it and strode to the window, pulling the drapes back with a jerk. He winced and turned his head away as the morning light flooded the room.

The phone rang again. And rang and rang. Alex stared at it for a full two minutes before answering. Kenni's voice sounded hesitant.

"I hope I didn't...um...sorry to wake you."

"I'm up," he said, trying to slow his breathing.

"Well, I...I mean we...." Alex frowned as she stuttered. Then her next sentence came out in a rush.

"I thought you'd be pretty bored sitting in that hotel room so uh...would you like to get out for a bit?"

"Sure." He heard the word come out of his mouth, but wondered why he'd said it. She told him George would pick him up. When he hung up he stared at the receiver for a few minutes. Then he went into the bathroom and splashed his face with cold water.

○ ○ ○

Kenni stared at her cell phone and groaned. *Kendra Adams, what are you doing?* She didn't try to answer herself as she dialed George's cell. When she asked him to pick Alex up his reaction was about what she'd expected.

"A little unprofessional, isn't it?"

"I know but...."

"Let me guess. You feel sorry for him."

"Well, how would you feel, being in a strange city under these circumstances?"

George sighed. She waited for another lecture about always picking up strays, but all he said was "Alright. I'll pick him up."

○ ○ ○

Alex's heart was still racing when the phone rang again.

"Hi." George's voice sounded far away. "Kenni tells me you're joining us."

"I guess. Time for some Seattle hospitality."

"Don't expect it to be the kind you're used to." Before Alex had time to comment George asked, "Had breakfast yet?"

"No."

"Well, get yourself something fast. I'll be there in forty-five minutes."

"Where we going?"

"You'll see. Be ready in forty-five. Oh, and bring what you need for overnight."

Alex hesitated. "Maybe I don't want to go."

George sighed. "Nobody's holding a gun to your head." Alex tensed in the silence. George's voice seemed more contrite when he broke it. "It'll beat hanging out in the hotel."

"I'll meet you out front," Alex said.

"Forty-five minutes."

Alex wasn't surprised to see the lawyer pull up in a shiny black convertible. He slid into the leather seat and looked around him.

"Nice. This yours?"

"Yup. One of my concessions to decadence. I love this car."

The vehicle lunged forward as George told him to buckle up. Alex pulled the seatbelt across his chest and tried to relax. The haze of the day before had cleared and the morning was bright, the air smelling more and more of the sea as they sped toward the harbor.

"Ever been sailing?" George asked.

Alex shook his head. "Never." For some reason he didn't like the way George grinned.

The convertible glided through a gate and stopped near a large sign—Shilshole Bay Marina, The Premier Sailing Center of the Northwest. George parked and locked the car. As they made their way Alex scanned the boats. They were lined up at ninety degrees to the docks, sailboats of all sizes, pleasure yachts and even a few houseboats. *They'd be easy pickings for someone who knew what was worth taking. Someone like me.* All of them gleamed in the sun as seagulls wheeled above, their raucous cries punctuating their frenzied search for food.

He followed George onto the dock. As the ramp bobbed in the water two people at the far end turned and waved. Alex's heart rate quickened as Kenni stepped forward to greet them.

"Ready for a day on the sound?" she asked.

"I am," George replied, "but Alex here has never been out." He turned to him with a grin. "We'll have to take it easy on him."

Alex wondered how George would look dripping with the oil-slicked water that lapped below them. He shoved his hands into his pockets.

Kenni smiled. "It's fairly calm today. I'm sure you'll love it, Alex."

He scanned the sleek sailboat bobbing gently at the dock, noticing "The Angel" written in large flowing letters on its side. "Whose boat?"

"Mine." The gray-haired man standing behind her took a step forward. He was dressed in navy and white, looking like he'd just stepped out of a sailing magazine. Alex was once again conscious of his T-shirt, jeans and shaggy hair.

"Alex, this is Drew Adams, my father." She slipped under the man's arm. "This is Alex Donnelly, Dad."

The man's handshake was firm, his blue eyes more startling than his daughter's. "Good to meet you, Alex. Kenni has told me a lot about you."

"Oh?"

Drew winked at Kenni and squeezed her shoulder. "She's the best researcher we've got." He dropped his arm. "But let's stop jawing on the wharf. The day's a-wasting." They moved to board as Drew turned toward the bow. "Cast off for us, will you, George?"

George bent to untie the ropes securing the boat to the dock, then leaped onto the deck as it began to drift away. Drew turned the key and the engine rumbled instantly. He maneuvered the craft out of the harbor, and before Alex realized it they were out in the open, the bow cutting cleanly through the water.

"Alex, over here." Kenni waved him toward her. He moved slowly, joining her just as she took a step down into the hold. She smiled up at him. "Come on in."

Alex peered down the short staircase. He couldn't see anything beyond her, just a dim space. He felt the color drain from his face as he took a step back and shook his head, his fingers massaging the raised white line on his neck.

"I'll stay up here," he said.

Kenni frowned slightly. "Okay. Sure. I'll be right up."

She returned a few minutes later carrying four life jackets and a windbreaker, which she held out to him. "You might find it cool." Alex pulled it on and buckled the life jacket over it, pulling the straps tight. When he was done she smiled at him as she slipped into her own life jacket. "Good. Now if you fall in, we won't lose you."

"I can swim," he countered, wishing he hadn't sounded so defensive.

"Great. But the water's a little cool for swimming, out this far."

She must think I'm a dolt. He watched her move easily along the deck, helping George unwrap and hoist the rigging.

Drew cut the motor and tacked into the wind. "Here we go!" he yelled as the sails filled. "Watch your head, Alex."

The boom swung toward him as the sail billowed out. The boat tilted and Alex grabbed for something to hang onto. Kenni was suddenly by his side again.

"Do you want to sit up front or back here?" She waved at a low bench in the stern.

He chose the stern. Once seated he tried to relax by watching the sails billow and snap. The boat cut the water smoothly, a fine salt spray reaching them now and then. After a while he stopped watching the sails and watched Kenni instead.

She was obviously enjoying herself, a slight smile playing on her lips. She'd pulled her long honey-colored hair into a ponytail, making her look a lot younger than she did at the office. He noticed she had a kind of turned-up nose lightly sprinkled with freckles. Her eyebrows had a reddish tinge, but her eyelashes were long and swept up with a flutter as she lifted her eyes to the sky. He'd watched her for quite a while before she seemed to notice. When she did, the smile spread.

"How do you like it so far?"

Alex shrugged. "Are we going somewhere, or just around in circles?"

"Didn't George tell you? We're heading for my parents' beach house. Only a few miles up the sound, but we probably won't get there 'til late this afternoon if this wind keeps up. Dad likes to take advantage of a day like this."

"So you're the boss' daughter."

"Well, he's one of the bosses, yes."

"And you're following in his footsteps?"

She shook her head. "No. I have no ambition to be a lawyer. I like doing the research though, digging out the details and finding out about the people behind the cases."

"Cases like mine?"

"Yes, but...actually I got roped into your case."

"Oh? How so?"

"George. He hates doing that kind of research. I owed him one." She sat straight. "But...well...I didn't mean that your case wasn't interesting. In fact, I was hooked from the first time I opened the file."

"Why?"

She turned to face him more directly. "Because I could relate. In-between all the facts and figures, the names and addresses, the dates—I could read between the lines. Before long I'd put together the whole picture. And I knew what to expect."

"Really. And am I what you expected?"

She tilted her head slightly, then nodded. "Pretty much."

"And that is...."

"A hard nut with a soft streak. Someone who's been hurt a lot by a lot of people, but still wants to be a decent person, only—maybe he doesn't exactly know how so he hides."

"Got me all figured out, hey?" Alex felt a biting pain as he clenched his jaw.

Kenni's reply was soft, but firm. "Yes. I think I do. You're also claustrophobic. I can guess where that comes from."

Alex snorted. "And how did a girl from the Ivy League get to be so savvy?"

"Because I...." she hesitated. "I've learned to read people and the details of their lives. It's surprising what you can learn from just a bunch of facts and figures."

"Right." Alex's sneer was mocking. "Well, maybe you'd better try reading between the lines some more. I think you lost the thread along the way."

He pushed himself off the bench and strode away. Thinking his stomach might need to flush out the bile he headed for the rail. He was glad for the spray that cooled his face as he took a few gulps of air. *Wish I could get away, off this boat, away from these people. I should never have come to Seattle, never started this. I should've known what it would do to me.* He was staring at the deep green surf below them when he felt a hand on his shoulder and turned to see George grinning at him.

"Feeling a little queasy?"

Alex glanced back at Kenni and caught her watching them. She turned away quickly.

"I'm fine."

"It might help to go below for a bit."

"I said I'm fine." The loud pitch of Alex's voice made Drew turn toward them.

"Okay." George held up his hands, palms out. "Just offering friendly advice. I know what it's like to be seasick." He leaned on the railing. "We'll be heading in closer to shore soon. The chop won't be so bad then."

Alex patted his pockets and muttered a curse. "Don't suppose you'd have a smoke?"

George's eyebrows hunched together. "No, I don't."

Alex gripped the thin railing. They both turned at the sound of Alex's name to see Drew beckoning to him. Alex wanted to ignore him, but knew he had no excuse for being that rude. He left George at the rail and moved toward the older man.

"Would you like to take a turn at the helm?"

"What?"

"Take the wheel." He stepped back, motioning for Alex to take his place. Alex hesitated for another moment, then reached for it. He felt the pull on the rudder instantly and grabbed on with his other hand.

"Just keep her tacked into the wind and hold her steady. She'll do the rest."

Alex planted his feet more firmly. He liked the feel of it, liked the power he felt as the boat surged under him. He suddenly realized he was in control. A wrong move and he could spill them all into the sea. He grinned to himself. *What would Miss Kendra Adams think of me then? Maybe it would be something she'd expect me to do. After all, she'd read between the lines.* He was wondering how much it would take to make this thing flip over when he felt a hand on his shoulder.

"Feels good, doesn't it?" Drew Adams was smiling, but Alex had the feeling he'd read his mind.

Drew looked up at the billowing sails. "Feels like you're in control, like it's all up to you." He dropped his eyes back to Alex's. "But it's all an illusion. Believing we're in control is always an illusion." He turned away, his eyes roaming the sound. "But it's a temptation on a day like this."

Alex kept the boat tacked into the wind, the sails full.

It was hard to avoid Kenni for the rest of the trip, especially when she passed out sandwiches and sodas for lunch. Alex managed not to make eye contact. He wasn't into making idle conversation with George either so he stayed with Drew at the helm, learning how to maneuver the boat until they moored it late in the day below a large boathouse.

The Adams' "beach house" was a sprawling cedar home, its front mostly high windows extending to a steep roof. Alex felt like he was walking onto a movie set. And he was the only prop that didn't fit. As they left the dock he noticed a woman waving from the deck. She came to meet them as they walked through the front door, giving Drew a peck on the cheek and Kenni a hug. She reached out and squeezed George's hand. Kenni didn't make any attempt to introduce him, and Alex noticed Drew waited for her to do so until it was obvious he would have to.

"Alex, this is my wife, Marie."

"So you're the famous Alex Donnelly." Alex thought he heard Kenni groan. Her mother extended her hand and Alex was struck by how different the two women were. In contrast to Kenni's slim figure, Marie was short and well into the stage of middle-aged spread. Her hair was blond, though Alex suspected it wasn't natural. But he was drawn into her warm smile.

"Or maybe infamous," he said in a flat tone.

Marie chuckled. "Well, if we were truthful, we'd all have to admit to a bit of infamy, wouldn't we?"

Alex didn't smile, but met her steady gaze as she chattered on.

"I hope you're hungry. I've been cooking all afternoon. Do you like seafood, Alex? I've made Drew's favorite, Dungeness crab. With a chocolate mousse for dessert. It's fairly light and quite fun to make. And we have some wonderful coffee some friends just brought us from Brazil. Do you drink coffee? I hope so. It'd be a shame not to taste it."

Without waiting for him to answer her questions she turned to her husband. "You don't need to change, do you, dear? It's almost ready. You don't mind an early supper, do you?"

She turned to Alex again. "We don't dress for dinner here, Alex. When we're at the beach we keep things informal. I like it better that way, don't you?" Alex opened his mouth to reply, but she'd already turned to George.

"So how was the day, George? Did Drew let you take the helm?"

"Alex was our pilot for most of the day," George managed to squeeze in. He flashed a look at Alex that made him frown.

Marie's eyebrows shot up. "Ah, you're privileged indeed, Alex. Drew doesn't let just anyone handle the Angel."

"He did a fine job," Drew said.

"Well, you all must be starving. I always get so hungry when I've been out on the water, don't you? Kenni, why don't you show Alex where he can wash up? I've got to get back to the kitchen."

Kenni pointed toward the back of the house without looking at him. "Down that hallway, to your right."

Alex followed the directions without comment.

George was waiting for him when he came out and he wasted no time coming to the point.

"What did you say to Kenni?"

"What?"

"She's in the worst mood I've seen her in for months. What'd you say to her?"

Alex scowled. "Maybe you should ask her what she said to me."

"Kenni's the most considerate, compassionate person I've ever known. So don't—"

Alex snorted. "I thought you said you had no attachment."

George's frown deepened and he lowered his voice a notch as he leaned forward. "We're friends, Alex. Maybe that's a word you don't understand, but I'm warning you...."

Alex's hands clenched into fists. He felt the familiar rage building. Part of him wanted to let go and slam his fist into George's face. Part of him tried to hold back. He forced his fingers to straighten as Marie's voice floated out to them from the other end of the house.

"Dinner, everyone. Come to the table please. Kenni? Find those boys and get them in here. I don't want this to get cold."

They heard Kenni's footsteps approaching.

George stepped around the corner to meet her. "Alex is coming," he told her. Their footsteps faded away.

Alex slumped against the wall, reached for a cigarette, and cursed under his breath when he remembered he didn't have any. He lingered in the hallway until he heard Drew call his name. He pushed himself away from the wall and joined them.

At the table, set with linen and gleaming silverware, Alex again found himself feeling like a cracked mug in a cabinet full of expensive china. The feeling intensified when Drew asked George to say the grace just as Alex picked up his knife and fork. He laid them down, the soft thud clanging in his ears.

George immediately bowed his head. Alex watched as Drew reached for his wife's hand. Then he watched George's face as he prayed.

"Father, we thank you for this day, for safety on the water and for good weather. We thank you for friends and the fellowship we can have together." George was quiet for a moment and Alex thought he was finished until he started up again.

"And, uh, we ask your forgiveness, Father, for…for doing and saying things we know we shouldn't. We thank you most of all for who you are and what you've done for us. Help us to be mindful of you and act according to your will in all things. We ask that you bless this food now, to your use in our bodies. Amen."

George opened his eyes and Alex quickly averted his, but in that second he thought he saw a flash of regret mixed with something else. He wondered what George was thinking. The others echoed the Amen and began passing bowls.

Alex watched them as he ate, his heart rate slowly returning to normal. They laughed and chatted, eating slowly and commenting often on how good it was. *Are these people for real?*

He remembered the table where he ate as a kid. It was cold gray metal and never covered. The plates were mismatched, some of them cracked. It was a table where Wild Bill took huge bites of steak, stuffing his mouth with more before swallowing what was already in it. Alex and the other kids ate freezer-burned hotdogs and over-cooked macaroni. They always knew what food they were not allowed to touch, and God help them if they dared to take what was not designated "foster food."

Alex blocked the memories by listening to the conversation and managed to enjoy the meal—so much so that he couldn't help complimenting Marie on her cooking.

"That's one of the best meals I've ever had, Mrs. Adams."

She beamed. "Thank you, Alex. It's always nice to receive a compliment."

Drew pushed his chair back. "So I suppose it's up to us to clean up your kitchen now?" He winked at Alex. "Marie is the best cook on the West Coast, but she makes the worst mess while she does it."

"Well, since we have a guest I could let you off the hook tonight." Marie smiled at her husband.

Kenni stood and reached for her father's plate. Alex saw her eyes flick toward him, then dart away again. He watched the soft curves of her body sway as she walked away. George picked up his plate and followed her, blocking his view.

"How are you with a tea towel, Alex?" Drew was already heading toward the kitchen.

Alex stood up. "Uh, okay I guess." He hoped he didn't drop anything as he joined the line at the sink. When they were almost done Drew invited him into the living room. Kenni was still putting leftovers away. He noticed George stayed behind.

Drew took a large recliner and waved Alex on to the long sofa. Alex sat on the edge for a moment, then tried to relax and pushed his body back into the soft cushions. He buried his hands in his armpits. They felt too thick, too rough and stiff to be exposed. He stretched out his legs, then pulled them in again. His feet seemed too big, his shoes too scarred and faded. He let his shoulders hunch forward and tried not to make contact with Drew's piercing blue eyes.

"So what are your plans, Alex, if you don't mind my asking?"

He shrugged. "I don't really have any yet."

"In a few days you'll have some huge decisions to make."

"Maybe."

"You still think this is all a mistake?"

Alex looked up. "I find it more than a little hard to believe, yes."

"I suppose I can understand that."

"Can you?"

Drew lifted his chin. "I wasn't always a wealthy man."

Find that hard to believe too.

"Mind if I offer a little advice?"

Alex shrugged again. "Sure."

"Get yourself a good financial advisor. I can recommend a couple. You'll want to start thinking about investments or charitable donations. I can recommend a few good organizations that use their money wisely and well."

Alex sighed and slumped back. "Maybe I'll just give it all away and be done with it."

Drew chuckled. "Well, that would make your life a lot simpler, I suppose, but wealth can be a great advantage. You could do a lot of good, bless a lot of people."

When Alex didn't respond Drew leaned forward. "Can I pray for you, Alex?"

The question so startled him that Alex just stared.

Drew smiled. "It's been my experience that prayer helps a lot when it comes to making decisions, whether they're about money or careers or just life in general. Praying about it can make all the difference."

"You sort of have to believe in a god first, don't you?"

The older man chuckled again. "That does help."

"I only believe in what I can see."

"Oh? But you believed in something unseen today."

"What do you mean?"

"The wind. We couldn't see it, but we believed it was there."

Alex smirked. He'd heard this line before—from Pastor T. "Because of the evidence. The sails were full."

"Exactly. There's all kinds of evidence that God is here."

"Maybe for you. I haven't seen any."

"Maybe you just aren't looking at things the right way."

Alex felt a pain knotting between his shoulder blades, but decided to play along. "For instance?"

Drew waved his hand toward the windows. "What do you see?"

Puget Sound lay calm and gleaming in the late day sun. Small waves rippled up onto the shore below them. Alex could hear their sighing between the cries of high-wheeling gulls.

"Water and birds," he answered.

The chuckle came again and Alex turned back with a glare, thinking the man was mocking him. But Drew was smiling in a way that made Alex's anger seep away.

"It's an ocean teaming with life, Alex. Fish of all kinds and colors, fish that aren't fish at all, but mammals—mammals that communicate and live communally. Organisms so small and so complex scientists are still puzzled by them after years of study. And plant life just as diverse. Do you think it all just happened?"

Alex shrugged. "I never really thought about it."

"And take your coming here to Seattle. I believe He led you to us and us to you."

"I thought that was Kenni's good research."

"Kenni lost your trail at one point. Completely. When you went to the Yukon you almost disappeared off the map. You don't use a credit card much, do you?"

Alex shook his head. "I prefer cash."

"Why did you suddenly use one two months ago?"

"Two months ago? I didn't—" Alex stopped. "Oh, yeah. Dog food."

"Dog food?"

"My supplier said he'd give me a real good deal if I bought a huge order. I figured I could sell some at a profit back in Dawson so I went for it. I had to use the card. What's that got to do with it?"

"Do you realize that's the first credit card purchase you made since moving to the Yukon?"

"So?"

"Interesting that you did it just when Kenni had lost your trail. That purchase led her right to you."

"Coincidence," he said, but cursed himself for using the plastic. He should never even have gotten one. He swallowed to try and settle the churning in his gut. He needed a smoke.

Drew shook his head. "I don't think so. And I don't think it's a coincidence that it was Kenni who was assigned to track you down."

"What do you mean?"

Before he could answer, George walked into the room and the conversation was diverted. Within minutes they were discussing a case George had just been assigned, and became so engrossed in it that Alex slipped away and walked out onto the deck. He stared out at the sound again, the huge expanse of water turning gold under the setting sun.

There was something good in the way Drew talked about it. Something...what was it? Respect. Awe. Passion. Alex sighed. He'd never felt that way about anything. He'd never allowed himself to. He was trying not to analyze why when he heard a sound behind him. He turned to find Kenni standing in the doorway. He dropped his eyes briefly, then leveled them to meet hers.

Her words tumbled out as though afraid that if she hesitated, she wouldn't say them. "Alex, I want to apologize. I've felt rotten all day." She took a few steps toward him. "I had no right to say I had you all figured out. It was arrogant. I barely know you. It's just that—"

"You were right," Alex interrupted her.

She looked up at him. "Pardon?"

"You nailed me to the wall. Guess that's what made me so mad." Alex dropped his eyes. "Or you could chalk it up to lack of nicotine."

Kenni's eyes smiled. "Well, maybe if I'd had a bit more tact...."

Alex shrugged. "You might've noticed tact isn't exactly my strong suit either."

The smile moved from her eyes to her lips and she put out her hand. "Friends?"

Alex shook her hand briefly, then frowned and looked away. "George just accused me of not knowing what that word means."

Kenni frowned. "George is a little...um...overprotective."

"Maybe he's right."

"Don't be so hard on yourself."

When he glanced sideways at her he was surprised to see tears brimming at the corners of her eyes. He wondered what she'd do if he kissed her, and maybe he would've found out if George hadn't walked out onto the deck right then. *The man sure has great timing.* He took a step away from Kenni. George's eyes flashed from one to the other, then focused on Kenni.

"You okay?"

Kenni nodded as she blinked the tears out of her eyes.

George peered into her face. "You sure?"

"Yes. Yes, I'm fine. I was just apologizing to Alex for something I said earlier."

"Oh."

Alex couldn't help looking smug. George ignored him.

"Your mom wants us all to come in for coffee."

Kenni chuckled. "Ah, yes, the special Brazilian roast."

Alex tried to focus on the coffee and dessert as his hosts chatted and laughed, but his eyes kept wandering back to Kenni. They were fixed on her when George asked about going to church. Alex almost dropped his fork.

"The service is at 10:00," Marie said, "so we can all go for lunch afterward before you young people head back to the city."

"Why don't you stay for a bit, Kenni?" Drew suggested. "George can take your car in and you can ride back with me. You've been working a lot of overtime. I think you deserve a break."

Kenni grinned at her father. "You don't have to tell me twice."

"Wonderful, dear," Marie said.

"You're welcome to stay too Alex, if you like." Drew drained his coffee cup. "I don't know if it's more comfortable than the hotel, but," he winked at his wife, "I'm sure the food is better."

"Uh...well I...." Alex was flustered. He hadn't expected this.

Marie jumped in. "Oh yes, stay, Alex. We'd like the company. Wouldn't we, dear?"

Drew nodded. "Wouldn't mind another man around. We can take the Angel out again or maybe do some fishing. You like to fish?"

He nodded. "Yes, but—"

Marie burst in again. "Oh good. I hate it. Hate to see the poor things pulled from the water. That will get me off the hook." She chuckled. "No pun intended. Then I can stay home and be ready to cook when you get back."

"I can guarantee a good catch, Alex," Drew added.

Alex saw George flash a look at Kenni, then at Drew. "Maybe Alex would rather see more of the city," he said.

Alex shook his head. "I've had enough of the city."

Drew stood up. "Good. Then it's settled. We'll drive back on Tuesday."

Alex couldn't help but gloat when George refused Marie's invitation for him to stay.

"I have a new case to get going on," he said in a chagrined voice. "Thanks for the invitation, but I should head back tomorrow afternoon."

"Well, you know you're always welcome, George," Marie effused. "Anytime at all."

George said, "Thanks," and gave Alex a look that made his fists clench.

Chapter Six

Inspector Sorensen towered over the young policeman and frowned. "You like digging, Rookie?"

"Depends on what for."

"How about a snake in the grass?"

"The officer grinned. "My favorite. What are we looking for?"

"Similar M.O." Sorensen handed him the slim file. "This is a cold case—five years ago. It keeps giving me indigestion. I want it solved before my retirement hits. See what you can find."

The rookie nodded. "Will do."

Sorensen returned to his desk and pinned the enlarged photo to the bulletin board behind it. Then he took a thick red marker and drew a bull's eye over Alex Donnelly's face.

○ ○ ○

Alex woke early and walked the beach to rid himself of the surreal shadow that always dogged him after another nightmare. He'd dreamed about the red-eyed snake again. This time it was coiled under the stairs in the cellar. He shivered and tried to distract himself by looking out at the bay. He shoved his left hand into his pants pocket to keep it from moving to his neck. "That was then," he whispered. "Stay in today." A low sun hid behind a smudge of cloud. Alex thought it looked like a huge thumb had tried to blot it out. Not bothering to roll up his pants he waded into the light surf, sucking in his breath as the cold lapped at his legs.

He breathed in the smell of the sea, the rich abundance of it, the smell of life breaking down and life coming into its own. He'd grown up near the sea, but had hardly noticed it. There was so much he'd blocked, so much he hadn't let touch him. He thought again about what Drew had said. *Could it all be just an accident? Was I an accident? Or was there more, something I'm missing?* He kicked at the waves. It seemed like there were always pieces missing. Glancing up at the Adams' house a burning resentment turned his empty stomach to bile. He turned away and spat into the water. *What am I doing here with these people? I should leave now, just disappear. He squatted and watched the lapping water. But in a few more days maybe I'll know....Know what? Answers?* He scoffed at himself. He wasn't even sure what the questions should be.

He lingered on the beach until his stomach started to growl, then jogged back to the house, slipping in quietly. He assumed everyone would still be asleep, but he found Kenni on the deck, alone. She had a small book in her lap and another larger one open on the table, a coffee cup beside it. He watched her for a while. She wrote something in the book on her knee, then closed it and shut her eyes. She lifted her face and her lips moved slightly. Alex backed up when he realized she was praying. Then he moved forward again when he saw her smile, almost like she was dreaming. She sat completely still as though listening.

Alex suddenly felt her goodness in a way that stunned him, recognizing it was what he'd been searching for, longing for—that something good he'd heard in her father's voice, the goodness in her eyes that made him want to move close to her and made him want to run at the same time. And as he recognized it he knew it was not a goodness that was her own, but something that had come to her and her father. He knew it had never, would never come to him. The longing rose up in him and as he felt it, the rage returned.

Kenni stirred and drew the other book onto her lap. Alex took another step backward, his heel brushing the leg of a chair. It scraped on the tile floor. Kenni looked up and smiled.

"'Morning, Alex."

He swallowed his emotions and stepped through the doorway. "You're up early."

"I love the morning, especially here. It's so quiet, peaceful."

"What are you reading?"

"Psalm 103."

"Oh."

The smile faded as she looked down at the Bible.

Alex suddenly wanted to please her. "So—what does it say?" he asked.

"That we should never forget to praise the Lord for all the good things He's done for us, because...." She smoothed the page with her hand. "Can I read it to you?"

He shrugged. She read. "He ransoms me from death and surrounds me with love and tender mercies. He fills my life with good things. My youth is renewed like the eagle's! The Lord gives righteousness and justice to all who are treated unfairly. Psalm 103, verses 1 to 6." She let the book rest on her lap and looked up. "This is my mom's Bible. A different translation than I usually read, the New Living Translation, but I kind of like it."

"Do you believe what it says?"

Kenni sighed. "Most of the time, though I admit there are times when it isn't easy."

"You've seen...what's it say? Righteousness and justice?" He fought to keep the anger out of his voice, but couldn't hide the cynicism.

Kenni's voice dropped to almost a whisper. "Not always. But I try to hang onto the hope that I'll see it, someday."

"Ah," Alex mocked. "In some pie in the sky heaven."

Kenni flipped the Bible closed and stood up. "No, Alex. Here. Now." Her eyes flashed. "You think you've got something better, then tell me about it."

Alex grinned at her. "Pushing some buttons, am I?"

Kenni turned toward the door. Alex moved quickly to block her way. He saw the pink tone pushing up her neck as she glanced at the opening. She'd have to squeeze by him to get through. She took a step back and opened her mouth to say something, then closed it again. He could see she was struggling for control. She took a deep breath, then dropped her eyes. When they flashed up again Alex stopped breathing. "Please move," she said.

He stepped back to the railing. For a second he'd seen something in her eyes, something that sparked his own desires. But when she turned toward him again he saw something there that bordered on sorrow. He didn't need anyone feeling sorry for him. He wanted to yell at her. And he wanted to kiss her. He knew he should apologize, but couldn't make himself say the words. He glanced at the Bible. "If you need to believe in something, I guess that's as good as anything."

Kenni held the book up. "When I read this...." She hesitated. "It's taken me a while, but I'm finally beginning to understand what real peace is like."

Alex turned his back to her, planted his elbows on the railing, and looked out. The sound was a flat gray slate, barely a whisper of breeze disturbing its surface. He was aware of the contrast as his stomach twisted into a knot. *Peace.* Another word he didn't know the meaning of. *Maybe it's just for people whose parents have beach houses and yachts.*

"It can give you peace too, Alex. God can give you peace." Kenni's soft voice pulled at him like the turning of a strong tide. He didn't dare look at her.

"And what does this god want in return? That I live like a monk?"

Kenni shook her head. "He just wants you, a relationship with you."

"A relationship." He turned to face her, feeling the rail on his back. "How can you have a relationship with something you can't even see?"

Kenni smiled. "I know it seems strange, and it's definitely a mystery, but it happens."

Alex wanted to pull his eyes away from hers, but he was riveted. The longing surged up in him and he was afraid he was going to moan out loud. When he spoke he barely trusted himself enough to mouth the one word.

"How?"

"Just admit you need Him. Admit you can't make life work on your own. Believe me, Alex, if there's one thing I know it's that you can't make life work well without Jesus."

"So...what do you do to make *your* life work?"

"Admit I've made a mess of it on my own and invite Him to take over."

"Take over? That sounds a bit drastic."

"What I mean is I stop trying to control everything. I try and let God be in control."

Alex frowned. "Like some kind of puppet master?"

"No." Kenni gave an emphatic shake of her head. "It's not like that at all. It's...." She exhaled slowly. "It's really hard to explain." She moved closer to him. "It's all about trust."

Alex turned away from her clear eyes and shoved the longing

back deep inside before it overwhelmed him. His voice took on a hard edge again. "Trust doesn't come easy," he said.

"I know," Kenni replied softly. "I read between the lines, remember?"

Alex stared out at the sound. A breeze had sprung up, building into wind that would soon lift the water into foaming whitecaps. A flock of gulls wheeled and screeched, then plunged toward the surf.

"Right," he said. "You know all about me." He turned back to face her. "And I bet I can tell your life story in a nutshell."

"Oh? So now you've got *me* all figured out?"

"What's to figure?" Alex smirked, but something inside him cringed as the words came out. "Rich daddy, all the toys and all the boys."

For a moment he thought she might slap him. Instead she clutched her book, turned, and walked away.

○ ○ ○

Once out of sight Kenni fled to her bedroom and closed the door. She felt like throwing something—something aimed at Alex Donnelly's head. She tossed the Bible onto her bed. *How dare he mock me like that?* She clenched her jaw and paced to the window and back again. *Be angry, but don't sin. Be angry, but don't sin.* She repeated the words to herself as she paced and tried to reason with herself. *He's a total stranger. Why am I letting him upset me like this? Why did I even invite him here? Because....* She stopped in the middle of the room as the thought came. *Because God told me to.*

She paced back to the other side of the room and stared into the large mirror on the wall. *Okay,* she prayed. *You want me to be involved in this man's life, but you know how dangerous that is for me. You know my need to be needed and how that can mess things up. I see the pain in him and it makes me want to hold onto him and then he makes me want to smack him.*

She groaned and plopped down on the edge of her bed. Maybe this wasn't God. Maybe it was just her. She closed her eyes and prayed again. *God, I'm going to need your help with this. I'm scared. I don't need another emotional roller coaster.* She picked up her Bible again. **Stay close to me.** She took a deep breath and nodded. "Okay," she whispered.

○ ○ ○

At breakfast Marie passed Alex a plate of toast and homemade peach preserves as she asked, "Would you like to come to church with us, Alex?"

Alex jerked his head up, but she didn't seem to notice as she kept talking.

"The music is very contemporary and the sermons usually aren't long, and they're quite good. Pastor Eckelston always makes you think, doesn't he, dear?"

Drew nodded. "He does have a way of making you do that, alright. I think you'd find it stimulating, Alex."

Alex glanced at Kenni, but she kept her eyes on her coffee cup. He turned to Marie and made his decision. "Well, uh...I don't have a suit or anything so...I think I'll just hang out here, if that's okay."

"Oh, you don't need a suit. This is just a small country church. No one dresses up, do they, dear? You can come as you are, Alex. And don't be afraid of being the only stranger there. There are always new people attending at this time..." Alex caught the look Drew gave her as she hesitated, then finished her sentence "...of year." She blinked and stammered a bit. "But...but of course there's no pressure at all. We can zip back and pick you up for lunch, if you just want to stay here. No pressure at all."

Alex glanced at Kenni again and this time her eyes were focused on him. He could hardly bear the hope that was in them. He turned away and shook his head. "You don't have to come back for me. I'll be fine."

"Oh, of course we will. No trouble at all. But it might be as late as 1:00." She glanced at her watch. "Oh goodness, I'd better go and get ready. Kenni, will you clear the table please?"

"Sure, mom." Her voice was low. Alex noticed her shoulders had slumped a bit. He watched her gather the plates. Then George stood, reached for the platter of left-over toast, and followed her into the kitchen. Alex thought he looked a bit too smug. *How bad could it be?* He turned to Drew.

"Uh, maybe I'll come along after all. Then you won't have to double back to get me."

"Whatever you like, Alex, but we really don't mind coming back for you."

"No, it's okay. Who knows, maybe something will rub off."

Drew chuckled. "You never know."

As he turned away Alex heard him add in a much softer voice, "What the Lord might do."

Chapter Seven

Night had fallen by the time Gil reached his cabin. He stood on a small rise of land and studied it. A sliver of moonlight gave it an other-worldly look. *You could paint a picture of it, "The Log Cabin in the Wilderness." But there should be smoke rising from the chimney and light in the windows, maybe even a face peering from one.* Gil sighed and tromped toward it, his head down. *The reality looks too harsh, too cold, too lonely.*

At least the trap line was laid out and ready to go. Maybe he'd be able to make some money at it this year, if he could figure out a way to sell the furs without attracting too much attention.

He was about to go through the door when he heard a strange sound. It was almost like a whisper, but with an electric crackle to it. He looked up. The sky was shifting with color. Gil turned and lifted his head to watch as streaks of blue, red, and purple light slashed across the heavens. He pulled his toque off to hear the sighing sizzle more clearly. Aurora borealis—the northern lights. He'd seen them many times since coming north, and they never ceased to make him stand in awe.

As he watched the play of light he couldn't help but think that someone was trying to get his attention. *So that men are without excuse.* The line from Romans 1:20 came unbidden, unwanted. A surge of violet suddenly twisted, wavered, and dove straight down toward him. He almost ducked. Then he turned back to the cabin. "Good try, Lord," he mumbled as he opened the door and closed it behind him.

○ ○ ○

The church looked like a picture postcard—small, white, and rectangular with a high steeple and narrow stained glass windows. But as they pulled into the parking lot Alex noticed there was an addition on the back that extended to one side, forming an L where it joined the old building. People were filing in through the two high front doors, shaking hands with a middle-aged couple as they moved into the sanctuary.

Alex stepped into the pew between Kenni and George, hoping he could follow their cues for sitting and standing throughout the service. The last time he'd been to a church service it was a funeral for a high school classmate. He'd felt like a yo-yo that day, jumping up and down every other minute. The service had been long and full of strange words and somber music.

He peered at the people gathering around him. They were all ages, but a surprising number of them were young. Some had small kids with them. There seemed to be a fair number of teenagers. *Guess that accounts for the keyboard and drums.* He was surprised to see them at the front, and even more surprised when a young man stood up and played a loud jazzy rendition of "Amazing Grace" on the trumpet. *Kenni's mother was right about the music.*

Another young man went forward to welcome the crowd and read a few announcements. Then six people leaped to the front and took up their instruments. Alex found himself enjoying the music for the first while, though the tunes and words were unfamiliar. Then the tone changed. Here and there people started to raise their hands in the air. Alex squirmed. As the chorus of the last song began the musicians stopped playing and the people sang without accompaniment. Most of them had their eyes closed. Alex glanced sideways at Kenni. Her eyes were closed too, her hands extended in front of her, palms up. He had the same feeling watching her on the deck the day before. He closed his eyes, not in worship, but with the ache of that strange longing as the sound of voices rose and fell in harmonies, reaching out to him from all sides. Suddenly, he realized his face was wet with his own tears. He wiped them away quickly. He wanted to get out, to run from this place and away from these people. But George was standing beside him blocking his way and to leave would only call attention to himself.

The song ended and a hush fell. Alex gripped the rounded top of the pew in front of him and gritted his teeth. It was all he could do to keep from moaning out loud. The guitarist who had led most of the singing finally broke the silence. His voice was clear and strong, but soft. "Lord, we worship you alone. We ask that you open our ears, our hearts, and our minds as Pastor Jim speaks. We ask that you speak to us through him as he yields to your Holy Spirit. Amen."

Everyone sat without being told. Pastor Jim Eckelston moved to the small wooden pulpit, placed the pages of his sermon on the stand, and then smiled at the congregation. "Good morning," he said.

Alex was surprised at the resounding response. The pastor's grin widened. "Ah, everyone's awake this morning. Good! I hope you can stay that way for the next half hour or so."

The collective chuckle took Alex by surprise again. This church was not at all like the last one he'd been in. He tried to relax.

Pastor Jim took a sip of water from a glass on the podium and began. "This morning I'm going to vary from the series we've been doing in Ephesians. I began preparing a message on the next passage in Chapter 5, but for some reason it seemed the Lord didn't want me to preach that message today. That's always a bit scary for a preacher, especially one like me who likes to know where he's going from week to week. But I've learned not to fight it when I feel that kind of block in my spirit. The last part of this week hasn't been exactly easy as I've tried to figure out what God *did* want me to say to you this morning. Sometimes He can seem a million miles away, can't He? Have you ever felt that way?"

Alex saw heads nod here and there.

"Sometimes that's our own fault. Our sin blocks our ears and our hearts, especially when we stubbornly refuse to let go. But God is never far away, even when He seems distant. He's always standing right beside us." The pastor paused. "It took me a long time to realize that. I was what someone once called a 'hard nut.'" Alex glanced at Kenni, remembering the words she'd used on the boat the day before. She smiled slightly, but didn't turn toward him. The pastor continued.

"It took a violent death to wake me up to the fact that Jesus was there, waiting for me to open the door. When I look back now I realize there were a lot of times when He invited me to open it, but I refused. I was too scared. I believed that if I invited Jesus into my life, He'd laugh and walk away, or more likely smack me in the head and walk away. I thought God would reject me because I wasn't good enough to be loved by Him, or by anyone. And I didn't want to risk that rejection because if God rejected me, who was left?" The young man took another sip of water.

Alex was close enough to see small beads of perspiration rising on his lip. *He's scared now.* Alex leaned forward.

"Most of you know that I was raised in a religious home, a home where God was mentioned a fair bit. I was sent to a private school that had the best reputation. All kinds of good things were supposed to happen there. But when I look back on that time now all the memories are colored by one event. It's a dark thing that makes everything else seem just as black." Pastor Jim took another sip of water. "I know some of you don't want to hear what I'm about to say. Some of you will think this isn't the time or place, but all I can say is God wouldn't let me say anything else today, and believe me we had a battle over this one. Even now, right now, I'm not sure I can do this. In fact, on my own, I know I can't so I think we'd better pray."

The pastor pulled a handkerchief from his pocket and wiped the perspiration from his face, then closed his eyes and prayed. It was a short prayer, a simple prayer, asking for God's help. He stuffed the handkerchief back in his pocket and gripped the sides of the pulpit with both hands. Then he lifted his pale face to the congregation.

"I was ten years old when it happened. I was on the swim team at school. We had three coaches, all of them respected teachers and spiritual leaders in the community. One of those men was what is called today a 'pedophile.'"

Alex put a hand over the scar on his neck. It felt like it was burning.

"Not many people used that word back then. As a little boy I probably couldn't have pronounced it. But I learned what it meant. I experienced what it meant. That man sexually abused me and…." He stopped and took another deep breath. "And terrorized me for six years."

Alex released the breath he was holding, slowly, watching the man's face, feeling as though every word were stabbing him. His heart raced. He could feel his pulse pounding in his temples and his stomach trying to disgorge what churned inside it.

He wanted to run, but something kept him rooted in his seat.

Pastor Jim swallowed another gulp of water. "Those years were difficult for me and my family. I was so full of rage I acted out in every way imaginable. No one understood. No one could, because no one knew. I started doing drugs and got into trouble with the law. Small things at first, vandalism, petty theft. Then one night one week after my sixteenth birthday my best friend, Dylan, picked me up and told me to open the glove compartment of his car. I'll never forget the feeling I had when I saw what was inside it. The gun felt so good in my hand." He held his hand out, turning it, pointing the imaginary weapon. "So powerful. It made me feel invincible. Dylan had everything figured out. We'd rob a liquor store and take off, just the two of us, across the country."

Jim took another deep breath. "We had a big argument about who would carry the gun. He won. I've often wondered what would've happened that night if it had been me. Maybe I would've been the one who ended up with three bullets in my back." Another gulp of water and he continued. "Dylan didn't die instantly. He crawled toward me, writhing in pain. I had nightmares about that for months, and every time I did I'd wake up in a cold sweat and realize it could've been me. Sometimes I wished it had been.

But I ended up in a courtroom. I expected to go to jail, but somehow I was put in the custody of my father's brother, my Uncle Pete. I don't know what happened exactly. Maybe the judge thought Uncle Pete could straighten me out because he was a military man, a Marine, for most of his life."

A small smile appeared on the pastor's face. "Living with him was a lot like boot camp for the first while, but Uncle Pete was also a deeply spiritual man and one of his gifts was discernment. It took him six months, but eventually he got me to trust him enough to tell him everything about the abuse. Then he led me to a point where I was willing to trust God again. Then he led me toward the extremely painful process of forgiveness.

I'm still going through that. There are still times when the memories overwhelm me and the rage boils up. It's like a volcano, always simmering under the surface. But I'm learning to take every thought captive, as the Scripture says, to resist the anger and turn away from the fear. It takes more energy and effort than I can generate sometimes, but when I feel like I just can't do it the Lord is there. It's like I'm drowning and then...." Alex followed the man's hand as he extended it out into the air. "Then He reaches down into the water and grabs my hand."

The pastor turned his head slightly and seemed to look right into

Alex's eyes. "I can't tell you what it's like to feel that freedom, to be free of the rage and pain and guilt. It feels like flying, like I'm weightless, but full of energy. It feels like anything is possible." His focus shifted and his face lit up in a smile. "And that's what I want to tell you today. That's what I believe God wants to tell you. With God anything is possible." He was beaming now. "Even getting up in front of your church and talking about something that makes your knees knock like castanets."

He picked up the notes he'd left on the podium, notes he'd never looked at, and nodded to the band leader. "As the worship team comes up there's only one more thing I'd like to say. If there is anyone here who believes like I did that God could never accept you, I want to say you're right. He can't accept someone who refuses to accept the forgiveness Jesus offers. But He's waiting to accept everyone who does receive that forgiveness. It's a forgiveness that has no strings attached. He wrote the contract in His own blood and He'll never take it back. All you have to do is say 'yes.' If you want to know more, come and talk to me." The man's face beamed with a boyish grin again. "I'm easy to find. Just follow the sound of the knocking knees." He raised his hand. "Will you stand with me as we pray?"

Alex remained seated, his elbows on his knees and his head hanging in his hands, as the congregation rose to its feet. He felt as though the people were crushing him. He didn't hear the prayer or the closing song at the end of the service. There was just a rushing noise in his head. He couldn't breathe. When George stepped into the aisle opening a space between them Alex leaped to his feet, pushed by him and through the people to a side door. Panting for breath as he burst into the sunshine he emptied his stomach onto the grass, then slumped against the building and waited for his heart to stop thumping.

He was almost back to normal when Drew found him.

"Alex? Are you alright?"

Alex stared at him. Accusations whirled in his head. *Had Drew done this or was it Kenni?*

George rounded the corner of the building just as Alex was about to demand answers.

"Everything okay?" George asked.

Alex dropped his eyes, straightened and nodded. "Yeah. Just got a bit light-headed in there."

Drew studied his face. "Light-headed?"

"Yeah. I...I'm a bit claustrophobic." Avoiding the men's eyes he pushed himself away from the wall of the church. "Just needed some air."

"You're sure? We can head home...."

"I'm fine." Alex realized he'd raised his voice. He lowered it and added, "No need to change the plan."

They found the others waiting by the car. Kenni glanced his way, but Alex continued to avoid eye contact. No one said anything about his hasty exit. As they climbed into the car Alex glanced back at the church. Pastor Jim was standing on the steps, looking in their direction. Alex hesitated, then ducked his head and got in.

He spoke only when he had to during the lunch and was glad when it was finally over. They were all quiet on the ride back to the house. Alex was afraid to speak, afraid his rage would rip out of him. He'd been betrayed before, but this made his blood boil. They'd exposed him, put him on display to a man who then tried to use the information to manipulate him. He stared out the car window and concentrated on keeping his breathing even, his heart rate normal. He barely succeeded. *How dare she talk about trust?*

Chapter Eight

Drew spoke a soft word to his wife, then headed directly to his office, closing the door behind him. He went to the window, the urgency of what he knew he had to do filling his mind. He got down on his knees and swayed as the prayers surfaced. He'd prayed this way before, but never with such a sense of need. His lips moved as the words came, words of petition and intercession for a young man he barely knew, and a young woman he called his daughter.

○ ○ ○

Alex watched from the deck as Kenni said goodbye to George. They talked for what seemed to Alex like a long time. He tried to read their body language, wishing he could hear what they were saying. *Are they talking about me? Is she telling George the details of my life? How could she know them? No one knew. She must've guessed.*

The depth of that discernment stunned him.

George leaned toward Kenni. *Is he warning her away from me?* Alex's jaw clenched as he watched the young lawyer climb into Kenni's car and speed away. Kenni watched it go too, then slowly turned back to the house. Alex gripped the railing and tried to get his anger under control.

Deciding he needed to move he headed down to the beach. He kicked off his shoes and strode away from the house. He'd only gone a few strides when he started to run. It didn't take long to reach the far end of the beach. Stopping to bend over and let his hands rest on his knees to catch his breath he saw a cigarette butt. It was on dry sand, and looked like it had just been dropped. Almost half of it was still usable. He picked it up, wondering if someone in the Adams' house had a secret. He sniffed it. It smelled fresh. He sniffed it again and his hand shook a bit. Fishing a lighter out of his pocket he lit the butt and inhaled deep and slow. Then he strolled back down the beach toward the house.

Walking out onto the dock he peered out at the water, then up at the house. The cigarette smoldered between his fingers. *I could clean them out before I disappear. Yeah. That'd be sweet justice.* He was about to turn away when the boathouse doors swung open and Kenni poled a sleek speedboat out and tied it to the dock. She startled when she saw him, but recovered quickly.

"Hi," she said.

He narrowed his eyes and flicked the stub of the cigarette into the water. "Going somewhere?"

She shielded her eyes. "Uh…yes, just for a ride…uh…want to come?"

Several disturbing thoughts rolled around in his head. He shrugged with feigned indifference. "Why not?" he said just as she was about to speak again. "Where to?"

"Um…well, we could just go up the shoreline a bit, I guess.…" Her face was pink and her eyes didn't meet his. She stepped lightly to the back and waved him on board, tossing him a life jacket. "Buckle up."

He threw it into the boat and stepped in after it. "I don't need it," he said, sat down, and turned away from her.

The boat roared away from the dock, its bow leaping high, then leveling off as it planed through the water and gathered speed. Kenni's long hair streamed in the wind. Once the boat was level she glanced at Alex over her shoulder. He turned away. She reached for the key and flicked it to the off position. The motor cut out, throwing Alex forward as the boat wobbled violently and tossed in its own wake. He grabbed the gunnel.

"What are you trying to do, drown us?" he yelled.

Kenni whirled the seat around and stood up, her legs spread apart for balance as the boat settled, her hands on her hips. "I might do just that if you don't tell me what your problem is!" she retorted.

"My problem! What about yours?"

"Mine?"

"Yeah, yours. You called that preacher, didn't you?"

Kenni's jaw dropped. "What?"

"Come on, Kenni. Admit it. You set me up."

"I didn't! I hardly know the man! Even if I did, I'd never tell a pastor what to preach! I had no idea what he was going to say this morning!"

Alex stared. "Swear to me you didn't call him."

"I did no such thing!"

He frowned. "Then how...?" he stopped short. "He kept looking at me, like—it was like he was talking only to me."

Kenni sat down in the pilot's chair. Her voice dropped back to normal. "That's what happens when someone speaks from his heart. God uses the words to touch others."

"To hurt others, you mean." The words were too soft for Kenni to hear.

She dropped her eyes. Alex turned away as she turned back to the wheel, flicked the key, and eased the boat forward again. She glanced over shoulder. "Apology accepted!" she yelled over the motor.

Alex hesitated. *Was I wrong?* "Okay. I apologize." He cursed under his breath. If he were wrong, then he'd just told her what he wanted no one to know. He clenched his teeth and wished he had another cigarette.

Kenni responded by gunning the motor. The boat leaped forward again. Alex slumped low, staring at the streak of silver water flashing below them. He didn't look up until he felt the boat decelerate and settle deep again. Kenni aimed the boat directly at the broad beach spread before them and beached it expertly with just enough speed. They leaped out, their feet sinking into smooth round stones.

As they ambled in silence Kenni kept stealing glances at him. He ignored her, watching the small shore birds skittering away from them, until she finally peered right at him. "You believe me, don't you? I really didn't tell Pastor Jim anything, Alex. Even if I'd known—any-thing—I wouldn't do that to anyone."

"I thought...." He stared at his feet. "I thought you really were good at reading between the lines."

She stopped and reached out a hand toward his arm, but drew it back without touching him. "I've only been guessing at what your life was like. I really don't know much more than dates and a few facts."

He cocked his head to one side. "You think George did it? Or your father?"

Kenni shook her head. "No. I think it was a God thing."

Alex frowned. "What? You think God...." Alex felt the color drain from his face. He clenched his jaw and reached for the scar on his neck.

Kenni's voice was soft. She didn't look at him. "God just told him to tell his own story." She started walking again and dropped her voice even lower. "Sounds like it's pretty close to yours."

Alex kept in step. "Close enough," he mumbled.

It was a while before Kenni responded. "Have you ever talked to anyone about it?"

"No."

"Maybe...I can give you Pastor Jim's number, or my dad would...."

"No." Alex sighed. "Digging it up just....No." He shook his head hard. "I don't want to talk about it."

They walked in silence again, the waves lapping at the stones just beyond their feet. Then Kenni stooped down and picked up a few pebbles. "My mom and dad brought me here for a picnic to tell me the adoption had been finalized. It's been my favorite place ever since."

Alex stopped and stared at her. "Adoption?"

She nodded. "I was twelve."

As she bent to pick up another stone Alex thought of the way he'd taunted her about being a little rich kid. He watched her turn a stone over in her hand.

"I love walking here, just looking at these stones. It amazes me how every one is so different." She held her hand out and showed him a flat oval one. "Some are great for skipping." She positioned the stone in her hand, winged it sideways out over the water, and counted the number of times it skipped over the surface until it sank.

Alex picked up another and copied her. His stone skipped twice more than hers. "Aha." Kenni grinned. "A challenge. Watch this one." She let another one fly. Alex was already searching for another. They continued until Kenni called a halt, laughing as she held her aching arm. "Okay, okay, I concede. You win."

Alex grinned and let the last stone fly. It skipped twice, then hit a small wave and sank with a plunk. Kenni laughed.

"Not a great finale," Alex said, "but I accept the victory."

Kenni turned away and strode quickly toward the steep cliffs soaring above them. She climbed onto a huge driftwood log and sat down.

Alex peered up at her. "You were adopted when you were twelve?" He let his curiosity show.

She nodded. "My father was...he died when I was a baby and my mother not long after. I was put into foster care when I was four."

"You were fostered?" Alex couldn't hide his surprise.

She nodded. "We have a lot more in common than you might think."

Alex leaned his back against the log, peering out at the incessant movement of water. He was going to say that he doubted she'd had anything like the experience he'd had, but kept silent, then pushed himself away from the log and wandered away from her. It wasn't long before he heard the pebbles grinding together as she caught up to him. He wondered if she'd tell him more, but he held his questions back. He had no right to ask.

"I used to spend hours here," Kenni said quietly. "It was almost an obsession for a while. I kept searching for the perfect stone." She turned a pebble over in her hand. "One that would fit my hand exactly, like it was cut from it. Every now and then I'd find one that came close and I'd take it home." She smiled. "I still have a jar of them at the house. But I never found the perfect fit and that always depressed me. It was kind of like my life. I kept searching for something that fit, that I could hold onto, something that would satisfy. Nothing—no one—ever did. I was always alone, always the one on the outside."

She stopped and stood close to him. He shoved his hands deep into his pockets to keep from touching her.

"I was going about it all wrong," Kenni continued. "I was trying to fit something to my shape, my way of thinking, my way of dealing with life. It took me a long time to realize I was the one that had to fit. I was the small round stone that had somehow fallen away and had to find its place again, in God's hand. I *do* fit there. Always have. Always will."

Kenni held out the stone and Alex pulled his hand out of his pocket to let her drop it into his palm. It was oblong and black, smooth but not polished and warm from the sun. He curled his fingers around it as she turned away.

"I've been reading about David lately," she called back to him, stooping to pick up another pebble.

Alex thought she'd changed the subject. "David who?" He started after her.

"King David, in the Bible. His story starts in the first book of Samuel. He knew what it meant to be rejected by everyone but God. He hung onto Him. Even when he was hiding in caves and being hunted like an animal he still praised Him and thanked Him. David's faith was unshakable. You should read his story sometime."

His hand tightened around the stone as he watched her. She turned and waited for him, her body outlined by the shifting sea. A single gull cried and swooped close. Alex fought to keep the longing from overwhelming him. He almost lost.

"David slept with a married woman, then arranged for her husband to be killed."

Alex frowned. "Nice guy." He slipped the stone into his pocket.

"God called him a man after his own heart."

"That's logical."

Kenni chuckled. "He did one thing right. He always admitted his sins. He always asked God to forgive him."

"Convenient," Alex mumbled.

Kenni stopped and turned to him. "A wise person once told me you'll always be a victim until the day you see your own sin. David saw his for what it was. And it set him free. It takes courage to face yourself—even more to recognize your sin and do something about it."

Before he could say anything she turned and started pushing the boat back into the water.

Chapter Nine

The blue neon light blinked through the bedroom window from the *convenience store across the street. The boy focused on its rhythm, blink, blink, pause, blink, blink, pause. He tried to crawl into the intense blue of it, make himself melt into it. But the pain always interrupted, always kept him from escaping. The man's weight forced the breath out of him. He tried to wriggle free, but large hands pinned him down. The stench of the man's breath and the chill of his sweat made the boy want to vomit. But he swallowed hard to prevent the bile from spilling out. He knew that would invite another beating. When it was over he lay completely still, his face turned to the wall. He could feel the man standing over him, hear the harsh rub of jeans on his legs as he pulled them on. "Remember who you are, kid. They'd never believe a little punk like you. They'd lock you up and throw away the key. So you keep your mouth shut, you hear me?" The boy didn't move as the man's knee pressed a hole into the space on the bed beside him. Then a large hand clamped over his mouth. "Keep it shut. Or I'll shut it for you." The man's next words were hissed in his ear. "Like this." The hand moved and covered his mouth and nose, blocking off the air. Another hand tightened around his throat. The boy squirmed, but couldn't free himself. He writhed in panic, feeling himself falling deeper into the darkness, feeling it close over him like the lid on a coffin.*

Alex woke, his body jerking, gasping with the effort to breathe. It took him a few moments to realize he was alone, in a large bedroom. There were no hands trying to suffocate him. There was no small window, no blinking light. The only smell was from his own body, the feral smell of his own fear. He lay back in the bed and stared at the ceiling. *That was then. Stay in today.* He repeated the words over and over to himself until exhaustion pulled him back into the darkness.

He woke with another jerk when he heard someone knocking on his door. "Fish bite in the morning, Alex."

He opened the door a crack, rubbing his eyes and trying to focus. Drew grinned at him. "Marie's got breakfast on the table. I'm going down to the boat. Whenever you're ready...."

"Be right there," Alex mumbled. He showered quickly, gulped down the eggs Marie served him, and trotted down to the dock.

Drew was sitting in a good-sized fishing boat, sorting tackle. He glanced up with a grin. "Morning. Sorry to wake you so early, but I like being out on the water at this time of day." He closed the tackle box and nodded at the rope tying the boat to the dock. "Cast us off and jump in."

Alex did as he was told, and pulled his jacket close against the cool morning air that became a wind as the boat picked up speed. They traveled a short distance down the coast, then Drew cut the motor and handed Alex a rod. They trolled for a while, checking their lures to make sure they were rolling well. A fine mist skimmed the water, hiding the shoreline and making it seem as though they were floating. Alex slumped in his seat, clutching his rod to try and keep his hands steady as he watched the thin fishing line dissect the water as they moved. His stomach twisted. He needed a cigarette.

Drew broke the silence. "You look like you had a rough night."

Alex sat up a bit and turned the reel on his rod slowly. "Strange bed, I guess," he said.

Drew didn't reply for a while, then said quietly, "I heard you cry out."

Alex's hand stopped, then resumed turning the reel. He shrugged. "Just a dream."

"A dream? Or a nightmare?"

Alex looked up. Drew held his gaze. "Yeah. It was a nightmare."

"Want to talk about...."

"No." Alex shifted away from him, regretting the harshness of his voice.

Drew stayed quiet, moving only to turn the motor slightly as the boat puttered its way along. Alex was nodding off when the tip of his rod snapped up, almost jerking it out of his hands. He cursed and clutched the rod tightly, pulling it up hard.

"Easy," Drew cautioned. "That rod is designed to snap up when the fish bites. Just don't let it go slack or you'll lose him."

Alex let the rod straighten a bit, feeling the fish as it took the bait and fought the hook. He reeled the line in slowly, watching the rod bend, then straighten, then bend again. Suddenly, the surface of the water erupted with a flash of gleaming green speckled scales.

Drew whooped. "He's a big one! Oh yeah, a chinook, and he's got 'dinner' written all over him! Bring him in easy, Alex."

Alex was standing now, the rod burning his hands as he continued to reel the fish in. At last they could see it, swimming docilely beside the boat. Drew leaned out and dipped a large net into the water.

"C'mon, old boy. Come to papa." He slipped the net slowly under the fish, reached out with his other hand and heaved. The fish writhed as the net breached water. Drew wasted no time as it flopped on the bottom of the boat, landing a hard blow to its head that killed it instantly. He tugged the hook free and beamed at Alex.

"I think this one deserves a picture, Alex," he said. He moved to the cabin and returned with a small digital camera. Alex lifted the fish by its gills, grabbed its tail, and faced the camera. "Smile," Drew said and Alex forced his mouth into a grin.

Once the catch was packed in ice Drew baited the hooks again and turned the boat. "One more and we can call it a good day," he said.

Alex baited his hook and let the water take it as he released the reel. They were silent for some time, and Alex's head had started to nod again when Drew's question caught him off guard.

"What did you think of Pastor Jim's sermon yesterday?"

Alex looked into the man's face. *Was it you?* He searched his eyes for any sign of guilt. There was none. *And how could you know?* Alex decided to take a risk. "It felt like he...knew me," he said quietly.

"Sometimes truth is universal. Makes it seem like it's meant just for you."

"Did you call him?"

Drew's eyebrows shot up. "Call him? No. Why would I...?" His head lifted with understanding. "No, Alex. I didn't call him."

Alex dropped his eyes. "Kenni said it was a God thing. I guess that's the way you see it?"

"If Jim's sermon touched you, yes, that was a God thing. He has a way of getting our attention like that sometimes."

It touched me alright, Alex thought. *About the way this hook touched that chinook.* "Maybe He should just leave us alone instead of stirring the pot."

"Sometimes He has to disrupt our lives to move us out of a place that isn't good. It's usually not easy, but He always wants what's best."

Alex felt the anger rising. "If that's true, why does He...?" He stopped and shook his head.

"Let bad things happen to innocent people?"

Alex turned away, his jaw working. *Why does he let the scum of the earth rape ten-year-old kids?* The words snarled in his mind. When the silence lingered he looked up at Drew again. The pain in the older man's eyes made him want to moan.

"I wish I could give you an answer that would help," Drew said slowly. "But I don't have one. All I can tell you is that God weeps when things—bad things—happen. With all the ugliness in this world His pain must be overwhelming."

"Then why doesn't He stop it?"

"When you were young did someone ever try to stop you from doing something destructive?" Drew didn't wait for him to answer. "Did you listen?" He sighed. "It's called sin, Alex, and it's never pretty. God does try to stop us, but He won't force us to do what's right and reject what's evil."

"What's He good for then?"

"What's He good for?" Drew smiled suddenly. "For days like this when the fish are biting." The smile faded. "And for days when you're so low you feel like putting a gun to your head. For days when everything goes right and days when everything goes wrong. But it's not just that He's good for something. It's that He's good. Absolutely good." Drew's voice dropped a notch. "And He does love you."

Alex turned away. "He has a strange way of showing it."

"Love doesn't always mean hugs and kisses, Alex. Sometimes it's painful."

Alex stared into the water, noticing the snap of the pole Drew had set in a holder. He lifted his chin toward it. "Looks like number two is on the line."

Drew sprang to the rod, grasping it just as the fish plunged deep. The reel spun and Drew whooped. "Here we go again!"

Alex couldn't help but grin. The man sure loved to fish.

They had the catch cleaned and cut into steaks by the time lunch was ready. Marie and Kenni had the table waiting.

"Well, did you men get your fill of fishing for now?" Marie asked, immediately turning to Kenni and asking if she wanted a cup of tea.

Drew grinned. "I suppose, though we could go out again if you ladies insist."

Marie waved her hand at him. "You know I won't."

"Me neither, Dad," Kenni said. "I think I'm just going to veg this afternoon. Read, maybe even have a nap."

"What about you, Alex?" Drew asked. "You like to read?"

He looked up from his soup. "Yeah. I read a lot."

"Well, Drew has an extensive library of westerns, if you like that sort of thing." Marie's wrinkling nose indicated it wasn't her preference.

Alex looked at the older man. His surprise must've shown in his eyes. Drew grinned.

"They're a minor obsession, I'm afraid."

"I don't mind a good duster now and then," Alex said.

Drew nodded. "Just finished a couple I liked. I'll see if I can dig them out for you."

Alex followed him from the dining room to a study on the other side of the house. One wall was all window, facing the sea. The other three walls were covered with shelves floor to ceiling and were full of books. Alex stood in the doorway and stared. He could spend six months in here and die happy.

Drew shifted a few books around. "Hmm...here we go. These were pretty good." He handed them to Alex. "I think you might relate to the main character. They're written by a Canadian, by the way, from Alberta I think."

Alex took the books. "Thanks. Guess I'll go find a comfortable chair."

"You can stay right here if you want," Drew replied. "I've got some puttering to do." He left Alex standing in the middle of the room. He chose a large leather chair by the window and tried to settle in. The first paragraph of the book grabbed his attention, but it didn't take long before images intruded into his mind like a relentless camera flash. He stood up and paced for a while, tried the book again, then finally went looking for Kenni.

He found her on the deck stretched out on a lawn chair, a book opened on her chest, her eyes closed. He started to back away when she stirred.

"Hi," she said, then frowned at the look on his face. "You okay?"

"I...I'd like to talk to that pastor. You still have the number?"

She jumped up and found it for him. Then she left him alone to make the call.

Pastor Jim didn't seem surprised to hear from him. "I can meet you in my office in half an hour," he said.

Alex borrowed Drew's car and wasted no time getting to the church. But then he sat in the parking lot for a long time, arguing with himself. *What are you doing, Donnelly? You know this won't help. This will only make it worse. But maybe...maybe he'll understand. He's been through it. So what? You need sympathy from some religious freak? You're pathetic.* Then he remembered Kenni's last few words on the pebble beach. "You'll always be a victim until...." Before the interior monologue started again he jerked open the car door and strode to the back door of the church.

The pastor greeted him warmly and got right down to business as he waved Alex to a large armchair.

"What can I do for you?"

"I just wanted to talk to you about...about what you said yesterday."

"You were with Drew Adams and his family, weren't you?"

Alex nodded. "I've been sort of visiting with them for a few days."

"I see. And you have a question about the sermon?"

"I want to know...have you really forgiven him?"

The pastor looked directly into his eyes. "It's a journey. I'm still on the road. But yes, I think I have forgiven him." When Alex didn't reply Jim added softly, "And I've been praying for you."

Alex's eyebrows shot up. "What?"

"I heard you toss your breakfast out the side door."

Alex dropped his eyes. "Yeah," he admitted. "That was me."

"Does that mean what I think it does?"

Alex shifted in the chair, looked up, then dropped his eyes again.

But he decided to get to the punch line. "Yeah. What happened to you...." He looked up for only a second. "It's pretty close...." He took a deep breath and faced the pastor. "But I don't want to forgive him." He felt his nails cut into his palms as his hands clenched into fists. "I want to kill him." He was aware of how easy it was to say those words and how much he meant them. As he dropped his eyes to the floor again he fought with the emotions raging inside.

Pastor Jim stayed silent until Alex made eye contact again. Then he quietly said, "Tell me your story."

Chapter Ten

Kenni paced the deck, staring out at the ocean without seeing it. She wished she didn't feel other people's pain the way she did. It seemed like she was pulled toward them like shards of metal pulled by a powerful magnet. Sometimes she'd just notice someone's posture, or look into their eyes and know they'd been through the same pain, tormented by the same guilt and fear.

She'd known that about Alex the moment he raised his eyes to hers in George's office. The question was what did God expect her to do about it? She knew the Lord had brought Alex into her life for a reason and she wanted to help him, but.... She groaned out loud. This was something more than just wanting to help. *Get a grip, you just met the guy. And he's dangerous. Anybody that needy is dangerous. You're falling into the needing to be needed trap again. You can't fix Alex Donnelly. Just like you couldn't fix all those kids in high school who cried on your shoulder and manipulated you so easily.* She went into the living room and flopped down on the sofa. *Just like you couldn't fix your parents.* She closed her eyes and prayed that prayer that had become so automatic for her—*Oh God, help.*

Her dad's car pulled into the drive and Kenni went to the door. Rain smeared the windows so she couldn't see Alex clearly. But she could see that he didn't move. Her heart started to pound. She wanted to go out to him, but held back. It seemed like an hour before he heaved himself out of the vehicle. He didn't raise his head and moved as though he were an old man—an old man in mourning. He jerked back when he realized she was there, then handed her the keys.

"Thanks," he said staring over her shoulder.

"Alex?"

When his eyes met hers she almost winced at the pain she saw there. All her confusion melted away. She responded to his pain, giving a small cry as she wrapped her arms around him. He stiffened at first, then put his arms around her and buried his face in her hair. They stayed that way for a long time until she finally took a deep breath and pulled away. She searched his eyes. "It's going to be okay."

"Is it?" His eyes were blurred. "All I know right now is that it's hard. Maybe too hard."

She started to reach for his hand, but stopped before she touched him. "Come in. I'll make some coffee."

Alex sat on the long sofa, facing the windows. Kenni sat in the big chair angled toward him. The rain pelted down, blurring the green and brown of the land with the surging colors of the sea. "You know you can stay as long as you need to, Alex."

He nodded. "Your dad said the same thing." He took a sip of his coffee. "But I don't think I'd be very good company."

Kenni ducked her head and gave him a sidelong glance. "You mean you won't be your usual engaging self?"

Alex winced. "Ouch."

Kenni chuckled. "Sorry, I couldn't resist." She was pleased to see that made him grin a little.

"Guess I'll just have to work hard at redeeming my reputation," he said.

"That might take a while." She smiled at him, but his face darkened again.

He stood up suddenly. "Kenni, I...I can't do this." He stopped and exhaled loudly, then strode to the other end of the living room, turned and paced back.

She watched him, her heart racing, wishing this didn't have to be so complicated. "It's okay, Alex," she said.

He stopped and looked at her. "No. It isn't okay. It will never be okay."

"Alex...."

He held up his hands. "Don't." The one word was barely a whisper.

She wanted to respond to the look in his eyes, but she just put her coffee cup on the table and said, "I won't pretend to totally understand what you're going through, but I know you're right. Dealing with this kind of pain is going to be hard. But I believe it will be worth it in the end. I know it is. It takes courage and a lot of faith, but it's worth it." She watched him slump into a chair.

"Courage. Maybe that's another word I don't know anything about."

"I wish I could do something to make it easier," she said, then smiled suddenly. "My mom used to say, 'If wishes were stars, there'd be no night.'" She turned away and stared out at the ocean again. "But we need the darkness sometimes."

Kenni tried to make her voice sound more optimistic than she felt as she turned to face him again. "It will work out, Alex. I'm sure it will." She leaned toward him. "I'm praying it will." She watched his eyes close briefly. When he opened them again she shivered at what she saw there.

"You must've had a pretty easy time in foster care if you still believe in prayer." He almost spat the words.

She forced herself to hold his gaze. "No," she said softly. "It wasn't easy." She turned away and heard Alex groan.

"I'm sorry," he said. "I didn't mean...I'm sorry," he said again.

Kenni took a deep breath and sat up straight. "I know a lot about *you*." Her voice was almost a whisper. "Maybe it's time I told you *my* story."

Alex slumped deeper into the chair opposite her. "If you want to tell it," he replied.

His voice was so weary she hesitated, studying his face. "Maybe this isn't the right time," she said.

Alex pushed a hand through his hair. "Maybe not." He met her eyes. "But they say misery loves company, so go ahead."

Kenni looked out the window again. "It all seems so far away now, like it wasn't my life at all, really." She shifted and looked back at him. "Do you ever have that feeling?"

Alex shook his head. "For me it's like it all happened yesterday."

Kenni sighed. "Maybe it's because my life changed so completely when I came here." She took a deep breath and began. "My parents were both addicts. My father was shot by police in a drug raid not long after I was born. I was four when they finally took me away from my mother. She died of an overdose a year later. I was in a pretty good foster home at the time, but for some reason when she died they took me out of that one and put me in a group home for a couple of years. It was okay there, but, you know, institutional."

Alex grunted. "Yeah. I know."

"Then I was placed in a foster home in Tacoma. There were four other kids there, three boys and one other girl. That's when life got ugly."

She was aware of Alex's intense gaze, but couldn't bring herself to look into his eyes. He leaned toward her and she thought he was about to speak, but then he sat back and waited for her to continue.

She dropped her head and her hair fell forward, covering her face. She stayed that way for a moment, then raised her eyes and brushed her hair back. "It started with one of the older boys. They used to leave him in charge of us younger ones a lot."

She was quiet and dropped her eyes again. Alex didn't move. Finally she raised her head and continued. "Then my foster father caught him with me one day. He flew into a rage and beat us both. That boy was gone the next day, but then about a week later my foster father started coming into my room." She stopped again, forcing herself to block the memories. "That went on for five years until they suddenly took us all out of there and charged him. I don't know how they found out, but he was doing it to all of us, girls and boys." Kenni paused again, shivered, and wrapped her arms around herself. But when she spoke again her voice was lighter.

"I met my mom the first day we had to go to court. I was so scared. I ran away, into a park across the street from the courthouse. Mom was waiting there for Dad. When I ran past her she followed me to a bench and asked me if I was okay." Kenni looked up with a slight smile. "She didn't wait for me to answer the question." Alex responded with a slight grin and she continued. "But she started talking to me, in that soft voice, and before I knew it I'd told her my whole story. Some things I'd never told anyone. Then she took my hand and walked me back into the courthouse. She sat there through the whole thing. When I got scared I'd look at her. She'd smile and I'd know everything was going to be okay. It was like I had my own personal guardian angel."

Kenni leaned forward. "I believe God did that, Alex. I don't think it was an accident that Dad had business there that day, that Mom decided to go with him. She rarely did."

Alex deflected the comment. "They adopted you right away?"

She nodded. "As soon as the trial was over I moved in with them. The adoption went through a few months later."

"And everyone lived happily ever after."

She ignored his tone. "I was in counseling for a long time. Mom and Dad got help too. They'd never had a troubled teenager around before. We've had our struggles, but yes, we've learned to live with one another and we've been happy."

Alex was silent for a while. Kenni watched his face. He dropped his head and his dark hair fell over his eyes. She wanted to reach out and brush it away, but she sat still and waited. She stiffened when his bitterness spilled out.

"Your own personal angel," he said. "Guess my angels were the two cops I had to run from when they came to drag me out of Wild Bill's." He snorted. "Go figure."

Kenni leaned toward him. "Alex, God...."

His head jerked and he stood up. "Don't talk to me about God!" The hard edge had returned to his voice. His hands were clenched into fists. "It's great that you've ended up with the soft life, Kenni," he blurted. "But some of us just aren't that lucky. Some of us have to make it on our own."

Chapter Eleven

The boy stopped reading when he heard the phone ring and Wild *Bill's voice answering it. He put the book down when he heard the thud of footsteps on the stairs. The house shook. He tried to back into a corner, but they kept disappearing, the walls kept shifting. The door burst open. A window shattered.*

The belt was already in the man's hand. It slithered on the floor and the boy whimpered as a snake's eyes gleamed red from its end. The man cursed, grabbed the boy's arm, twisted it behind him, and pushed him face down on the bed. He felt the man's hot breath and the spray of spittle on his face as he hissed into his ear.

"You've been whining to that teacher again, haven't you? Didn't get enough to eat, huh? Didn't get no breakfast? Well, you can forget about supper tonight too. Didn't I tell you what would happen if you opened your mouth?"

The boy buried his face in the rough blanket as the belt struck again and again. He crawled to the edge of the bed. It was floating in mid-air. The walls, the floor had disappeared. A black chasm surrounded him. A swarm of small red eyes blinked at him from the darkness below. If he moved another inch, he'd plunge into them, to his death. Fear of what would happen when the blows stopped paralyzed his mind. Then he felt Bill's big hand grab the back of his shirt and lift him. His eyes bulged as his legs flailed in the air. The black chasm yawned beneath him. Then the man threw him down. The boy felt his heart stop when he landed hard on his back at Bill's feet.

"Strip!" He bellowed.

The boy froze until the heavy boot struck. He watched his hands tremble as they moved to the button on his pants. Then they turned into claws and he couldn't force them to push the button through the hole or grasp the zipper. His frantic attempts made the claws gouge long scars into his own flesh.

Alex woke drenched in cold sweat. His breath came in short pants, his head pounded with his own pulse. He forced himself to breathe normally, then got out of bed and went into the hall, stopping briefly to listen before slipping into the bathroom. He gulped air to keep the bile from rising in his throat. Running a trickle of water into the sink he wet his face, trying to be as quiet as possible. When his breathing was even he headed back to his room, but stood staring at the door for several minutes. He repeated his mantra to himself. *That was then. That was then. Stay in today. Stay in today.* But he couldn't make himself push the door open. He went into the living room.

The house was quiet, the night sighing with the sound of the sea. He stepped out onto the deck, shivering as the ocean breeze cooled his body. A full moon shone bright, highlighting the white foam of cresting waves. He went down the steps to the shore and broke into a run. He ran with only the moon for light, just beyond the pulling curves of the surf.

○ ○ ○

By morning the longing ache inside him was like a physical pain. He groaned and stretched out on the bed. A pale dawn light was rising through the bedroom window. He listened to the ever-present sound of the sea surging toward him. The silence in the house made him want to rush out at once and wake Kenni and her parents, made him want to find someplace to curl up and hide. Or curl up and die. By the time the sun was fully up he was dreading the day. *God, when will it end? When will I be free of it?* He sat up and reached for his pants, cursing himself again for coming here, for talking to that pastor. The nightmares were getting out of control.

Something clunked against the wooden footboard. He put his hand into his pants pocket and took out the smooth black stone. He passed his thumb over it. It still felt warm. Kenni's face floated into his mind. Half of him tried to make it fade away while the other half studied it with the intensity of a man saying good-bye to the one he loved before going off to war. *Love. Another word I don't know the meaning of.* He wanted to let himself love her, wanted to stay here with her and her family, wanted.... He shook his head and stood up. Kenni's face vanished. *No. I want to get out of here. I'll leave today, get the information I need, and leave for good. Then I'll forget all about Kenni Adams.*

A knock on his door almost made him drop the stone. Drew's voice boomed at him. "Up and at 'em, Alex. Breakfast is on the table."

He tossed the stone onto the bed, dressed quickly, and threw his few belongings into his small duffel bag. His hand was on the doorknob when he hesitated and looked back. The stone lay like a lump of coal on the white sheet. He snatched it up, shoved it into his pocket, and went into the dining room.

The smell of pancakes gave him a calming sense of reality and the smell of coffee made his nostrils flare. His stomach growled. He sat down and they all instantly bowed their heads as Drew prayed.

"Father, thank you for a new day. Whatever it brings our way, Lord, we ask that you help us to know you're with us. We ask that you teach us today, Lord. Teach us how to love as you do, how to live according to your will. We thank you now for the food you provide. Bless it to your use in our bodies. Amen."

Alex dove into the pancakes, barely hearing the conversation floating around him. He gulped his coffee down, sat back and fidgeted with the silverware, suddenly impatient to be gone from this house.

Drew glanced at Kenni, cleared his throat, and stood up. "Guess we should get going," he said.

As Alex stood he paused, turning to Marie. "Uh...th...thanks, Mrs. Adams," he stammered and turned away in embarrassment.

Marie came around the end of the table and engulfed him in a mother-bear hug. "God bless you," she whispered in his ear. He knew, to her, those words signified the bestowing of the blessing itself. And they were spoken with a certainty that made a lump rise in his throat. He forced it back down as she stepped back. "And come back and visit anytime."

Alex glanced at Kenni and mumbled, "Thanks," again.

As they headed out the door Drew held out the two books Alex had left in the study. "Take these with you if you like," he offered.

Alex nodded and stuffed them into the bottom of his bag.

In the car Drew told him the firm had called with a message that the results from the police were waiting for them.

Alex's stomach flipped.

"That was quick," Kenni commented.

Leaning forward from the back seat Alex tried not to sound too anxious. "Did they say what the results were?" *Will they be waiting for me at the office, handcuffs ready?*

Drew shook his head. "No. But Mr. Ferrington will be waiting for you in George's office."

"Ferrington?"

Kenni twisted in the seat to face him. "He was the lawyer who handled your parents' case, Alex. He's pretty much retired now, but wanted to come in to hand things over to you, to tie up the loose ends, I guess."

So now I'm a loose end. But he said nothing and Kenni didn't try to make any more conversation as he slumped back into the seat and stared out the window.

○ ○ ○

Drew turned to Alex in the lobby of the building. "I'd like to be with you, but I have an important meeting in about five minutes." He extended his hand and Alex gripped it. "Max will take good care of you, but if there's anything you need, don't hesitate to call me."

Alex nodded, suddenly unable to speak as he tried to shake the feeling that he needed to hang onto this man for dear life. He turned as Kenni said goodbye to her dad, and headed toward the elevators. They rode up in silence. He felt her glance his way a couple of times, but didn't acknowledge it. He just wanted to get this over with.

Maxwell Ferrington pushed himself to a standing position as they entered the office. He was a tall thin man with a thick patch of white hair and small dark eyes behind round glasses. George stood beside him, but Ferrington extended his hand without waiting for an introduction.

"Max Ferrington, Alex. It's a pleasure to meet you."

Alex shook hands and glanced at George. He didn't meet his eyes.

"What's wrong?" Alex's heart raced. Had they discovered...?

George looked up quickly. "Nothing. The prints matched, Alex. You're the person we've been looking for."

Alex let his breath out.

Ferrington turned to Kenni, then George. "Ms. Adams, Mr. Bronsky. If you'll excuse us now please?"

As she passed, Kenni gave him a low wave. For a moment he thought she was going to touch his hand, but she just smiled and followed George from the room.

When Alex turned back to Ferrington the lawyer held the large envelope in his hand. "You look a lot like your mother, Alex."

As the words registered Alex realized he'd stopped breathing again. He exhaled. "You knew her?"

"Yes. I was your mother's legal counsel. She was a lovely woman, a strong woman."

Alex stared at the envelope in the man's gnarled hands. Then, trying to keep his voice from shaking, he reached for it. "I guess that belongs to me."

The elderly lawyer pulled it back slightly. "Before I give this to you I want to warn you. It contains some information that anyone would find disturbing. Considering your past you may find it particularly upsetting."

"Okay, you've warned me." Alex didn't try to hide his impatience as he extended his hand again.

"Your parents loved you, Alex," Ferrington said as he handed him the envelope. "I know you'll have questions after you've read this. If you'd like to sit at the desk...."

"No." Alex gripped the envelope. "I...I need to get some air." He whirled around and strode from the room. He saw George and Kenni standing by the water cooler, but ignored them. As he turned in the elevator he saw George heading toward him. He didn't try to stop the doors from closing.

He'd just climbed into the taxi when George jumped into the seat beside him.

"Hey." He was panting hard. "Want some company?"

Alex glared at him. "No."

"Uh...maybe it's not a good idea to be alone when—"

"I said no, George. I'm a big boy. I can handle it."

"Well, uh, it seems we're going in the same direction so...."

Alex gave him a nasty look, but told the driver to take them somewhere where he could see the ocean, and sat in silence until the taxi pulled into Waterfront Park. George followed him as he made his way to a bench facing the water. He sat with the envelope in his lap and focused on the sounds around him—the gentle lapping of the water, the screeching cry of the gulls, the rhythmic slap of joggers' feet and the click and whir of bikes on the walkway behind them. He watched the boats glide across the water beyond the high metal railings.

Max Ferrington's words echoed in his mind. "You look like your mother." Such a simple statement of fact. It made Alex want to moan and scream. But he sat still, staring. Finally, he looked down at the envelope.

"I could just throw it into the sea and walk away."

Before George could respond Alex ripped open the envelope with such violence the lawyer startled. Alex pulled the papers out, but his hands were shaking so badly he couldn't read them. He shoved them into George's hands.

"Read it to me," he said.

George held the document up and read.

"Further to the Statement of Claim brought by the plaintiff, Ms. Janis Marie Perrin, against the defendant, Dr. Donald Albion, MD, claiming damages caused by the defendant's medical negligence and carelessness in failing to perform his duties in term...." George stopped and his eyes flicked to Alex's face. When he continued his voice was a notch lower. "...in terminating the pregnancy of the plaintiff, this is to certify that the Court finds in favor of the plaintiff, and grants to the plaintiff general and special damages in the amount of $250,000."

Alex was aware of George's look as he flipped the page to the next document. "This is the Trust document." Alex nodded and George continued reading.

"This is to certify that Alexander Gabriel Perrin, born July 30, 1982 at Virginia Mason Hospital, Seattle, Washington is hereby designated as sole recipient of the amount of $250,000 to be held in trust in his name until he reaches the age of twenty-one, at which time he'll be in receipt of that amount and any and all interest which may accrue."

"There's a small envelope too," George said and handed it to Alex. He ripped it open and pulled out a long key tagged with a number and the address of a bank.

"Looks like the key to a safety deposit box," George offered.

Alex turned it over in his hand. "Read it again," he said. "The first page."

George hesitated, but then did as Alex asked.

They sat still for what seemed like an hour. Then Alex dropped the key into the small envelope, stuffed everything back into the bigger one, handed it to George and stood up. He didn't look at him. "Go back to your office," he said and walked away.

When he realized George was following him he whirled around. "Leave me alone, Bronsky!"

George skidded to a stop. "Okay. Okay. Just...call me when you're ready to talk."

Alex strode away leaving George to stare after him.

Chapter Twelve

Kenni sank down onto the small couch in her apartment and clutched the document George had given her. "Oh, God," she moaned. "God, hold onto him."

George sat down beside her. "I checked his hotel room before coming here. He's not there."

Kenni jumped up. "It's been almost twelve hours. We need to find him." She paced. "But where would we start? He could be anywhere."

"The bars, most likely." George clenched his fist and groaned. "I shouldn't have left him alone."

Kenni whirled around. "I'll get my coat."

They searched the bars closest to the waterfront first, but saw no sign of him. Giving a description to the bouncers and bartenders yielded nothing as they made their way from one sleazy liquor outlet to another. At 4 a.m. they gave up.

It was 8 a.m. when George rolled over, looking for the source of the ringing. He fumbled for the phone and finally succeeded in putting the right end up to his ear.

"Hullo?"

The silence was the kind that told him there was someone listening. "Hello, who is this?"

"Guess I need a lawyer."

"Alex?" George swung his legs out of the bed, the cold floor making his feet recoil. "Where are you?"

"Uh, West Precinct, on Virginia Street."

"I'll be right there."

It took him less than half an hour. Filling out the paperwork and getting him released from the drunk tank took a while longer. Alex didn't say anything until they were outside standing beside George's car. He glanced down at himself. His shirt was torn and blood-soaked. A yellowish green stain was crusted down one leg of his jeans.

"I'll grab a cab," he said and backed away.

George shook his head. "Get in the car, Alex."

"I'm a mess."

"Just get in."

He slid into the seat without another word. George hit a button and the ragtop slid down. He gave Alex a sidelong glance as he gingerly touched his left eye. It was almost swollen shut. Blood from a cut above it was clotted in his hair. His hands shook.

"What's the other guy look like?" George asked.

"Worse." Alex winced as the cut on his lip burst open. He cursed and dabbed at it with part of his shirt.

"You're lucky they aren't going to lay charges."

"More than you know," Alex mumbled.

George turned the key in the ignition. "The other guy was apparently just as drunk, and fortunately you'd already been kicked out of the bar so there were no damages to property. You'll have to pay a fine for being drunk in a public place, but I think you can afford it."

Alex snorted. "I guess an unaborted rich man can handle that. Is that a word, unaborted?"

"Alex...."

"Just take me to the hotel, okay?" He slumped down and put his head back.

Neither of them spoke until they pulled up in front of the building. "I'll call you later. I need some sleep."

George nodded. "Better put some ice on that eye. I'll be at the office til 6:00." Alex started to get out of the car. George leaned toward him. "Use my cell number after that."

He leaned further as Alex got out. "Alex." When he leaned down to look at him George continued. "You can ignore the messages from Kenni. I'll let her know you're alright."

Alex dropped his eyes, said "Okay," and slammed the door.

○ ○ ○

Once in his room Alex called the front desk and ordered a bucket of ice and a bottle of painkillers. Stripping out of the filthy T-shirt and jeans he threw them in a pile on the floor. He stayed in the shower until his knees felt weak. When he stepped out he toweled himself dry slowly, wincing at his bruised ribs. "Stupid," he mumbled. *If they'd finger-printed me....* He shuddered, dropping his head as he put both hands on the counter. When he looked up his reflection was clouded by the condensation on the mirror. He wiped a spot and leaned forward. His left eye looked worse, but the cut above it was clean. "You look like your mother." The words taunted him. Alex cursed and swept his palm across the wet surface.

○ ○ ○

Kenni was relieved when George told her Alex was alright. "Are you sure he doesn't need to see a doctor?"

"I'm sure. He's going to sleep it off. Said he'd call later. He looks pretty rough, but he'll be okay."

She couldn't keep the irritation out of her voice as it rose a notch. "How can anyone be okay after discovering something like that? You don't know what it would mean to someone who's always wondered, always imagined...."

George sighed his exasperation. "Okay, I guess I don't, but he said he'd be fine. What more do you want me to do?"

Kenni sighed too. "I'm sorry. I didn't mean to snap."

"He did say he'd call," George mumbled.

As if on cue his cell phone rang. He signaled to Kenni when Alex said hello.

"Hey. How you feeling?" George tried to keep the edge out of his voice

"Like I got hit by a Mack truck. I need to talk to that old guy, Ferrington. Can you arrange it?"

"Sure. I'll pick you up in the morning."

"Okay. But, uh, not too early."

"Ten or so?"

"Maybe make it 11:00."

"Okay. See you then."

"Uh, George? Have you seen Kenni?"

"I'm with her now. Do you want to talk to...?"

"No. Just tell her...never mind."

The phone went dead. George turned to Kenni. "He wants to talk to Max."

She sighed, stung that he didn't want to talk to her. "I hope that's a good sign," she said.

Chapter Thirteen

Kenni glanced at her watch, at Max Ferrington, then at her dad. "I'm sure they'll be here any minute," she said, but her voice was not as confident as her words. She picked up a pen, put it back down, and looked at her watch again. She jumped up when George walked in, alone.

"Alex is gone."

"What?"

"He left me a note at the hotel saying he should've let the past stay there." He handed Kenni a small envelope with her name scrawled across it. "And he left this."

Kenni read the note quickly and sank back on the chair. There was nothing in it to tell her his intentions. "Did he say where he was going?" she asked.

"No. My guess is back up north."

"That won't be far enough." George and Kenni both turned to Drew. A faint smile played on his lips. "God is after Alex Donnelly. There's nowhere he can run where God can't find him. We just have to keep praying."

Max snorted. "He'll be back. He hasn't signed the papers yet. He can't get at the money until he does."

Drew shook his head. "As hard as it might be for you to believe, Max, this young man doesn't care about the money."

Max headed for the door. "Everyone cares about money." He turned with his hand on the doorknob. "By the way, what was his reaction to the letter?"

George frowned. "Letter?"

"Yes, the letter from his mother."

"There was no letter. Just a small envelope with a key in it."

Ferrington frowned. "There should've been a letter with the documents."

George moved to the other side of the desk and removed the contents of the large manila envelope. "This is all there was, Max. This is all Alex read."

"Then he only knows half the story." He turned to Kenni. "We have to find that letter."

She nodded and swept past him out the door. "I'm on it."

He looked over at George. "And we'd better find Alex too."

George responded over his shoulder as he followed Kenni. "I'll call the hotel. Maybe someone overheard where he went."

His office now empty, Drew Adams started to pray.

○ ○ ○

Kenni entered the archive vault where Alex's documents had been kept. She searched for the numbered file drawer, lifted out the entire rack, and took it to the table where she so often worked. She flipped through the files, but there were none marked with the appropriate names or numbers. She went back to the drawer and searched inside. No small envelope was there. Sitting down she started going through each file, flipping each piece of paper in hope that the envelope had gotten stuck in the wrong place. She prayed with each flip of her fingers. An hour slipped away, but she found nothing. Just as she was shoving the drawer back into place George arrived, frowning.

"Any luck?"

"Not yet. I've gone through every file in this drawer."

George peered at the columns of drawers. They were high and wide. He sighed. "I'll take the one above," he said and reached for it.

Kenni pulled out the drawer below and began the same process all over again.

"Any luck finding out where he went?" she asked.

"The airport. Eight o'clock this morning." George heaved the rack of files onto the table. "Probably ran back to his hidey-hole in the bush."

Kenni stared, annoyed at the tone in his voice. "You don't sound very sympathetic."

George pursed his lips. "Well, somewhere in-between putting up with his attitude, staying up til dawn looking for him, bailing him out of jail, and now having to go through this...." He tugged at a handful of files. "I'm running a bit short on sympathy."

He tugged again and the files flew out of his hand, scattering across the floor. George said a word he normally wouldn't. Kenni squatted beside him and helped pick up the papers. He glanced sideways at her.

"Truth is," he continued, "I'm glad he's gone. I hope he stays gone. Maybe things will get back to normal around here."

Kenni stood up and put a handful of papers on the desk. "You don't have to be so...involved if you don't want to be."

"But you do?" George stood and moved to the other side. When Kenni didn't answer he snorted, "Guess that's kind of obvious."

Kenni felt her face burn. "George Bronsky, that's...." she whirled around and sat down. "It's none of your business!"

His face was mottled with red blotches as he stared at her in silence for a moment, then said more quietly, "You're right. But I...I just don't want to see you get hurt. This guy's bad news. You should know that better than any of us."

Kenni started to speak, but stopped.

"You've fallen for him, haven't you?" George asked.

She sighed. "I don't know." She almost groaned. "I do feel—a connection to him. I guess because I know what it's like to be in the prison he's in. It's like I'm standing on the outside, with the key, watching him suffer and it's—it's really hard."

It was George's turn to sigh. "Just...be careful, Kenni. Don't let your compassion blind you. A lot of Alex Donnelly's pain is of his own making. You can't rescue him."

"I know, but...."

"What?"

"Maybe it's no accident Alex Donnelly came into our lives. Like my dad said it seems like God is after him and somehow I think we have a part to play in His plan. I'm just trying to sort out what it's supposed to mean and how I'm supposed to deal with it—deal with him."

George sat down beside her. "And I guess it doesn't help when your best friend suddenly throws an adolescent tantrum."

Kenni grinned. "You really are overprotective, you know."

George shuffled the papers in his hands, but said nothing. He stood up quickly. "Just...just be careful. I really don't think you should get involved with someone like Alex Donnelly."

"But I already am." Kenni sighed. "We all are."

George stared at the stack of files again and groaned. "Right. So I guess we'd better get back at it."

They searched the files all afternoon, then called for others to help and continued into the night. No small envelope was found.

○ ○ ○

Exhausted, Kenni stepped into her apartment and flicked on the light. She tugged off her jacket and noticed the note from Alex sticking out of the pocket. She sank down in a chair and unfolded the page.

Kenni,

Sorry, I just can't deal with any of this right now. Maybe I never will. Please say thanks to your parents. Those couple of days at their place were—well, at least now I can picture what peace is like. Maybe some day I'll figure out how to find it.

Alex

Kenni put her head down on her arms and let the emotions pent up inside flood out.

○ ○ ○

The next morning George reread the note addressed to him.

George,

I should've let the past stay in the past. Thanks for trying to help.

Guess I'm just a hopeless case. Maybe you are too. Don't be a fool like me—you have a diamond sitting in front of you. Hold onto it.

Alex

He was still staring at it when Drew walked into his office. "Kenni's going after him, George. I want you to go along."

George blinked. "What?"

"I can't talk her out of it so unless you can, you're on your way to the Yukon again."

George sighed. "I don't think she'll listen to me either. But this is a wild goose chase. If Alex doesn't want to be found, the Yukon's a perfect place to hide."

"Kenni thinks he'll just go back to his cabin, but she's anxious to get going and try to catch up with him."

George nodded and stood up. "Okay, when do we leave?"

"You'd better talk to her. She said she was going to book the first flight she could get."

George was already heading out the door. He found Kenni on the phone and interrupted her. She covered the mouthpiece as he told her to book two tickets. She started to object, but George reminded her that he'd already been there and knew how to find him. She made the bookings.

"The flight leaves at 9:45 tomorrow morning. There aren't any connections from Whitehorse to Dawson for a few days so I arranged for a rental. Are you sure you want to do this, George? I can go alone."

George shook his head. "Not a good idea. I'll go with you, but don't be surprised if we can't find him."

"What do you mean? You said that's where he went."

"The Yukon's a big place. If he doesn't want to be found...."

"We have to try."

"And if we find him, then what? How will you convince him to come back?"

Kenni sighed. "I'm hoping the letter...."

George's eyes widened. "You found it?"

Kenni shook her head. "Not yet, but we have every available person looking. It has to be here...it's just a matter of time."

It was George's turn to shake his head. "I don't know, Kenni. I don't think Alex wants to know anything more than what he does already. And I can't blame him."

"Suddenly you're sympathetic?"

"Just realistic."

Kenni sank down into her chair. "We have to try," she said again, then glanced up at George. "I have to try."

He nodded with a sigh. "Okay. I'll check on things down in the archives, see if they've turned up anything."

George smacked the Down button in the elevator and slumped against the wall. Kenni was like a sister to him—at least that's what he'd always told himself—but maybe he *was* being overprotective. Maybe he should back off and let her go chasing after Alex Donnelly on her own. As he stepped from the elevator he knew he would not, could not do that. And he thought maybe it was time he examined why.

Chapter Fourteen

September 1

Alex walked into a bank on the main street in Whitehorse and punched his PIN number into the ATM. When the screen lit up with his account information he groaned. "Not enough," he grumbled and crumpled the small slip of paper in his fist. He thought briefly about the money sitting in a Seattle bank—money that could be in his bank account. He scowled and punched more numbers into the machine, grabbed the twenty as it slid out and headed for the bar. *Maybe I could pick up some work there.*

He was in luck. A mining company was looking for someone to watch over their site for the winter. He called the number and made an appointment to meet with the man in charge of hiring. Within the hour he had the job and by mid-afternoon sat in a helicopter on his way to the camp. He wanted to make a trip to Dawson and his cabin first, but the boss insisted he get up to the camp immediately. His cabin wasn't on the way. Alex didn't want to risk being fired before the job even started so he'd agreed.

"There's a griz hanging around the camp," the boss explained, "a six footer at least, probably around 1500 pounds by the signs we've seen. Your job is to make sure he doesn't do any damage. I've seen griz tear up a whole campsite til there's nothing left but bits of wood and metal. And they'll track a man so watch your back.

"There's a dog there," he continued, "He'll be outta food and water about now. His name's Titan. Keep him chained up til he gets used to you, then let him roam. He'll let you know when the griz is in the neighborhood. His food's in the shed behind the house. I'll see about arranging for a relief caretaker in a few weeks."

Alex only had time to buy a few items of warm clothing, a new winter parka and boots. His hands had stopped shaking and the nausea was gone so he decided not to buy cigarettes. Maybe a few months in the bush without smokes would break the habit once and for all.

He didn't even have time to look anyone up in Whitehorse, not that there was anyone he desperately wanted to see. He tried to call Sal, but there was no answer so he left a message telling her he'd send money for dog food and he'd see her in a few weeks. Then Kenni's face floated before him. He tried to block her from his mind, but it was no use. He remembered how she'd held him that day, how soft her hair felt, how much he'd wanted to keep holding her, how just being with her made him want to forget everything else. He closed his eyes tight for a moment, trying to shut her out. He knew she was beyond him, as much as a swan in flight was beyond a baying hound. Bitter bile rose in his throat.

○ ○ ○

The helicopter vibrated irritatingly, but most of the machine's noise was blocked by the headphones the pilot had given him to wear. Alex stared at the landscape as it streaked by. The trees had started to change while he was gone, the gold and rust of poplar and birch beginning to soften the dark green spikes of spruce, giving the landscape an unusual light that flickered in a mesmerizing pattern below him. But he knew it would be brief. The leaves would be down soon and snow not far behind. He hoped the camp had a few books around and regretted, again, that he hadn't been able to get to his cabin.

The first sight of the camp took Alex by surprise. It was bigger than he expected, with several bunkhouse-style trailer units arranged in a circle around a large bare yard. The biggest building was a huge tin shed, probably sheltering the Cats and other equipment. At the other end a good-sized log house sat on a small rise of land. Thick bush hugged the circle, scraggly spruce, and a few stunted poplar hemming it in on all sides. He could see the scar of the cut line over another long hill to the north where they'd scraped away the topsoil to get at the bedrock and the gold beneath.

The boss had given him keys to all the buildings and told him to use the house and the office for his needs. "Everything's there," he'd said.

"Freezer full of meat in the house, radiophone in the office. There's a list of emergency codes by the phone. The rifle is over the door, ammo in the desk drawer. Hope you like the sound of your own voice 'cause there isn't anybody else around. 'Cept Titan and the grizzlies."

"I'll manage," Alex had said. As he crouched low and dashed away from the helicopter he thought he would. But when it lifted and careened away he felt an uneasy chill race up his spine. The growing silence as the chopper beat its way south left him feeling bereft. He shook himself, hefted his pack, and turned toward the camp.

Titan welcomed him with a low growl once he stopped barking. He was a big malamute, mostly white, his thick fur tipped with brown guard hairs outlining his ears, massive square head and thick legs. His bushy tail curled up over his back, but it didn't wag. His blue eyes stared as Alex filled the water dish and food bowl. Alex didn't try to get any closer than necessary. He had a feeling it was going to take a while for Titan to warm up to him.

He spent the rest of the afternoon exploring, starting with the bunkhouses. Most were completely bare except for the beds and small tables furnishing each unit. He pulled a couple of drawers open and found a few magazines, most of them of the pornographic variety. There were no books.

The office was in one half of a trailer unit at the top end of the row. It consisted of a large desk, a comfortable chair and tall file cabinet. The diesel heater sat against the wall dividing the trailer into two rooms, its heavy oily smell making Alex's nose twitch. The radiophone sat on one end of the desk—a square gray metal box with a small round microphone the size of his palm attached to it by a coiled cord. Alex flicked on the toggle switch, but only static blared out at him so he switched it off again. He knew there wasn't much chatter during the day. He'd try again in the evening when the conversations would get interesting. He pulled the desk drawer open and discovered a John Grisham novel. "One book," he said aloud. "Guess I'd better save it for a rainy day." He tossed it onto the desk, stood, and opened the door to the other half of the bunkhouse. A pile of sheets and heavy blankets sat on the end of a double bed, and there was a dresser and table against one wall. He threw his pack into a corner. "Home sweet home." He spoke aloud again, but felt no comfort from the sound of his own voice.

He decided to check out the house before unpacking. As he climbed the small hill, his boots thudding as they gripped on hard-packed dirt, he turned back to survey the yard. He could imagine the rumble of heavy equipment coming from the cut line over the hill, the hiss and flash of welders' torches in the shed, the methodical comings and goings of men in the dusty yard at shift change. But now it lay bare and still, the only sound the muffled thump of the diesel generator. The plain gray bunkhouses needed painting. The weathered wooden porches needed repair. The air was still and bitter with cold. Alex shivered and continued the short climb.

He roamed through the house feeling like an intruder. The interior had been left natural, the round logs shiny with varnish. There was a toy tractor on the floor in the living room and a complete set of exercise equipment assembled and ready to use. Another diesel heater sat in one corner, a large stone fireplace on the opposite wall. The air smelled faintly of pipe tobacco. His hand twitched and he regretted not buying any smokes. He moved into the kitchen, the only room with flat walls painted a bright yellow. An assortment of dirty dishes sat in the sink. Alex ignored them and opened the fridge. There were six dozen eggs and a carton of milk on the shelves, plus an almost empty container of orange juice. A large freezer sat against one wall. He lifted the lid and shifted the frozen packages around. Lots of meat and bags of frozen vegetables. "Like the man said, everything I need," he mumbled.

There were no linens on the beds, but a towel was still draped on the rack in the bathroom. Alex found himself back in the living room and breathed in the smell of pipe tobacco again. That stirred the craving again. He wondered if they'd left any around. The room was well furnished with what looked like handmade tables, comfortable chairs and a large overstuffed couch. He scanned the coffee table and end tables, then noticed the mantel above the fireplace. There was an old pipe resting in a rack, but no tobacco. Beside it was a book with a black cover. Alex reached for it, recognizing what it was the moment he touched it. *A Bible*. He smirked. *Wouldn't you know it? Two books in the whole place and one of them is a Bible.* A thin notebook lay underneath it. He flipped it open and read the date at the top of the page—November 2, 2000. He scanned the small cramped writing. Curious, he sat down in one of the big chairs and started to read.

I've been alone here now for over a month, but I still can't shake the feeling that I'm being watched. Maybe it's just paranoia. Maybe it's guilt or a little of both. God knows I have enough to feel guilty about. Maybe I should start reading that Bible I found. One book in the whole place and it's a Bible! He does have a sense of irony. Who knows, maybe it'll help make sense of it all now, make sense of my screwed-up life. Hiding out here isn't going to make anything go away. Spring will come and then I'll have to face it all again. Or find another place to run to. Or just stop.

Alex stared into space. The similarity of the words and his own thoughts was eerie. He put the book down, wondering about the man who had written in it. *What had he been running from?* Alex picked up the Bible again, letting his callused fingers play over the soft worn cover. He remembered that day he and Kenni skipped stones on the pebble beach. He remembered her talking about David. *Where did she say that started?* He opened the Bible to the index and scanned the chapter titles. None of them looked familiar. He flipped a few pages, reading here and there, then scanned the subtitles until he found what he was looking for. He started to read from Samuel 1:1.

"There was a certain man from Ramathaim, a Zuphite from the hill country of Ephraim, whose name was Elkanah, son of Jeroham, the son of Elihu, the son of Tohu, the son of Zuph, an Ephraimite."

Alex stopped reading. He skimmed the rest of the chapter, but found no sign of David's name. He paged further, reading the headings until he found it. Chapter 16—Samuel Anoints David. He put his feet up on the coffee table and got comfortable.

It wasn't until the light in the room started to dim that he realized he'd been there all afternoon. He stood up and stretched. *Always was a sucker for history. And fantasy.* He carried the book into the kitchen and rummaged around for some supper. *Steak. Yeah. Might as well start this job off right.* He cooked the meat to medium rare, tossed two potatoes in the microwave, and sat down to enjoy the meal. He paged through the Bible as he ate, reading bits here and there. Some of it made no sense. Some of it intrigued him.

When he was finished eating Alex picked up the steak bone and went outside. He noticed the edge in the air, the kind of stinging cold that cuts through thin jeans and T-shirts. *Soon be time to wear that new parka.*

Titan stood up and watched him approach, his eyes on the bone. "Got a treat for ya, Titan!" Alex called, holding it up. "Left some meat on it too so you be thankful, ya hear?"

The dog yipped and Alex tossed it to him. He caught it in the air and lay down with the bone between his paws. Alex was about to turn back to the house when he saw Titan lift his head and sniff. The growl began low in his throat, but died away before it rose to his mouth. Then he lowered his head again and concentrated on gnawing the bone. Alex looked in the direction the dog had peered, realizing he'd left the rifle inside.

He remembered a story he'd heard about a grizzly that had rampaged through a cabin. It had bulldozed the door down and gone out through a window, taking half the wall with it. Cast iron pots had been found crushed and scarred with tooth marks. "No time to get careless, Donnelly," he chided himself and headed for the house.

○ ○ ○

The next day Alex tried out the exercise equipment, working up enough of a sweat that he thought about a shower, but decided to clean up the mess in the kitchen first. He had his hands in a sink full of water so hot it steamed the window in front of him when he heard Titan bark once and quit. It sounded almost like someone had clamped a hand over the dog's snout to muzzle him. He grabbed the towel on the counter and swiped at the window, leaning forward to peer out.

Two eyes peered back at him, pale eyes set deep under thick bushy eyebrows as overgrown as an untrimmed hedge. Alex leaped back. The face disappeared. He raced to the door, grabbing the flashlight as he went. Running around to the side of the house he let the beam scan the yard. There was no sound, no sign of anyone. Titan lay curled on top of his doghouse, oblivious. Alex scanned the yard again, then examined the dirt under the kitchen window. It was hard packed and gave no evidence of footprints. "Must be seeing things," he mumbled. He peered around the yard one more time, then went back inside.

He finished cleaning up quickly, returned the Bible and notebook to the mantel, picked up the flashlight and rifle, and trotted back to the office. He turned the volume up on the radiophone and listened to the chatter. It wasn't long before his eyes started to droop.

The sudden silence jerked him awake. The darkness made his heart race. He groped for the flashlight, then grabbed the rifle and stood still, the thump of his own pulse the only sound. *How long had the generator been off? Calm down, Donnelly. Maybe it just ran out of fuel.* He took a deep breath and stepped outside. The yard was pitch black and the feeble beam from the flashlight didn't help much. Alex stood on the porch for a long time, listening. There was no sound but the rustle of the wind in the bushes. He walked slowly toward the generator shed, turning and scanning with the light as he went.

He stepped inside the shed and let the door swing closed behind him. His ears rang with the silence as he leaned over the machine. Suddenly, a flood of cold air raced toward him as the door flew open. It caught him in the middle of his back and sent him sprawling. The rifle exploded when he hit the floor. The flashlight somersaulted through the air. Alex rolled, pumped the gun to reload, and fired a round through the open doorway.

Then silence descended and nothing moved.

○ ○ ○

Inspector Sorensen looked up when the file landed on his desk.

The young rookie grinned at him. "Nine cases," he said, "with similar M.O. Four in the lower mainland, one on the Island, three in the Okanagan, and one up north."

Sorensen reached for the file. "All in the last five years?"

"Yeah. One was fairly recent."

"Where?"

The younger officer took the file from Sorensen's hands, flipped the pages, and laid it back in front of him. He tapped a photo with his index finger.

"Whitehorse."

Chapter Fifteen

Kenni leaned toward the young man at the counter and tried not to let her frustration show. "I reserved the vehicle yesterday. Are you sure there's no record of it?"

The young man behind the counter shook his head. "Sorry. It's September. We just put most of our vehicles in for overhauls. The couple that were left are gone."

George turned away. "We'll have to grab a cab into town." He snatched up his bag. "This is turning out to be one of those trips."

At the hotel Kenni watched George's frustration grow. He glared at the desk clerk. "I can't believe there isn't a single car to be had in this town."

"Sorry," he shrugged. "It's September."

"Right. So doesn't anyone want to go to Dawson City in September?"

"If they do, they fly or take the bus."

"Great. Where do I call to book a flight?"

When he dialed the number Kenni tried to tell him it would just be a recording, but he ignored her. She knew he was listening to a slow recorded message listing the dates and times for flights around the territory. The next flight to Dawson was in three days. When he hung up Kenni reminded him that was why she'd rented the car, or thought she had. It didn't improve his mood.

At 7:00 the next morning they stood in front of a small building with a sign in the window that read "Greyhound Bus." There were no buses to be seen, and no people.

"I can't believe it's already so cold here." Kenni pulled her jacket tighter. "Shouldn't they be open by now if the bus leaves at 7:15?"

George didn't answer, just plunked his bag down and shoved his hands into his jacket pockets. At 7:10 a blue school bus pulled up in front of the small building. Kenni looked at George. "You don't suppose...."

The driver stepped down and nodded to them. "Mornin'. You folks goin' to Dawson?"

"I'm afraid so," George answered.

"I'll get you a couple of tickets." He stepped aside and waved toward the bus. "Go ahead and have a seat."

As they climbed aboard, a young native couple stared from the front seat. A few minutes later the driver appeared and handed ticket stubs out in exchange for their money.

"How long does it take to get to Dawson?" George asked.

"Oh, 'bout eight hours if the road's good."

Kenni groaned.

"You folks visiting somebody up there?"

"Sort of."

"Kind of a different time to visit. September's off season, ya know."

"No kidding," George answered morosely.

"Yup. Right after Discovery Days, Dawson rolls up the carpet. By the end of August it's almost a ghost town, 'cept for the locals of course. Who'd you say you was visitin'?"

"A guy named Alex. Alex Donnelly."

"Yeah, I know Alex. Sort of." The driver frowned. "Haven't seen him around lately, though. You sure he's there?"

Kenni glanced at George. "No. We're not sure. You haven't seen him lately?"

"Nope."

George sat back and slumped on the seat. "Great."

"That doesn't mean he's not there," Kenni commented as the driver returned to his seat.

"The word 'city' tacked onto the name Dawson is a bit of a misnomer. The place is more like a village. Everybody seems to know everybody who belongs, and everybody who doesn't."

Kenni bunched up a sweater, punched it into the corner of the window, and laid her head on it. "Well, I guess we'll find out in about eight hours."

The vibration made it impossible to sleep so she stared out at the landscape as it flowed by. Trees, rock and water. *What would drive someone to such a lonely place? A lot of pain, a lot of distrust. Maybe even the need to hide.* She shivered as the thoughts surfaced. She didn't move from her position at the window until the bus lurched to a stop at a highway lodge.

"Best cinnamon buns in the country," the driver assured them. He grinned to reveal a gaping hole on one side of his mouth. "That singer, you know, used to be on the folk festival circuit? Always forget his name. He wrote a song about this place, called it 'Cinnamon Bun Strip.'" He pulled the lever to snap the door open as the native couple got off. "We'll take 'bout half an hour here," he said and followed them.

George heaved himself up and groaned as he tried to stretch the stiffness out. Kenni echoed his groan as she sat up. "Not quite as comfortable as your car, is it?"

George held his hand out. "C'mon. I'll buy you one of the best cinnamon buns in the country."

The lodge was more like a roadhouse with six long wooden tables in a large open room, a small counter and cash register at the far end. They could see the shoulders and torso of the cook moving behind an opening in the back wall. Kenni plopped down at the end of one of the tables while George headed for the hole to order. He poured two cups of coffee from a pot on the counter and sat down. A few minutes later the waitress held up two plates and looked at George expectantly. He rolled his eyes, but got up and retrieved them.

The cinnamon buns were not only good, they were huge, each one covering a dinner plate. Kenni laughed as George picked his up and took a huge bite, leaving stickiness all over his face. He was chewing enthusiastically when the door swung open and his jaw dropped. He tried to swallow quickly as a tall young woman strode toward him.

"Hey. Fancy meeting you here. Gerry, right?" Her eyes flashed toward Kenni. "Where's Alex?"

George managed to get the mouthful of bun down his throat and wiped his face with a napkin. "Uh, I don't know." Kenni noticed he ignored the fact that she'd gotten his name wrong. "We're on our way to Dawson to try and find him."

The woman's eyebrows shot up. "Well, you're wasting your time. He's not there."

"You're sure? He might've just arrived yesterday."

She shook her head. "I just came from Dawson. If Alex was in town, I'd know about it." Her eyes flicked to Kenni again and narrowed. "How come you're lookin' for him?"

Kenni piped up. "We have a letter to deliver to him."

"Oh?" She stared at her.

George cleared his throat. "Uh, Sal, this is Kenni."

The woman said "Hi," but made no move to shake hands.

Kenni leaned forward. "Maybe Alex went straight up to his cabin, on the river?"

Sal shook her head again. "Nope," she looked into Kenni's eyes. "I'd know he was around. I'm still lookin' after his dogs."

Kenni dropped her eyes to her plate, the cinnamon bun suddenly looking greasy and unappealing.

George glanced at her, then back to Sal. "So you have any idea where he might be?"

Sal's eyes narrowed. "No."

George sighed. "Guess there's no use going all the way to Dawson, then." He swung around and called out to the driver, sitting with the native couple at the front of the room. "When's the next bus back to Whitehorse?"

The driver looked up from a huge sandwich. "Should be one through here 'bout midnight."

George groaned. "Nothing til then?"

"Nope."

Sal grinned at them. "You could hitch."

Kenni looked up at her, not appreciating the laughter in her eyes. "You heading south?"

Sal shrugged. "Maybe I could. For a price."

"How much?" George asked.

"Fifty bucks. Each."

"Okay." George stood up. "Let's go."

Sal held up her hand. "Whoa, cowboy. Haven't had my cinnamon bun yet."

Kenni pushed her plate toward her. "Have mine. I'm not hungry."

Sal glanced at it. "No thanks. I'll get my own."

She turned and walked toward the counter, poured herself a cup of coffee, and sat with the driver. They heard her say the word "cheechakos."

The driver's loud guffaw made Kenni scowl.

"I thought northerners were supposed to be friendly," she said taking a last gulp of coffee.

"It's September," George replied, the sarcasm thick in his voice. "Tourist season's over."

Kenni sighed. "Do you trust that girl?"

"Why would she lie?"

Kenni cocked her head slightly and gave him a look.

George frowned. "I...I don't think she'd do that." He took another bite of cinnamon bun. "But if you want to keep going to Dawson, it's your call."

Kenni's eyes flicked in Sal's direction. "Do you know if...?" She dropped her eyes, then leveled them on George. "Are they close?"

George's face turned pink. "I don't think Alex is close to anyone," he said.

Kenni sighed. It was an evasive answer, but she decided not to press the issue. She stared at the bottom of her empty coffee cup. "Maybe we should just go home."

George glanced over his shoulder. "Actually, it's good we ran into Sal. She'll know Alex's friends, where he hangs out. We'll find him."

Kenni's eyes flashed back to where Sal sat, then focused on George again. "I'll let you ask the questions."

George grinned. "Good plan."

The bus driver stopped at their table as he left. "So you're going to jump out here?"

George nodded. "Change of schedule."

The driver shrugged. "Suit yourself."

Sal was right behind him. "Okay, Gerry, taxi's leavin'."

"George," he said.

"Huh?" Sal frowned.

"My name is George."

"Whatever," she said. "You comin' or not?"

Sal's truck was old, but hummed reassuringly as they drove. George pumped her for information about Alex's habits in Whitehorse. She didn't volunteer many details, but did volunteer to deliver the letter. She gave them a skeptical look when they explained that they didn't exactly have it with them. By the time they reached Whitehorse they knew little more about Alex than what they'd already discovered. Before Sal dropped them at the Westmark Hotel George paid her for the ride and gave her his card. He scribbled his cell phone number on the back. "If you see him, Sal, will you call me?"

"Yeah, sure," she said and peeled her truck's tires when she sped away.

"I wouldn't hold my breath," Kenni commented.

They booked two rooms in the hotel and met in the lobby to decide what to do next.

"Alex took me to a bar the first night we were here," George said. "They make good pizza," he responded to Kenni's raised eyebrows. "I guess that's as good a place to start as any."

They sat at a small table for several hours asking everyone who came in if they knew Alex Donnelly. The few who did hadn't seen him and had no idea where he might be. They walked back to the hotel just before midnight.

"Guess you were right," Kenni admitted. "This is a wild goose chase."

"We'll have another go at it tomorrow," George replied. "Somebody has to have seen him. A man can't just vanish."

"Unless he wants to." Kenni's shoulders drooped.

"There's one thing we haven't done yet." He waited for her to look at him. "We haven't contacted the RCMP."

Chapter Sixteen

Alex shook his head, trying to relieve the ringing in his ears so he could hear whatever was out there. It didn't work. He got to his feet and shuffled around the small shed until he found the flashlight. The beam burst through the dark. *Breathe. Just breathe.* Then he took one step out the door.

"Stupid," he said aloud. He stared at the tracks within the circle of light at his feet. The paw print was long and wider than the span of his hand. The imprint of the claws was unmistakable. *Grizzly.* He followed them a short way, crouching down now and then to check for blood. He was relieved to find none. The last thing he needed was a wounded bear in the neighborhood. Firing a shot off into the dark without seeing what he was shooting at…. "Stupid," he said again.

He stood outside the shed for a few moments staring up at the long claw marks on the door and lintel above it. If that had been his back…. Alex shivered and pushed the door open. Striding quickly to the machine he removed the cap to the fuel intake and shone the flashlight down to check the level. He could see no gleam of liquid in the tank. He refilled it and pulled the cord. It roared to life and the lights blinked, then blazed. Alex wasted no time returning to the office.

○ ○ ○

George called the firm the next morning to check in. The letter had yet to be found. "But we're still looking," the secretary assured him. Kenni made a face when he told her, but said nothing.

"Let's go over to the police station," George suggested. "Maybe we can learn something there."

The officer took the information, but said they could do nothing unless they wanted to report Alex as a missing person. They both agreed it was too soon to do that. George left his cell phone number and they headed back to the restaurant.

"Okay," George said pulling out a pen and pushing his plate aside. "If he was going back up to his cabin, what would he need?"

Kenni started the list. "Food, warm clothes, boots, toiletries, dog food."

George nodded as he scribbled on the placemat. "Essentials," he said. "What else?"

"Books."

George looked up, then remembered the stack of books in Alex's cabin. Books, he wrote. "What else?" He chewed the end of the pen. "Skis?"

"Or snowshoes, maybe," Kenni said. "Batteries? Ammunition?"

"Maybe." George tore the list from the rest of the placemat and handed it to her, then wrote a copy and tore it off for himself. "Okay. I'll start at one end of the main street. You start at the other. Go into every shop that sells any of these items."

Kenni nodded. "Okay. Meet you back here when?"

George looked at his watch. "Noon?"

She nodded and scrambled out of the booth. Two and a half hours later they stared at one another across the same table. "Some people know Alex," Kenni started.

"But no one has seen him lately," George finished. He sighed. "We'll cover the other streets after lunch." This time they went together, but their success rate was the same. They had just come to the end of the street when George's phone rang. The voice on the other end had the somber controlled tone of someone trained in speaking the words that George heard. He responded with one syllable words and hung up. Then he took Kenni's arm. "We have to go back to the police station," he said.

"Why?"

"They have some information." He didn't tell her what.

○ ○ ○

They were ushered into a small room with a table and four chairs. The walls were concrete block, painted pale green. Kenni stared at the intersecting lines. They reminded her of the grooves made by small tunneling animals. It seemed a long time before a policeman entered with a file and sat across from them. He introduced himself as Constable Ray Ewing.

"I understand you're looking for a man named Alex Donnelly?'

George nodded. "That's right."

"Can I ask the nature of your interest?"

"He's my client."

"Client? As in, lawyer?"

"That's right."

"I see. Then as his lawyer you're aware of the warrant for his arrest?"

Kenni's eyes flew to the man's face. "Warrant?"

"Yes. He's wanted on a charge of sexual assault."

She felt the color drain from her face. "What?"

The officer's next words seemed to echo down a long tunnel. "Alex Donnelly raped and brutalized a thirteen-year-old girl in Vancouver five years ago."

Chapter Seventeen

The policeman continued. "We had no idea he was in this vicinity until today. Interesting." His eyes narrowed. "You brought his name to our attention at the same time we were alerted to the possibility that he might be in Whitehorse. This is going to be a priority for us." He opened the file he'd brought with him. "Do you have a recent photograph?"

Kenni opened her mouth, but no words came out. George took her hand. "No," he said. "No photograph."

The officer flipped a page in the file. "We'll use this old one then." He slid the photograph across the table. "This is the same person you're looking for?"

George looked down at the picture and nodded. "Yes. That's him."

The officer retrieved it. "This will be circulated throughout the territory. Is there anything more you can tell me about him?"

George glanced at Kenni. She didn't look at him. He shook his head. "No. That's all we know."

The constable stood up. "We'll contact you when we have anything of interest. Thanks for coming in."

○ ○ ○

Kenni shook her head all the way back to the hotel. "I don't believe it."

George leaned over the table toward her. "Kenni, think about it. You hardly know him. And considering his background...."

"His background is the same as mine, George." Her eyes snapped.

129

"And you've had a lot of help to get over it. Alex hasn't."

Kenni shook her head again. "No. I just won't believe it." She gripped the edge of the table. "Not until I hear it from his own mouth." She almost glared at George. "We have to find him."

George sat back and sighed. "I think we'd better let the police handle—"

"No!"

The pitch of Kenni's voice made him frown. He stared at her. They sat in silence for a few minutes. Then George took a deep breath and made a decision. "Okay," he said. "Let's try that bar again. This is about the time we went there," he reasoned. "Maybe the same bartender will be working. He seemed to know Alex fairly well."

The logic paid off.

"Yeah, Alex was here, just the other day." The bartender leaned forward, his tattooed biceps bulging as he stroked his beard and grinned at Kenni. "He looked pretty rough, like he'd been at the wrong end of somebody's fist."

"Do you know where he went?" she asked without smiling.

"Nope. He was lookin' for work. Disappeared pretty quick so I guess he found somethin'. Haven't seen him since."

George leaned forward. "Where would he find work at this time of year? Construction? The mines?"

The man shrugged. "Could be. Faro's always hiring. Or maybe he scored a caretaking job."

"Caretaking?"

"Yeah. Some of the gold companies, this time o' year, they hire guys to go live at the mine site to guard their equipment. Usually it's just a bear watch to make sure some griz doesn't come along and trash the place. Pay's good."

Kenni put her hand on George's arm. "That sounds like something he'd go for," she said.

George nodded and turned to the bartender again. "Can you tell me the names of some of these mines?" He scribbled as the bartender rhymed off several names.

"That's all I can think of. What's the big rush to find Alex anyways?"

"We have a letter to deliver to him. An important letter." George asked for a phone book and they sat at a table searching for the mining companies' numbers. A few of them weren't listed. None of the others had heard of Alex Donnelly.

George asked the bartender about the unlisted companies. He explained that their head offices were probably out of the territory, in Vancouver, Edmonton or Calgary. George started calling long distance. Several phone calls later a secretary's bright voice said, "Oh yes, we just hired an Alex Donnelly to caretake our properties in the Yukon."

George wondered if she'd ever heard of the privacy act, but didn't mention it. "Is there a phone number where we can reach him?"

Her laughter bubbled across the line. "Oh, no. That camp is in the middle of nowhere. There's a radiophone, but it has to be turned on of course."

"Can I have that number please?"

She gave it to him without hesitation. "Bingo," he said as he flipped his cell phone closed. Then he frowned. "Kenni, I really think we should tell—"

"No." Kenni was emphatic, but her voice was now calm. "Not until I have a chance to talk to him."

"This is against my better judgment, but...." George offered his cell phone to her across the table. "You want to try calling or shall I?"

Kenni took the phone and glanced at the number. "How do I punch this in?" she asked, frowning. The number was only four digits but included two code words.

"Try the operator," George suggested.

Kenni hit zero, gave the information to the operator who transferred her to another, and in a few moments Kenni heard the woman's voice giving the call sign. "Calling, Beacon Hill 4-8-9-0, Beacon Hill 4-8-9-0 come in please." She repeated it three more times then said, "I'm sorry, ma'am, that phone is not receiving."

Kenni's face fell. "Thanks," she said and hung up.

They returned to the hotel and tried calling the number every half hour for the rest of the day and into the evening. They were having supper when Kenni's exasperation spilled out. "Oooh, if Alex Donnelly were here right now, I'd...strangle him!"

George snorted. "I'd help, gladly."

Kenni sighed. "What if we can't get hold of him, George?"

"Then I guess we'll have to wait for the police to do it for us."

Kenni shuddered. "There must be something else we can do. Maybe we can find out where that camp is and fly out there."

George cut into the steak in front of him, then looked at her. "Maybe tomorrow. Let's try and enjoy our meal right now, okay?"

She sighed again, but nodded and put the cell phone away.

○ ○ ○

Kenni didn't try calling again until she was back in her room. After several calls she was ready to give up. She ran a hot bath, soaked until she felt like she could fall asleep, and decided to try one more time.

"Calling Beacon Hill 4-8-9-0, come in please." The refrain was becoming so familiar she thought she'd hear it in her sleep. "Calling Beacon Hill 4-8-9-0, come in please."

"Beacon Hill 4-8-9-0, go ahead."

Kenni leaped to her feet. It was Alex's voice, loud and clear. She heard the operator's voice say, "Stand by one, Beacon Hill. Go ahead, ma'am."

"Alex?"

There was silence for a minute, then a click and one word. "Kenni?"

She wanted to laugh. "Yes. It's me. You're a hard man to track down, Alex Donnelly."

Silence again. Click. "Maybe I don't want to be tracked down. Over."

She ignored that. "Alex, you only know half the story." She heard a click again, but kept talking. "There's a letter, a letter from your mother. We haven't found it yet, but it exists. You have to come back."

Again the silence seemed long, the click a welcome noise. "I only caught part of that, Kenni. You have to say 'over' when you're done. I have to hit a button on this end to talk and when I do I can't hear you. All I caught was that I only know half the story." His voice dropped. "That half was enough. Over."

"There's a letter, Alex," she repeated. "A letter from your mother. You have to come back. Over."

"Not possible. Just got this job. I need the money. Over."

Kenni felt like screaming. "You have enough money to do whatever you want, sitting in a bank in Seattle." She almost forgot to say over.

"Just for your information the entire territory and at least half of Alaska can hear your conversation so watch what you say. Over."

"Alex, please. I have to talk to you, face to face." She wanted to blurt out the question haunting her. She wanted to warn him, but then remembered what he'd just said about others listening in. "There's something...something else we have to talk about. It's important. Over."

"Like I said...." Static blotted out his words. Then she heard, "...not possible. Over."

"I'm not leaving until I see you. Over."

No click. No answer. Kenni couldn't stand the silence. "Alex? Are you still there? Over."

Click. His voice was gentler, not as cold, but the words made her shiver. "Leave it alone, Kenni. Go home. Over and out. Beacon Hill clear."

Static blared into her ear. She flipped the phone closed and tossed it onto the bed. She wanted to scream at him, but she wanted to see his face, wanted to look into his eyes. She wanted more than anything to hear him say he hadn't raped that young girl. She groaned and flopped onto the bed, then got up and paced. *Why did God make men so stubborn and so...unreachable? And why do I feel so helpless? I don't even know what to pray anymore.* She wiped the tears from her eyes with quick angry strokes.

Chapter Eighteen

Alex picked up the Grisham novel he'd been reading, scanned the page for the last sentence he remembered, and when he couldn't find it threw the book across the room with a curse. He picked up the microphone and thumbed the switch, listening to the static, empty of voices. *Quit dreaming, Donnelly.* He put the microphone back into its holder. Then Kenni's words echoed in his mind.

"There's a letter, Alex. A letter from your mother."

He couldn't deny how his heart had leaped when she'd said that, but then he remembered the words in that legal document. "Terminating the pregnancy of the plaintiff." Alex's hands clenched into fists. *So why would I want a letter from her? Why would I want anything at all from a woman who wanted me dead before I was even born?*

And what was it that seemed to nag at the edge of Kenni's voice? What else did she want to talk to me about? A sick dread rose inside him. He tried to push it away, but couldn't shake the anxiety.

A long low howl made him jump. *Titan.* Alex listened as the dog's voice increased in volume, then intensity. He leaped up and grabbed the gun from over the door, checked to make sure it was loaded, grabbed the flashlight, and stepped out into the darkness. The dog was lunging at the end of his chain. Alex shone the light toward him, noted the direction in which he was barking, and scanned with the flashlight. He was just in time to catch the bear's huge rear end disappearing into the bush.

Alex strode toward the dog. "Good boy, Titan!" he called. The animal growled. Alex grinned. "Hey, don't blame me, I didn't invite him here." He scanned the bush with the flashlight again, then let its beam swing out over the compound. There was no sign of the bear or anything else, but the hair still bristled on Titan's back. Alex put a hand to the back of his neck. His hair was bristling too.

○ ○ ○

Gil stood still behind the screen of branches and waited until the man went back inside. He nestled his rifle in the crook of his arm and stood for a time watching the yellow glow of light from the window. He took a step forward, stopped. Then he turned and moved silently back into the bush.

○ ○ ○

George watched Kenni pick at the eggs on her plate. He laid down his fork. "You can't make a horse drink, Kenni."

"Yes you can," she said. "You rub salt on his lips."

"Well, that trick didn't seem to work with this horse."

"I know, but I still think we should hire a helicopter and go find him." She looked up. "I feel like I'm abandoning him."

George shook his head. "Helicopters are expensive. And how would you convince him to come with us?" George knew his exasperation was leaking into his voice, but he didn't stop. "We don't have the letter. And even if we did, he doesn't seem to want to know what's in it. We can't even prove the letter exists. And now there's this other thing—and if it's true—Kenni, we have to tell the police. Even though I'm not licensed here, I still have an obligation—we have an obligation to—"

"I know," Kenni cut him off sharply, then softened her voice. "I know, but...I can't do it, George. I can't betray him like that."

It was George's turn to sigh. "My dad used to always say 'There's only one way to change an impossible situation. Pray.'"

Tears welled up in Kenni's eyes. "I have. That doesn't seem to be working either."

George's stomach twisted at the look in her eyes. He dropped his voice a notch. "Maybe God has a plan that doesn't include Alex coming back to Seattle."

Kenni shook her head hard. "I can't believe He'd let us find him in the first place, and lead us through all this for nothing."

"Maybe it hasn't been for nothing. Maybe there are things we're supposed to be learning. I think there are one or two I've been picking up on."

"Such as?"

George swallowed. "Such as how do I keep from wanting to smack Alex Donnelly with a two-by-four?"

Kenni's grin was brief. She dropped her eyes.

"And," George continued, "maybe more to the point, why do I really want to?"

Kenni's eyes flashed up just as the waitress arrived with their bill.

George continued when she was gone. "And maybe God has other purposes in this."

Kenni reached for the bill. "What do you mean?"

George hesitated, then blurted out what he was thinking. "Maybe God wants Alex to face up to what he's done. Maybe we've just been agents in that."

Kenni's eyes narrowed. "You've tried and convicted him already, haven't you?"

"Kenni...."

She didn't give him a chance to finish. "If we're going to catch the plane back to Seattle, we'd better get going."

Chapter Nineteen

The boy blinked against the dim light. He could see the small curve of *the girl's cheek, wet with tears. She turned her head toward him, her eyes pleading, but all he felt was the rage, the rage that made him want to destroy everything in his path. A long slim snake slid over the girl's shoulder, its red eyes unblinking. Alex's mind froze and instinct took over.*

Then he was running, sirens screaming in his ears. He looked over his shoulder and into a gaping maw, teeth dripping with blood. He screamed and fell headlong, tumbling over and over, the images of the girl, the snake, the bear swirling in his mind.

○ ○ ○

Alex woke with the vague unsettled feeling that told him his dreams had been disturbing. Again. At least he couldn't remember much of this one. *Small mercies.* He opened his eyes as those words flitted through his mind. Pastor T used that expression a lot. "Be thankful for small mercies," he'd say. Alex snorted and rolled over.

There was no reason to get up early when the first rays of light edged through the window so the morning was all but gone before he crawled out of bed. The events of the last few days seemed almost like a dream too, but when he twisted to look at his back in the small mirror on the wall the large dark bruise told him it was real.

He knew the conversation with Kenni had been real. Her voice lingered in his mind. And the mixture of hope and dread returned. *What was the other thing she wanted to talk about? Could they have found out? Maybe he should get out of here. Maybe he should call her. Had she left Whitehorse yet? Was George with her? Would he take his advice and make a move?* He groaned, pulled on his shirt with a quick jerk, and shook himself. *Don't go there.* He finished dressing quickly, picked up the rifle, and went outside.

Titan greeted him with a quick yip as if to say, "It's about time you got up."

Alex grinned at him. "Hungry, old boy?"

He went to the shed and was about to open the door when he glanced down at his feet. There was a large imprint beside his own. It looked like a man's footprint, but without the clear stamp of a boot or shoe. Alex crouched down to examine it more closely. The edges were round, smooth. *A moccasin? Didn't notice these tracks yesterday. Maybe I just wasn't paying attention.* He glanced around, suddenly feeling the same way he had the night the generator went dead—like something—or someone—was watching him. He cradled the rifle in one arm and stepped into the shed.

Titan started to bark as Alex scooped the chunks of dry food into a pail. Then the dog suddenly went quiet. Alex listened for a moment, heard a soft whine, then nothing. He stepped out and around the shed. Titan was laying calmly in the dirt, staring off toward the bunkhouses. Alex followed his gaze, but saw nothing. He rattled the pail and the dog leaped up and started to bark again.

After giving Titan the food Alex walked toward the bunkhouses. He walked around them, then stood still and listened. There was no sound other than the muffled thump of the generator and the soft whisper of leaves as the wind stirred in the poplars and sighed through the spruce.

Alex shook his head. "I'm getting paranoid already," he said aloud, "And it's only week two."

He returned to his chores and gave Titan a bowl of water. He had already gulped down most of the dog food. The rest lay scattered on the ground.

"You're a messy eater, Titan," he said and crouched down, balancing the rifle across his knees as he slowly reached out his hand for the dog to smell. Titan extended his head, then pulled it back. His blue eyes didn't waver as they stared.

Alex chuckled. "Don't trust anybody, do ya?" He stood up, Pastor T's voice echoing in his mind again. "I know you're afraid to trust anyone, Alex." He remembered the anger burning inside him at those words. He'd wanted to scream, "I'm not afraid!" but he'd kept a stony silence until the pastor finally quit talking and let him go. Alex fingered his earlobe and let his thumb trace the line of the scar on his neck. *Why do I keep thinking about that pastor?* He remembered feeling safe with him, even wanting to be around him, except when he'd start with the lectures and the anger would return. Alex sighed. He knew it was always that anger that got him into trouble and kept him from letting people like Pastor T into his life. *The guy sure had tried to help me.* Just like Kenni and her dad and George. He fingered the scar again and tilted his head. *Yeah. They're all alike. Do-gooders.* He snorted and watched Titan lick at the bits of dog food laying in the dirt.

As he turned away he realized his stomach was rumbling. *Time for some breakfast.* He had his hand on the doorknob of the back door to the house when he saw another set of those strange footprints. *Must be from one of the crew or maybe the people who had lived in the house. I just haven't noticed them before.* He pushed open the door to the kitchen.

He noticed the Bible immediately. It was lying open on the table. Alex stared down at it. He was sure he'd put it back on the mantel. He moved into the living room. Nothing seemed changed, but he thought the smell of tobacco was stronger than the day before. *Probably just the nicotine craving kicking in.* He went back to the kitchen, rummaged in the freezer, and found a pound of bacon. Chopping off a chunk he fried it up and made himself an omelet to go with it. The last bite of eggs was halfway to his mouth when he heard a floorboard creak above his head. The fork remained suspended in the air as he listened. It was in his mouth when he heard the sound again. He went to the bottom of the stairs and stood still. There was no sound from above. He took the stairs two at a time and moved quickly through the rooms. No sign of anyone.

Alex frowned. *Enough to make a guy believe in ghosts.* He turned and started to descend the stairs, then stopped and sniffed. The strong smell of a pipe was undeniable. He continued down, headed for the front door, and made a lot of noise getting there. He opened the door and slammed it shut again, then waited. Nothing moved. No floorboards creaked. No man, or ghost, appeared. Alex forced himself to wait for three long minutes, then grunted. "Ghosts," he said aloud and went back to the kitchen.

The Bible caught his attention again. It was open to Psalm 145. A psalm of praise. Of David. Alex picked it up and read the first two verses: "I will exalt you, my God the King; I will praise your name for ever and ever. Every day I will praise you and extol your name for ever and ever." Alex's heartbeat quickened. He knew he hadn't read those words the night before. He stared at it for a few moments, then whirled around and opened the refrigerator. Scanning the contents he tried to remember what was in it the last time he'd looked. *Were there four dozen eggs, or six?* He couldn't remember. Turning back to the counter he saw the rest of the pack of bacon sitting on the cutting board. He counted the slices, wrapped it loosely, and put it in the fridge. Then he counted the eggs left in the carton and put it beside the bacon. *If this ghost gets hungry, I want to know about it.*

He went into the living room and spent the next hour on the exercise bench, showered, and returned to the kitchen. He left the breakfast dishes for later and headed for the office. Titan raised his head as he went by, but made no sound. Alex went directly to the radiophone and scanned the list of numbers beside it. The name of the company that owned the mine site was first on the list. He snatched up the microphone and pressed the Call button. The operator responded in a few minutes. Alex gave her his call sign and asked her to connect him to the number of the company. He replaced the microphone and sat down to wait for her to call him back. He was engrossed in the Grisham novel when her voice boomed from the speaker.

"Beacon Hill 4-8-9-0. Beacon Hill 4-8-9-0, come in please."

Alex grabbed the microphone and responded. It took the secretary a while to get the hang of how to talk on a radiophone, but once she did she assured Alex that she'd have someone call him back by 5 p.m. that day.

"Remember, it has to be someone who knew the men who worked here," Alex said.

"Yes, I understand that. I'll have someone call you as soon as possible. Over."

As Alex replaced the microphone he pictured the pale eyes that had looked back at him through the kitchen window. He tried to visualize the rest of the face, but couldn't make it come into focus. All he remembered were those eyes. But it'd be hard to forget eyes like that. He hoped the description would be enough to identify the man.

He was in the middle of the novel when the radio blared again. The man's voice on the other end was familiar.

"This is Bob Jeske, Alex. What's up? Please don't tell me you're quitting already, over."

"No, not yet," Alex responded. "Did you know the men who worked out here last summer? Over."

"Yeah, I knew them all. Why? Over."

"Was there a guy—maybe an older guy with gray hair and very pale eyes? Maybe the caretaker a couple of years ago? Over."

"I've only been with the company a year and a half, but I don't remember any old guys. Over."

"Nobody with pale eyes and bushy eyebrows? Over."

"Not that I ever noticed. What's this about? Over."

Alex thumbed the Reply button. *What should I say, that I've been seeing and hearing a ghost?*

"Uh, well, I was just wondering if maybe somebody stayed behind. Maybe without you knowing about it. Over."

"Not possible. We took everybody out a few days before you got there. Over."

"How about last year, or the year before? Over."

"You telling me you've got an unwelcome visitor out there? Over."

"Maybe. Or it could be...could be just my imagination. Over."

"Must be. I can almost guarantee there's nobody within a hundred miles or more of you. Over."

"Yeah, okay. Hey, any luck finding a fill-in? I'd really like to get out to my cabin to check on my dogs and get some of my stuff sometime soon. Over."

"Nothing yet, but I'll let you know. Anything else? Over."

"No, I guess that's it. Over."

"Okay. Talk to you again. Over and out."

Alex clicked the microphone one last time. "Beacon Hill, clear." He hung it on its hook and flopped back down into the chair. *No point holding my breath about a replacement. I'm here, doing the job. They won't be in any hurry to let me leave.* He picked up the Grisham novel and dog-eared the corner. *I could polish off the rest of the book in an hour, but then what?*

Those pale eyes floated before him again. *Is there a man out there somewhere, keeping himself hidden? Is it maybe the same man who had written in that small journal and left the Bible open on the kitchen table? Why wouldn't he show himself? What's he afraid of?*

Or is this all in my head? Maybe I left the Bible on the table. A breeze could've shifted the pages. Maybe I imagined that face in the window.

He sighed. His life seemed to be always full of questions—questions with no answers.

Chapter Twenty

George watched Maxwell Ferrington pace in the large office, then he glanced at Kenni. She was frowning at the small Zen pan of sand he kept on his desk. She'd given it to him on his birthday some time ago. The small rake was gone, but she trailed the tip of a pencil through it, tracing wavy lines around a single smooth stone. George's eyes lingered on the slender curve of her hand.

He became aware that Max had stopped in front of a large window overlooking the skyscape of the city. The elder lawyer's voice was low and he mumbled. George wasn't sure if he was addressing them or not, but he interrupted. "Sir?"

Max waved his hand. "I was just berating myself, George. I should've made a copy of that letter when it first went into the file. I almost did, but thought it was too personal and should be kept sealed. If I'd followed my first instinct, perhaps we wouldn't be in this predicament."

George shook his head. "I doubt that the letter would make any difference, Max. Alex obviously doesn't even want to read it. And, understandably, he doesn't want to be found." He looked over at Kenni, but she was still playing with the sand.

"We have to find a way to convince him, a way to reach him."

Kenni looked up. "What makes you so sure that what's in the letter will make a difference?"

Ferrington stared out the window again. "I knew the woman who wrote it. And I know that she loved her son and would've tried to communicate that to him." He turned to face them. "I feel an obligation to make sure Alex knows that. If he still wants to reject his past, that's his choice, but I have to make sure he knows the whole story."

George sighed. "So what do we do now?"

"We keep trying to contact him, keep trying to convince him to come back. And keep looking for that letter." Max strode toward the door. "We can also try looking into this sexual assault allegation. Find out the details and go from there." He gave a wave of his hand and was gone.

Kenni stood up. "We need to personally check with every lawyer, every secretary in every office in this firm. That letter has to be somewhere."

"We've already had them combing through their files," George said. "They won't be happy about being told to do it again. You know how busy everyone is."

Kenni gave a determined shake of her head. "I also know how easy it is to ignore a memo. I'm going to go to every office, in person."

"That will take a lot of your time, Kenni."

Kenni headed for the door. "If that's what it takes, that's what I'll do."

George stared at the Zen pan of sand holding the one smooth black stone. He opened Alex's file, read for a while, then picked up the phone and dialed. He had a favor he could call in. It might be enough to get them the information they needed to make a start.

○ ○ ○

Sorensen watched the rookie walk toward him, an evidence box in his hands. He waited for the young cop to leave the office before opening it. Lifting out the bagged clothing, one piece at a time, he stared at each item as though the small skirt, pink sweater, and under-garments could talk to him. Cindy Vilner's face floated before him. He remembered the interview as though it were yesterday. She was so tiny. So scared. She looked so much like his own daughter. He replaced the bags in exactly the same order and picked up the file again, flipping through it quickly. He frowned. *No DNA report. Strange.* He strode to the door and bellowed the rookie's name. When the young cop appeared Sorensen came right to the point.

"There's no DNA report on this clothing. Find it."

The rookie nodded as he took the file "Yes, sir, I'll add it to my list."

"You'll put it on the top of your list."

The rookie sighed. "Right." He returned to his desk and laid the file beside the one already opened in front of him. "Right after this one," he mumbled.

Chapter Twenty-one

October 15, Beacon Hill, Yukon

Alex frowned at the words in front of him from Psalm 39. Someone had underlined verses 5 to 7. He read them again. "Each man's life is but a breath. Man is a mere phantom as he goes to and fro; he bustles about, but only in vain; he heaps up wealth, not knowing who will get it. But now, Lord, what do I look for? My hope is in you."

Alex shook his head. David was a puzzle. He'd gone from being a shepherd boy to a king, abused his power, and slept with a woman who probably had no choice in the matter, then killed her husband, and yet he still hung onto his God and believed He would answer him.

"This guy's more of a loser than I am," Alex mumbled and closed the book.

He glanced out the kitchen window. It was only 4:30 in the afternoon, but it was already dark. Alex could hear the beat of the generator, cut off now and then by the howl of the wind as it swooped through the yard. Snow swirled on all sides. He picked up the Bible and notebook and went into the living room. Embers still glowed in the fireplace. He laid a few logs on them and blew them into flame, then went to the couch and settled in to read.

He'd finished the Grisham novel a month ago so he'd been reading excerpts from the notebook and the Bible ever since. The notebook was proving to be a guide—he'd read it and then find the passage of Scripture mentioned. Several times the comments the man had made helped him understand what he was reading. He wondered again about the writer. He'd seen no further sign of his ghost and decided it was his overactive imagination coupled with finding this journal that made him think there was someone out there.

He picked a page and read:

November 20, 2000

Read more in the Old Testament today. Enjoying the history. I'd forgotten what a bloody lot those Israelites were. And their God seemed to have a thirst for it too. He was brutal at times, even with the Hebrews. They kept doing the opposite of what He told them so He'd punish them somehow, but kept after them, kept giving them leaders who'd pull them back to what He wanted them to do, even though those leaders were flawed too. It does encourage me to know they were. Maybe there's hope for me yet.

Alex tossed the journal down on top of the Bible. He'd finished reading about half of the Old Testament. He'd even read parts of it twice. What the journal writer said was true. But there was something else that nagged at his mind. *Why did God bother? If any of it's true, why did He keep interfering? Why didn't He leave Moses alone after he left Egypt, for instance? He was happy—had a family, livestock, food in his belly. Life was sweet. Until that burning bush incident. Why didn't God just leave him alone?*

He shook his head, realizing he was thinking as though it had really happened, as though God really did talk to people. "You think too much, Donnelly," he mumbled. *And you're talking to yourself too much too. Maybe it's time to try and get out of here for a while.* There had been no word on a replacement. Alex decided he'd call the head office again and put a burr under somebody's saddle.

He pulled on his parka, gloves, and boots and stepped outside. Titan raised his head from where he lay on top of his doghouse. Alex had let him loose a couple of weeks after arriving, but he didn't go far, especially in this weather. The dog stood up and shook himself, stretched, and leaped to the ground. He padded after Alex as he hunched into the wind and made his way to the office. Alex turned at the door and looked down at the dog. They'd maintained a passable relationship over the past couple of months. He held the door open and Titan dashed into the heat.

Flicking the toggle switch on the radiophone Alex waited a minute, then pressed the Call button. It took several tries before there was an answer. He gave the operator the number and sat down to wait. The one-sided chatter was entertaining for a while, but as static crackled through the air Alex dozed.

Titan's growl woke him. The dog was staring at the door, head down, the growl slowly rising to his throat until it erupted in excited barking. The hair on his back bristled. Alex grabbed the scruff of his neck and pulled him back. "Okay, Titan, okay. Let me check it out." He peered out the window. The grizzly was standing in the full beam of the yard light, beside Titan's doghouse, head down, snuffling the food bowl. Titan lunged at the door again, his barking ferocious. Alex booted the dog away. "Down, Titan!" he yelled. The dog leaped at the window, his barking increasing in volume and intensity.

Alex reached for the rifle, made sure it was loaded, pushed Titan away again, and slipped outside. The bear had turned toward the noise and taken a couple of steps closer. Alex could see its nose moving, its small nearsighted eyes of no use. *Maybe it'll get a strong whiff of me and decide not to go man hunting today.* He was about to send a shot off to hurry it along, but the animal veered back to the dog bowl, tossed it in the air with a swipe of its large paw, and ambled off, its thick reddish fur rippling on its shoulder hump with the movement.

Alex let his breath out and went back inside, hoping the bear would soon realize it was time to hibernate. Titan had calmed down, but a low growl still rumbled in his throat. Alex grinned at him. "You're no match for him, old boy. One swipe and you'd be on your back." He scratched the dog's ears, replaced the rifle, and sat down at the desk again.

The static was interrupted by the operator's voice. "Calling Beacon Hill 4-8-9-0, Beacon Hill, 4-8-9-0. Come in.

Alex grabbed the microphone and responded, leaning forward, ready to insist that whoever answered pinpoint a time for his relief to arrive. The voice that sounded into the room made him sit back. He let his hand hang with the microphone in it and stared at the radio.

"Alex, it's Kenni. Over."

He didn't move.

"Alex? Please answer." Pause. "Over."

His thumb rested on the button, but didn't press it.

151

"I'm not giving up, Alex. I'm going to keep calling until you answer. Over."

Alex stared in silence.

"Okay."

He could hear the frustration in her voice.

"Then just listen. We've been looking into something." Her voice faltered. "Something that happened in Vancouver five years ago. Over"

Alex's spine stiffened, his pulse raced.

Kenni continued. "We think we can help, Alex. Please let us help you. Over"

Alex groaned and shook his head. "Don't, Kenni," he whispered. "Just—don't." The microphone was still in his hand, but his thumb didn't push the Talk button.

"And we're doing an exhaustive search of this whole firm to find that letter. Mr. Ferrington says it will make a difference. He says you need to hear what's in it. So we're going to find it. Over."

Alex stared at the radiophone, half hoping she'd keep talking, half hoping she wouldn't.

"We're going to find it, Alex," she repeated. "And when we do I'm going to find you. Over."

Only his hard breathing broke the silence.

"I'll call again. I'm not giving up on you, Alex Donnelly." Her voice dropped a notch. "No matter what. Over."

Alex didn't move. A sudden burst of static blared into the room and the operator's voice made his whole body jerk.

"Beacon Hill 4-8-9-0, are you clear?"

He raised the microphone to his mouth. "Beacon Hill, clear."

"What happened in Vancouver." Kenni's voice echoed in his head. But another face came sharply into focus in his mind—the face of a young girl with dark eyes, eyes that haunted him. He stood up and paced the room. All his instincts told him to run. But his mind fought them. *She won't tell the cops. She won't. Maybe I should call her. And tell her what? She works in a lawyer's office. She's probably heard it all. All the possible lies, all the arguments, all the excuses.* He wished he could call in a helicopter. Then he was glad he couldn't afford it. *Maybe I should just take off, hole up out in the bush somewhere.* He lifted his head as the wind rattled the window. *Right. With winter coming on like a hurricane I wouldn't last a week without proper shelter*. He picked up the microphone and almost called the operator again. Then he slammed it back into its holder. He groaned and slumped into the chair.

Titan had been following him with his eyes. The dog stood up, padded to his side, and laid his head on Alex's knee with a soft whine. He stroked the dog's head for a moment, then leaped up and headed for the house.

He'd spent an hour on the exercise bench when he realized the call from the mining office never did come through.

○ ○ ○

"The girl's name was Cindy Vilner."

George handed a yellow legal pad to Kenni. She read it and started to pace the length of his office. Then she stopped and gave him a weak smile. "Thanks for going after this, George. I know it's…" she hesitated and dropped her eyes, "well, against your personal feelings at this point."

George stared at the file on the desk. "I want to know the truth too." He looked up at her. "But you're right. I do have…personal feelings."

Kenni started to say something, but turned on her heel and resumed pacing. "So there's a Cindy Vilner living in Surrey, just outside of Vancouver?"

George nodded. "It sounds like it could be the same girl. She's the right age at any rate."

Kenni turned toward the door. "I'm booking a flight."

George sighed. "We don't have time for this, Kenni. I have other cases…."

"I'll go alone," she interrupted. "It's probably better that way. It'll be woman to woman."

George stood up and came around from behind his desk. He stepped in front of Kenni and put his hands on her shoulders. "Promise me something," he said.

"What?"

"If this Cindy Vilner is the right person, and if she says Alex Donnelly raped her, you'll call the police immediately and tell them where he is."

It took Kenni a long time to nod her head.

Chapter Twenty-two

The next morning Alex plowed through a fresh fall of snow to the house. He put the coffee on and had just started to rummage through the pantry for something to eat when Titan barked. Alex went to the window. He could see the dog staring at the house. The barking wasn't hysterical, but insistent enough to make Alex sigh. *Now what?* He turned the stove off, pulled on his coat, and went outside.

The air was still, the cold like a thin membrane around him, so fragile that if he breathed too hard or moved too fast it would shatter and he'd be left unprotected, vulnerable in a climate that could kill him. The thought made him tread lightly, his movements slow. He called Titan, but the dog only glanced toward him, then ran around the end of one of the trailers and disappeared.

Alex was about to turn back when he heard the dog bark again. He ploughed forward, mumbling to himself about chasing dogs chasing rabbits. He rounded the corner of the trailer and realized he didn't have the rifle. He hesitated, listening to Titan's bark. *Definitely not his bear bark.* Alex kept walking.

He followed the dog's tracks around the back of the trailer and around the other end. Titan lay in the snow, quiet now, his nose in the air, sniffing. Alex kept walking, staring in the same direction. When he reached the dog Titan wagged his tail and stood. "What's up, boy?" Alex reached for the scruff of the animal's neck, then froze, staring at the trail leading away from the trailer. The imprints were deep and evenly spaced. Alex took a few steps forward to get a closer look. There was no doubt. The tracks had been made by a man, a man wearing mukluks.

Alex peered into the bush for a moment, then whirled around and trotted back to the office. He checked the rifle for ammunition and trotted back to where the trail began. Titan romped in the snow around him as he headed into the bush. The path wound its way up a low hill, then down again into the valley and along the river. The snow wasn't deep enough yet to prevent a man from making good time. Alex followed the tracks for almost an hour, wondering how much farther they'd go. *And where was the guy headed? Did he have a cabin out here somewhere? He'd have to have some kind of shelter.* As Alex followed the trail away from the river he stopped and sniffed the air. *Wood smoke.* Now he was certain his boss had been wrong. *There is someone out here alright, and a lot closer than a hundred miles away.*

Titan stayed with him for a while, but then disappeared, off chasing rabbits no doubt. It was another half hour before he saw the cabin. It was small, smaller even than his own, tucked into the side of a hill that seemed to lean protectively over it. *Great place to hide.* As he got closer he noticed it was latched from the outside. There were no windows on this side, only one narrow slit to the right of the door. A pair of homemade snowshoes hung beneath it. He hesitated for a moment, then lifted the latch and stepped inside.

The heavy musk of animals hit him as the door swung closed. A rough table sat in the center of the cabin, a homemade stool pushed under it. Heat radiated from a small airtight stove on the back wall. There were hides everywhere—a large pile of rabbit skins in one corner, a few muskrat, beaver, coyote and one wolf. The thick fur of a lynx's hide was spread over one wall above a narrow cot.

As his eyes adjusted to the dimness he noticed a notebook on the table, a candle beside it. He leaned his rifle against the table and picked up the notebook, realizing immediately it was identical to the one he'd found in the house at the mine site. Turning it toward the stream of light coming in from a small window in the back wall he tried to read the faintly penciled words.

"I ran out of pens about a year ago."

Alex whirled around. A tall bearded man filled the doorway. He held a rifle in his hands and it was pointed at Alex's heart.

Chapter Twenty-three

October 17, Surrey, British Columbia

Kenni scanned down the list of names in the dim entrance of the apartment building. There were only two that started with V. She pressed the button beside Vilner 106 and waited. In a moment she heard a voice, distorted by the machine, but clear enough that she knew it was a woman.

Kenni spoke into the screened intercom. "My name is Kenni Adams, Ms. Vilner. I called a few days ago?"

She shifted her weight from foot to foot as the silence dragged on.

The intercom crackled. "I told you I didn't want to talk to you."

"Please, Cindy. I understand your reluctance, but...." *God, what should I say?* "Please. I just want to know the truth."

The silence lingered again.

"Truth costs," the voice said. "You got twenty bucks, I'll let you in."

Kenni took a deep breath. "Okay."

The harsh buzzer made her jump. She pulled the door open and moved quickly up three dirty stairs to the first floor. The hallway carpet was threadbare. There was a pile of garbage at the far end. The smell made Kenni want to turn and run, but the door to apartment 106 was ajar. As she raised her hand to knock it swung open.

The young woman squinted at her through a mat of white-blond hair and held out her hand, palm up. Kenni dug in her purse and held out the twenty dollar bill. The girl snatched it.

"Have they arrested him?" Her eyes darted everywhere, but never rested on Kenni's face.

Kenni shook her head. "Not yet." She kept her voice low. "May I come in?"

Cindy stepped away and led her into a small living room. There was only one chair so Kenni remained standing. The girl fingered the ring in her bottom lip and curled her other arm around her thin waist. Her large dark eyes were glazed, puffy, and outlined in black. They flicked to Kenni's face for an instant, then down to the floor.

"I won't testify," she said. "He'll kill me." The eyes flashed up again. "He really will."

"I don't believe Alex is capable of...."

"What would you know?" The words were so guttural they made Kenni start.

"Then—it was Alex who...."

The young woman's next words were ground out between clenched teeth. "I don't want to talk about it." She turned her back to Kenni and peered through a small grimy window. "He ran. I wish I'd had the guts to do the same."

Kenni had to swallow hard to make her voice come out normally. "I know it must've been terrible for you, but can you tell me...?"

The girl whirled around. "What part of the word 'no' don't you understand?" The fury in her eyes made Kenni take a quick step backward.

"I...I just want to know the truth."

The woman's frown deepened. "People only want the truth when it suits their purposes." She spat the words. "What do you really want, Ms. Adams?" The girl's lips curled over the name.

Kenni cringed. "I...I have to know...did Alex Donnelly rape you?"

Cindy's fists clenched as she took a step toward Kenni, her eyes wide, her whole body shaking. "Get out!" She screamed.

Kenni turned and fled.

She lurched down the stairs and onto the street, glad that she'd asked the taxi driver to wait. She sat in the back seat and tried to stop shaking. The girl's words pounded in her head. "What do you really want?" She put her hand to her mouth and choked down a sob. *God,* she prayed. *Help me to do what's right.*

When she saw that the taxi driver was watching her in the rear-view mirror she got herself under control. As her breathing settled back into an even rhythm she remembered her promise to George. Everything in her wanted to scream "No!" but she leaned forward and told the driver where she needed to go.

Chapter Twenty-four

"Put it back." The man motioned with the rifle.

Alex laid the journal on the table, keeping his eyes glued to the pale eyes staring at him. He raised his hands in the air. "I didn't mean to...."

"To what?" The man interrupted. "Snoop into another man's private belongings?"

"Seems like the pot's calling the kettle black."

The muzzle of the rifle dropped and the man's low chuckle suddenly filled the room. "Had ya goin' though, didn't I?"

Alex dropped his hands and took a deep breath. "Yeah, you could say that."

"Safety's on." He rested the rifle in a corner and took a step toward the stove.

"I'd offer you coffee but my supply's running kinda low." He stooped and tossed two logs on top of the embers, then crouched down and blew slowly into the stove until the wood crackled. Alex stayed where he was.

The man stood and extended his hand. "They call me Gil, Gilbert LaPierre."

Alex shook his hand and told him his name.

"Well, Alex Donnelly, I believe you have a couple of things that belong to me. Had to leave them there when the chopper dropped you off. You arrived a full month earlier than last year's caretaker." He scratched his beard. "I'd like them back."

"The other journal." Alex said.

The man nodded. "And the book—the Bible."

Alex was surprised at the tinge of possessiveness he felt in his gut.

159

He decided to go on the offensive. "Why have you been spying on me?"

Gil didn't meet Alex's eyes. "It's been a while since I talked to anyone. Wasn't sure if I should trust you."

"What did you think, that I'd shoot first and ask questions later?"

"Maybe." Gil's mouth smirked. "Bet you were just wondering the same thing."

Alex nodded. "Seems we both have suspicious natures."

Gil grunted. "Goes with the Territory."

Alex took a step toward the door. "I'm going back to the mine site. If you want your books, you can come and get them." He had his hand on the door latch, then looked over his shoulder. "I have lots of coffee."

Titan appeared at his side again when he reached the river, and he kept up a steady pace as gusts of wind bit at his cheeks. By the time he got back to the house he was chilled to the bone and ravenous. He found more bacon in the freezer, fried it up with the last of the eggs, and made some bannock. Pouring himself another cup of coffee he pulled the notebook toward him. Now that he'd met the man who'd written in it, he felt like he was stepping over a line by reading it, but he flipped its pages and picked up where he'd left off.

August 6, 2002

Just read 1 Kings 19 and promised myself I'll leave here for good, this fall. Maybe beg a ride out with the crew at the mine site. The walk out and back just about did me in last spring. Supplies are low. Don't want to live on rabbits for another year. If the garden hadn't frozen...but then maybe God wants me to go back. No maybe. I've known for two years what He wants me to do. That line in Ch. 19 was like a knife in my gut. But to go back—I know what that would mean. I'm too much of a coward.

"I can relate, old man." Alex looked at his empty plate. *Maybe I should make a gesture of friendship—take the man some meat.* He closed the journal. *No. The old guy obviously wants to be left alone. Let him make the first move.* He cleaned up the dishes quickly and decided to skip his workout. He tucked the Bible and notebook under his arm and headed for the office.

Settled into the large comfortable chair he flipped open the Bible to the Index and found the page number for 1 Kings. He'd already read it, but didn't remember much except that it was a good story. He was curious to know why Gil would pinpoint it. He put his feet up and started to read Chapter 19. It only took three verses for Alex to remember what he'd thought about the prophet. Jezebel spouts off and the man runs for his life. *Bit of a wimp.* He snorted. *Guess I can relate to him too.* He kept reading. The angel visitations were pretty cool. Unbelievable, but cool. Alex shifted in the chair. The next verse seemed to bounce off the page like sonar.

"What are you doing here, Elijah?" God asked.

Alex could almost hear the whiney voice the prophet used to spill his excuses. But God asked him again, "What are you doing here?" Alex saw the connection immediately. Maybe Gil thought God was asking him the same question. Or maybe he was asking it of himself. Again, Alex could relate. He finished reading the chapter, then closed the book.

"What are you doing here?" The words seemed to bounce from the walls and shout from the closed book.

He pushed it away and flicked on the radiophone. Static blared into the room. He flicked it off again, wishing he had something else to read. He got up and went into his bedroom. His duffle bag was still in the corner, half full. *Guess it's long past time I finished unpacking.* He dumped out the few clothes and started putting them in the drawers. When he started to stuff the bag under the bed he felt something solid in the bottom. He turned it upside down again and shook it. Two books tumbled out, the two books Drew Adams had given him the day he left the beach house. He'd forgotten all about them. Alex grinned as he picked them up. "Ask and you shall receive," he said aloud, and wondered where the expression came from. Back in the office he got comfortable again and opened the first book.

It was the middle of the next afternoon when he finished it, realizing as he closed the cover that he hadn't stopped for lunch. He stared at the back cover. Drew had obviously chosen these books just for him. Alex sighed. He did recognize himself in the main character, a man with things in his past that haunted him—a man on the run. He thought about how that fictional cowboy had been able to find the peace he thought unreachable. Standing in a country church all by himself, he'd surrendered.

Alex stared out the window. He'd spent a lot of energy trying not to surrender in his lifetime—to the loneliness, the fear, the need to know who he was. To surrender meant leaving your belly open for someone to stick a knife into it. *What would it mean to surrender to God?*

He shook his head. "I don't believe in any god," he said aloud, the bitter words hard in the quiet of the room. He put the book on the desk and paced the office. He'd wanted a diversion from his own thoughts, but the book had only stirred up the guilt that already smoldered inside him. And now his imagination was heaping more wood on the fire. He'd felt the burn of those smoldering coals too much, felt like they'd erupt into a blaze at any moment and consume him. He knew he couldn't let that happen. Yet sometimes the pull to let go was almost more than he could stand.

He remembered hearing Pastor T say something about that once. He was talking to another kid, but Alex had felt like the words were meant for him. "You can't hang on forever, letting that build inside you," he'd said. "You can't just keep trying to stuff it down or it'll erupt into something ugly. You have to get rid of it, and only God can help you do that."

He shook himself and decided it was time he took care of the growling in his stomach.

Your hunger can be satisfied only in me.

Alex stared at the Bible and backed away from the table. The words had been so powerful it seemed as though a voice had spoken aloud. He shook his head again. "Now I'm hearing voices," he mumbled. "I really do need to get out of here."

○ ○ ○

November 15, Beacon Hill, Yukon

Alex rolled out of bed to a gray day, a shroud of ice fog floating in the cracks of the land like the shirttails of a ghost. It was the kind of morning that made him want to stay in bed or stretch out by a warm fire and read. *Well, I've got one book left.* The familiar twist of guilt seemed to sizzle inside him like hot grease. *Better to leave it alone.* He scrubbed at his face and dressed. His stomach was growling by the time he reached the house, but he decided to do his workout before breakfast. He was on his back on the bench when he heard Titan. He scrambled to the window and saw the man trudging steadily toward him. He was draped in fur, his face hidden behind the ring of wolf on his hood, his body swathed in lynx and his hands shielded by rabbit. A rifle rested in the crook of his arm. The ice fog swirled around him as he came. *He looks like a Disney character.* Alex went into the kitchen. The bacon was sizzling when he heard the knock on the door. He yelled, "Come in!" and took two mugs down from the cupboard.

Gil stood in the doorway. Alex whisked the powdered eggs into a bowl of water, then looked up. "Close the door, man. It's freezing out there."

Gil put the rifle in the corner and pulled the fur parka over his head. "Smells good," he said.

"Coffee will be ready in a minute. Have a seat."

They ate in silence except for the click of their utensils and the slurping noises as they drank. Gil downed three cups of coffee.

"Thanks," he said. "It's been a while since I ate like that."

Alex nodded. "I'll get your books."

Gil stared at the Bible when Alex handed it to him. "You been reading this?" he asked, holding the Bible up.

"Some."

"Old Testament or New?"

"The first part."

"Try the second. That's where it gets personal." He handed the Bible back.

Alex took the book. "You've read it all?"

Gil nodded. "Yeah. At one time or another." His eyes lingered on it. "It used to...." His eyes flicked to Alex's face, then away. "It used to be just about the only thing I read."

"I was just reading about Elijah." Alex watched his face. A small tic played near the man's left eye.

"What did you think of it?"

"The spin was a bit much."

Gil cocked his head. "How so?"

163

"It was all just a little too convenient, wasn't it? The way God showed up at just the right time?"

"But what about Elijah? There wasn't any spin on him. The story shows his fear, even his cowardice."

Alex shrugged. "But he's not the main character, is he?"

Gil's eyes locked on his. "No. He's not."

Alex shrugged again. "It's entertaining reading when you don't have anything else."

Gil's nostrils flared. "Some would say it's the word of God. That's a long step up from entertainment."

Alex studied his face. "Sounds like you value it a lot more than I do. Maybe you should take it back." He held the book out to him.

Gil's shoulders slumped and he leaned back, raising his hand, palm out. "No. I...I don't want it." He turned away and grabbed his parka. "Thanks for the breakfast."

Alex watched him pick up the rifle and reach for the doorknob. "I'm having steak tomorrow," he said. "The eggs will be powdered, but the meat should make up for it."

Gil gave a jerk of his head. "Appreciate the invitation."

Chapter Twenty-five

When Gil didn't return that next morning Alex was surprised to realize he was disappointed. He looked for him for several days, and was thinking about making the trek to his cabin with a couple of steaks one morning when he heard Titan give a welcome yip. He looked out the window and saw Gil's fur-encased body roughhousing with the dog. He put the coffee on.

Gil's eyebrows shot up when he saw the cinnamon buns. "You're downright domestic," he said.

Alex shrugged. "I like cinnamon buns. Can't exactly have them delivered."

Gil nodded, his eyes never leaving the sugar-covered bread. He drew in an exaggerated breath and closed his eyes. "It's been a long time since I've smelled anything that good." His eyes flicked open and settled on the frying pan. "Except maybe steak frying."

Alex grinned and moved to the freezer. "I guess that could be arranged."

They ate in silence, both savoring the food. As Alex poured Gil a third cup of coffee he cleared his throat and said, "I've been reading that Bible." He glanced at Gil's face to gauge his reaction. "The New Testament part, like you said."

Gil leaned back in his chair. "So?"

"So...since you seem to know so much, I was wondering if you'd help me understand some of it."

"Such as?"

Alex put down the coffee pot and retrieved the Bible from the top of the fridge where he'd left it. He sat down again, opened it to the passage he'd been reading, and pushed it in front of Gil. "Like this. I don't get it."

Gil picked up the book, scanned the page, and put it down again. "Beats me," he said and stood up.

Alex frowned. "I thought you—"

"You thought I was an expert on this? Well, I'm not." The gruffness in the man's voice made Alex's frown deepen as he watched him pull his parka on and head for the door.

"Thanks for breakfast," he said and was gone.

○ ○ ○

November 20, Whitehorse, Yukon

Constable Ray Ewing scribbled on a notepad as he listened to the voice on the phone. Then he frowned. "Yes. You'll get the reward, if your tip leads to his arrest."

He listened for another minute, then interrupted. "No." The tone of his voice revealed his impatience. "It doesn't work that way. You'll be notified if you have anything coming to you."

He hung up and shook his head.

"Anything worthwhile?" The officer at the next desk looked hopeful.

"A tip—anonymous, of course—about the Donnelly case. Won't know if it's legit til I follow it up. Guy says Donnelly may have got himself a job caretaking." The officer groaned. "Looks like I'm going to be spending a few hours on the phone."

The other officer grinned. "And it's Friday. Good luck."

Ewing grunted and went in search of a phone book.

○ ○ ○

This was no rabbit. The pitch of Titan's howl had reached its peak. Alex grabbed the rifle, pulled on his parka in one movement, and was on the front step in seconds. What he saw in the yard below made his heart stop.

The grizzly was on its hind legs, its enormous front feet pawing the air. At first Alex thought there was some kind of animal on the ground below it, but then he saw a man's legs stretch out and try to push away.

As Alex started to run the scene played out in slow motion. He saw Gil cover his head with his arms and fold his legs up toward his chest. He saw Titan rush at the bear, darting in and back. The beast pivoted and swiped at the dog, but missed.

Alex could feel his heart pound as the animal took two fast steps back toward the prone figure on the ground, opened its maw and attacked. Gil screamed. Titan darted in again, distracting the grizzly only for a moment. It turned back and clawed at Gil's leg. Alex must've hollered then, though the only thing he could hear was the booming of his own pulse. He saw the beast swerve toward him, its huge shoulders rolling in one fluid motion, its powerful hindquarters gathered under it as it charged, its mouth still open and roaring. Within seconds it was almost on top of him. Alex skidded to a stop, raised the rifle and fired. The bear kept coming. He stopped breathing and fired twice more. He could smell the stench of the animal's hot breath as it roared and pawed the air less than five feet above him. The rifle boomed again and Alex saw a thin stream of blood seep through the thick fur of the animal's neck. He had to leap sideways as it dropped, its huge head lolling to one side.

Alex felt his legs go weak as he stared at the huge carcass, its fur rippling in the wind. He gulped for air and bent over, pressing the butt of the rifle into one knee to steady himself. Then he looked up and started running again toward the man writhing on the ground. When he reached him Gil was on his back, his right arm cradling his blood-soaked left. He turned to look up at Alex, slumped back, and started to laugh hysterically.

He passed out as Alex lugged him inside and peeled off the heavy coat. There were several punctures and one deep gash that oozed blood from Gil's arm. Alex felt his stomach flip over when he saw the bone protruding from it, but gulped air and tugged off his own parka, letting it fall to the floor as he ran to the kitchen for the first aid kit. He hoped it contained some strong antiseptic and something to kill the pain. When he returned Gil was awake, clutching his arm and groaning.

"He got your arm pretty good," Alex said crouching beside him. It was then that he realized his own pants were wet between his legs. He tried to ignore the chill as he ripped what was left of Gil's sleeve away from the wound. He pressed a cloth to it and told him to hold it as tight as he could. Tugging off Gil's torn pants he grunted, "Leg's not so bad," he said. "He raked it pretty good, but the scratches aren't too deep. But the arm's bad. It's broken and the gash is deep. We're going to have to get you out to a doctor. I'll radio—"

"No!" Gil lunged up, winced with pain and slumped back, but his eyes, pale eyes deep-set under bushy eyebrows, didn't leave Alex's face. "You can set the bone. Then use those bandages and wrap it tight. It'll heal."

Alex shook his head as he stared at the cloth the man held over his arm. It was already soaked, the blood oozing between his fingers. And Gil had started to shake. The shock was hitting. "No way. I've never set a broken bone before. And bandages won't do it. That gash needs stitches."

Gil took a gulp of air. "I'll tell you what to do. All you have to do is do it."

Alex continued to shake his head. "No way. It's too—"

"Then I'll do it myself." Gil grabbed the box, but his hand shook so violently the contents spilled out. He groaned and fell back, squeezing his eyes shut.

Alex put his hand on the bandage and applied pressure, watching the man's chest heave.

Gil opened his eyes again. "I could bleed to death by the time a chopper gets here. You have to do it."

Alex lifted the cloth from the wound. He saw that Gil was right. He nodded. "Keep the pressure on it," he said, then rummaged in the contents of the box, looking for some kind of anesthetic. *Nothing.* He looked at Gil.

"There's nothing to kill the pain."

Gil blinked. "I'm tough," he said. Between moans of pain he gave Alex instructions on how to set his arm.

A rivulet of sweat coursed down Alex's side and his hands went clammy. He gulped for air again, took the man's arm in his hands, and pushed it tight against his ribs. He saw the bone slip back into what he hoped was the right position. Gil screamed and passed out. Alex worked quickly, ripped open all of the alcohol swabs but one, and cleaned around the wound as best he could. His hands shook as he tried to thread a fine needle. It took several tries, but he finally managed to do it. He wiped the needle with the last swab and turned to the work.

Gil didn't wake up. Alex was thankful for that as he stitched the long flap of skin hanging from the gash, then tended to the punctures. He ripped a cotton sheet and bound the arm, then fashioned a sling to keep it nestled against the man's chest. As he finished, Gil woke and moaned. Alex cleaned the long scratches on his leg and bandaged the worst of them. Then he sat back on his heels. "You're a tough old buzzard," he said.

Gil let his head fall back and licked his dry lips. "So I've been told. Don't suppose there's any booze in this place?" He was still shaking.

Alex shook his head. "The best I can do is some no-name headache pills."

"I'll take a handful."

Alex tipped four pills out of the bottle, got a glass of water from the kitchen, and steadied the man's hand as he drank.

Gil squeezed his eyes shut for a few moments, then opened them and looked into Alex's. "I owe you," he said. "If you didn't come running...."

"Thank Titan," Alex said.

Gil nodded. "He can have the first steak."

When Alex frowned Gil lifted his chin toward the door. "You'd better get out there and start skinning before that dog tears the hide to shreds. Can't waste all that meat and his fur is prime. Salt it down good and I'll split the take with you when I sell it."

"Generous of you," Alex said, "considering I'm the one who shot it and I'll be the one to do the skinning and butchering."

"Don't mention it," Gil said and closed his eyes again. "Think I'll have a bit of a nap while you go at it."

As Alex draped a blanket over him he noticed how pale the man's face was, how the lines creasing it had deepened. He stood, repacked the first aid box, and pulled on his parka. He was at the door when Gil's voice stopped him.

"See if you can find my rifle while you're out there. I dropped it when the beast swiped me from behind."

"I'll find it," Alex said. "Be back in a bit."

He changed his pants first, then went into the office. The radio-phone blared static when he turned it on. He thumbed the Call button, but there was no response.

"Come on," he mumbled. "This is no time to take a coffee break."

After several more tries he replaced the microphone and turned it off. *I'll try again later.*

Later was a long time coming. It took him the rest of the day to get the animal skinned out and the meat hung. He'd seen a few bears dressed out and was always amazed at how much they looked like men. *Maybe that's all we are.* He started cutting into the meat. *Beasts. No better than wild bears.* As he did the work he groaned at the necessity of killing the animal, but consoled himself with the knowledge that it was old. Its teeth were worn down and broken, some of them obviously infected. Alex reasoned that was why it hadn't hibernated yet. A toothache that bad would keep any beast awake.

As he worked he wondered about the man in the house. He had a lot of questions, but also had a feeling Gil LaPierre wasn't about to answer them, even if Alex did break the unspoken code of the north and asked. He checked on him a few times as he finished dealing with the bear. Usually he found the man sleeping, or trying to. Alex tried the radio phone several more times too, but to no avail.

The day was closing into darkness as Alex rubbed the last of the salt into the hide, rolled it up, and wrapped it in an old burlap sack he'd found in the shed. Heading for the office he bent his body against a blast of wind that drove the falling snow horizontally and gave it an edge that cut. He tried the call again, but still couldn't raise the operator. *Even if I managed to reach someone now, no chopper would risk being in the air in a blow like this.*

Gil was awake when he came in. Alex bent down to look at his arm. "Bleeding seems to be letting up," he said. "How's the pain?"

"Feels like it's on fire. Otherwise, just fine." He shifted and groaned. Alex helped him sit up a bit, noticing he'd almost stopped shaking.

"I'll get some supper on. You feel like steak?"

Gil's head snapped up. "Sure. It's been a long time since I've had bear steak."

Alex headed for the kitchen. "How do you like it?"

"They say you should cook bear meat good," Gil said, "so I'll settle for well done."

When the steak was ready Alex cut it into chunks and took it to him. Gil savored each bite. Alex watched him as he ate his own plateful, then decided it was time for some questions.

"How long you been out here?"

"Five years or so. Worked at the mine for a couple of summers, then took on the caretaking for a winter."

"And now?"

Gil eyed him. "Now I just live."

Alex put a piece of meat in his mouth and chewed slowly. He swallowed. "You didn't do what you promised yourself." Gil's fork hovered. "You didn't take the last chopper out." Alex knew he was pushing him.

"I have my reasons," Gil said.

Alex stood up. "Well, there's no getting away from it now. I'll be calling the chopper tomorrow to get you out to a hospital."

Gil glared at him. "I'll be gone before it gets here."

"You need a doctor," Alex insisted.

"I need to be left alone," Gil replied.

"Why?"

Gil turned away. "I'm cold. Do something useful and light a fire."

Alex bristled at the tone of the man's voice. "You're not exactly in a position to give orders." He moved to the fuel heater in the corner and turned it up a notch, then went to the fireplace and began laying crumpled paper and wood shavings on the grate.

Gil grunted, put his plate on the floor, and pulled the blanket up. Alex took the plates to the kitchen, pulled his parka, boots and gloves on, and went outside. The wind was raging now, building into a full-blown blizzard. He loaded his arms with wood and went back inside. Gil wasn't on the couch. The front door was wide open. Alex dumped the wood and dashed out. The man didn't get far. He was only a few paces from the step, face down in the snow. Alex heaved him back into the house and dumped him, none too gently, back on the couch. He ignored the man's groan as he yanked off his mukluks again.

"Old fool," he mumbled.

Gil opened his eyes. "I *am* that," he admitted.

Alex threw the blanket over him and laid the fire. It didn't take long before its warmth reached out to them. He settled into the chair close by and stared at the flames. He was surprised when Gil suddenly started to talk.

"You ever been in trouble with the law, Donnelly?"

Alex went rigid. "Once or twice."

"Ever been in jail?"

Alex gave a quick jerk of his head.

"Then maybe you'll understand." Gil shifted and winced. "I can't risk calling attention to myself in a hospital. Don't have any ID. No driver's license. No health care card. Gilbert LaPierre doesn't exist."

Alex watched the man's face, but didn't speak.

"Another man," Gil continued, "Another man existed—seems like a long time ago. A man who was supposed to be a pillar in his community, a saint even." The pale eyes lifted to peer into Alex's, seemed to judge him, then dropped away again. "That man did something—something that can't be undone. You understand?" Gil looked directly at him again. "That man can never go back."

Alex felt a chill creep up his spine. He nodded. "I understand."

Chapter Twenty-six

"Gotcha." Constable Ewing smiled at the piece of paper in his hand. *Beacon Hill.* He didn't know where it was, but he knew it wouldn't take him long to find out. He glanced out a window. *Now if the weather would just co-operate....*

○ ○ ○

Alex watched the fire until he heard Gil's breathing deepen into sleep. Then he banked it, moved the heater's regulator down a notch, and went to his own bed. The wind howled through the night and Alex heard every moan. It was well before dawn when he got up and went back to the house, loading his arms with wood as he went in the back door.

He made enough noise to wake the dead as he stomped in and dumped the wood, but Gil didn't open his eyes. Alex bent over him, noticing the sheen on his skin. He pulled off his gloves and put the back of his hand on Gil's forehead. He mumbled a curse. The man was burning with fever. Alex knew fever meant infection. He went to the kitchen, filled a bowl with water, grabbed a cloth, and went back into the living room. Gil opened his eyes slightly as Alex wiped the perspiration from his face, but said nothing. He removed the bandage on the man's arm and cursed again. The wound was inflamed. An angry looking red line extended up toward the shoulder and spiked down toward the wrist. He changed the bandage and pulled the blanket up over Gil's inert body. Then he ran to the office. He stayed as long as he dared, trying to reach someone, anyone, on the radiophone, without success. When he ran back to the house it seemed that the wind wanted to batter him to pieces.

He spent the rest of that day trying to get Gil to drink some water, trying to force more pills down his throat. The man fought him every time. Alex tried several more times to radio out, but finally gave up with another curse. There was no point trying until the storm let up. And it showed no sign of doing so.

He spent the night trying to sleep on the floor beside the couch where Gil tossed and turned. The man called out several times in the night, the raging fever making him delirious. Sometime around midnight Alex tried to get him to drink again, but most of the water spilled down his chest. Alex sat back on his heels. "Don't die on me, old man," he whispered, then said it loud. "You hear me? Don't die."

He went into the kitchen for more water. His eyes fell on the Bible. *Pray.* Alex took a step back. *Pray.* The word resonated in his mind like an ancient drum. He went back into the living room and stared down at Gil. He got down on his knees and lifted the bandage. The dark red line looked longer and redder. Alex wiped Gil's face with the cold cloth again. He opened his eyes. "Pray," he whispered, and closed them again.

Alex clenched his hands into fists. "I don't know how," he said. Gil didn't respond. Alex stood up and paced. He remembered praying when he was a kid—praying that someone would adopt him, praying that he'd get something to eat that day, praying that the beatings and abuse would stop. The night he was forced to run he even thought of praying for the courage to kill Wild Bill, but by then none of his other prayers had ever been answered so he didn't bother. The image of Kenni praying on the deck of her father's house came into his mind. He groaned aloud as that now familiar longing rose inside him. He wished he could reach her, wished he could talk to her and ask her to pray. He had no doubt Kenni's prayers were answered.

He stood over Gil again, then knelt beside him and stared into his fevered face. A curse formed in his mind again, but didn't make it to his lips. *Pray.* The word hit him with such urgency he opened his mouth and spoke the only words he could think of.

"God, don't let this man die. Please." He stared at Gil's face. "I know he's probably as much of a write-off to you as I am, but…." Alex struggled to think of something more, some reason that would make

God do what he was asking. He could think of nothing. His helplessness overwhelmed him. Tears streamed down his face and sobs wrenched out from his gut.

Gil shifted. His eyes barely opened, but his lips moved. "Pray," he whispered.

Alex knew he could never come up with a reason why God should help them. "Maybe he's no good and neither am I." He wiped at the tears blurring his eyes. "But please, God, don't let him die."

He put his head in his hands and took great gulps of air to try and stop his weeping, but he couldn't. All the sorrow and pain that had been building in him, all the sorrow and pain he'd turned to bitterness welled up and poured out. *You're pitiful, Donnelly.* He tried to get his emotions under control, but the sobs kept coming. And then the sorrow turned into something else. It wasn't self-pity anymore, or self-loathing, or even fear. It was that longing again, that deep yearning for something he couldn't name and couldn't reach. And suddenly, he knew the yearning was for God, for the Father he believed had abandoned him, for the goodness he'd seen in Kenni and Pastor T. He moaned and let the sobs come.

When the morning light started to ease through the living room windows Alex was still on his knees, his head buried in his arms beside Gil. He felt a jab and lifted his head. Gil grunted at him.

"If you think you can manage, without spilling it all over me, I'd like some water."

Alex blinked and straightened. He pulled the blanket down and examined Gil's arm. The skin was a normal color, the wound red but not inflamed. There was no red line leading to the man's heart. Alex stared, his mouth dropped open.

"Water, boy, water," Gil said.

Alex brought him the glass and helped him drink.

"Couple more of those pills too," Gil said.

Alex got the pills.

Gil tried to push himself up, groaned, and asked Alex to help him. When he was almost in a sitting position he asked, "What's for breakfast?"

Alex just stared at him.

"Wake up, boy. I'm hungry!" The man's voice boomed into the room.

Alex blinked, then went into the kitchen and started frying bacon. *Was last night a dream? Did I imagine the red line, that blood poisoning was crawling up Gil's arm and heading for his heart like a bullet for its target?* Alex frowned as he mixed the bannock. He knew by his own exhaustion that what he'd gone through in the night was no dream. *But if it wasn't a dream, then....* He stared down at the Bible still lying on the table.

When he carried the plates into the living room Gil dove into his immediately. Alex watched him eat, but left his own untouched.

"I prayed for you last night," he said quietly.

Gil's hand hesitated, then put a chunk of bannock in his mouth. "You figured I needed it?"

"You asked me to," Alex replied.

Gil snorted. "Must've really been out of it."

"And...." Alex thought of the voice in his head, but decided not to mention it. "And there was a line of blood poisoning heading straight for your heart. I figured you'd be dead by this morning."

Gil stared at him. "Then I guess I owe you, again."

"I didn't do anything. There wasn't anything I could do. I just prayed."

"Then you can thank God for me."

Alex stared at his plate. "I didn't think I believed in God, until last night. But now...maybe I've believed in Him all along. Maybe I've just been too mad at him to admit it."

Gil shook his head. His mouth curled into a sardonic grin. "The Lord does have a sense of irony."

Alex frowned. "What do you mean?"

"Here I am in the middle of the wilderness, hiding from cops, friends, enemies, and especially from God. And who saves my life? A pilgrim!"

"I wouldn't call myself that."

Gil snorted again. "Sounds like it to me."

Alex reached for the man's plate, the frown still creasing his forehead. "I wasn't looking for God when I came here."

Gil leaned back and sighed. "Take it from somebody who knows. He never stops looking for you."

○ ○ ○

Inspector Stan Sorensen smiled as he took the photo of Alex Donnelly off the bulletin board and put it in his briefcase. "Fee fi fo fum," he mumbled. The image of Cindy Vilner's face floated through his mind again. And again, his stomach burned. He opened a drawer in his desk, took out a bottle of antacid tablets, and tossed them in on top of the photo and the file. He snapped the briefcase shut and headed for the airport.

Chapter Twenty-seven

"Sounds like you're a bit of a pilgrim yourself," Alex said.

Gil shrugged with his one good shoulder. "Like I told you, I used to be a saint."

"Seems like God still thinks you're worth salvaging."

"Apparently so. Makes me think He's a poor judge of a man's character."

Alex nodded. "The Bible seems to prove that point."

Gil chuckled, then winced. "You got that right." He shifted and winced again. "Got any coffee going in there yet?"

Alex went into the kitchen and put the coffee on. He stared at the Bible for a while, picked it up, and went back into the living room. Gil sighed when he saw it.

"You got a favorite part?" Alex asked.

Gil closed his eyes. "John."

Alex heard the reluctance in this voice and watched him try to roll onto his side, his face to the back of the couch. Alex settled himself in the chair by the fireplace, found the Gospel of John, and started to read. He'd only read a few paragraphs when he heard Gil shift again. He could feel the man's eyes on him, but didn't look up until he heard his voice.

"Wouldn't mind if you read it out loud," he said.

Alex went back to the beginning and read straight through to the end of the sixth chapter. As he read verses 66-69 his voice dropped. "From this time many of his disciples turned back and no longer followed him." Alex cleared his throat. "You do not want to leave too, do you?" Jesus asked the Twelve. Simon Peter answered him, "Lord, to whom shall we go? You have the words of eternal life. We believe and know that you are the Holy One of God."

Alex looked up and was surprised to see that Gil's face was wet with tears.

"It's been a long time since I've heard the Word read," he said as he wiped his face with the heel of his hand. Alex stayed quiet.

It was some time before Gil broke the silence. When he did his voice was low. "You know, when I was staring down that old grizzly's throat I thought *This is it, I'm about to meet my maker.* The thing that surprised me was that it felt like God was...." He turned and faced Alex. "I could understand Him being angry, you know? But it seemed like...I could sense this unbelievable excitement, like a kid at a birthday party—like He just couldn't wait for me to get there. But I knew I wasn't ready yet." He sighed. "Maybe I'll never feel ready."

Alex didn't know what to say so he stayed silent. Gil's eyes seemed to bore into his.

"Are you?"

"Am I what?" Alex asked.

"Ready to meet your maker?"

Alex dropped his eyes. "Guess I've done some things I'm not proud of," he answered.

Gil nodded. "Most of us have. All of us have. And we usually blame God for all of them."

Alex cocked his head, but Gil shifted onto his back and continued before he had the chance to comment.

"I've been blaming God for everything. Somehow had it all figured out that if God had intervened and stopped me, it never would've happened. He should've stopped me from falling in love with my best friend's wife, stopped me from getting drunk that night and slamming the car into a telephone poll. And He should've kept her from dying. That, above all. It was all His fault." Gil let the tears course down his temples and drip into his ears. "Truth is, it was all my fault. God forgive me."

Alex stood up, grabbed the poker, and played with the ashes in the fireplace. "Do you think He will?" he asked quietly.

Gil grunted as he moved. "Yes." The strength of the man's voice made Alex look at him. "I was forgiven before I asked."

"I don't get it."

"Neither do I, son. Neither do I."

"But…you used to?"

"I used to think so. But I don't think I've ever really understood mercy and grace. All I know is that I've been on the receiving end of it, more than once. The first time I was just a teenager."

Alex leaned forward. "What happened?"

Gil's grin surprised him. "You want to hear my testimony?"

"What?"

"That's what they call it in the circles I used to run in. The story of how I became a Christian."

It was Alex's turn to grin. "You mean a saint."

Gil snorted. "That's what they said I was. Don't think I ever really believed it." He shifted again. "You want to hear the story or not?"

Alex shrugged. "I guess." He glanced out the window at the swirling snow. "We've got nothing but time." As Gil began Alex returned to the chair.

"Like I said I was a teenager. Full of hormones and not much brains. Didn't care about anybody but myself." He sighed. "I seem to have a particular bent in that direction." He stared at the ceiling for a while, then continued. "My dad was in the military. A spit 'n polish kind of guy. He was always on my case and it seemed like I could never get it right, like I was never good enough. He and I went head to head a lot. Most of the time he won, usually because he had a belt in his hand."

"I know what that's like," Alex mumbled.

Gil turned his head to look at him. "When I was fourteen he sent me to this camp. It was sort of a mixture of boot camp and a holy-roller's convention. I don't think he realized what the religious stuff was all about, but he hoped it would somehow straighten me out." Gil chuckled. "He got more than he bargained for.

I had a pretty wild time there, for the first week. Then one night a bunch of us got hold of a box of beer and took out one of the sailboats. This was on the Atlantic coast. We were having such a good time we didn't realize the boat was drifting out of the bay. When the storm hit we were so far from land we didn't even know where we were. When the boat capsized I thought we were all going to drown. I'd never been so scared and I'd never prayed like I did then. I promised God that if He got us out of there, I'd do whatever He wanted. I guess He was just waiting to hear me say that, 'cause about five minutes later a coast guard patrol boat showed up and pulled us out of the water. When we got back to the camp the whole lot of us got down on our knees and one of the counselors led us all in the sinner's prayer."

"The what?" Alex asked.

"Never heard of the sinner's prayer? It's the standard evangelical's way to get saved. They call it asking Jesus into your heart. Basically it's admitting you've messed up and need Jesus to get you right with the Father again." Gil pushed himself up with his good arm. "I'd heard that before, but something one of the counselors said got to me. He said we didn't deserve to have that coast guard boat show up, that we'd made some bad choices and should've drowned out there. We all knew that was true. I knew it—I'd been the one who got the beer and suggested we steal the boat. When I was bobbing in that cold water I figured I was going to die knowing I was responsible for my friends dying too. I knew I didn't deserve to be saved—didn't deserve anything but punishment. That counselor looked right at me and said that's what mercy means. It's getting what you don't deserve—forgiveness. And something in me snapped." His voice dropped a notch. "And after I'd prayed, something in me felt more whole than it ever had before."

Alex frowned. "What do you mean, whole?"

Gil stared at the fire for a while before answering. "The first year I came up north I helped this guy build a log cabin. It was shaped like an octagon—an eight-sided circle. The guy did everything by hand and when it came time to put the door in it was no different. We built it a foot and a half thick and beveled into the frame. When we hung that door and it swung shut it felt like an electric circuit had just been connected—like the circle was complete. When I let God in that night that's what it felt like—like there'd always been a hole—something was missing—and now it was filled—something was complete. Whole."

Alex let the silence settle for a bit, then asked, "So what happened then?"

"We had a party."

Alex's eyebrows shot up. "A party?"

"Yeah." Gil grinned. "They woke up the whole camp and had a holy-roller party, right then, right there." He chuckled. "By the time I went home two weeks later I was out to save the world and decided to start with my dad."

"How'd that go over?"

Gil sighed. "Eventually I somehow got him to pray the prayer, but it seemed like nothing happened. Then about a month later he came into my room one night and got down on his knees beside my bed and asked me to forgive him. He was a different man after that night. Guess I was a different kid too."

Alex stood up and poked the ashes again. *Can people really change that much?* "That feeling of being whole—is it still there?"

Gil didn't answer right away. Alex heard him take a deep breath and let it out in another sigh. "There's been a lot of water under the bridge since then," he said. "Some of it black and some of it bloody. But yes, I'd have to say that feeling is still there. I've tried to deny it, especially in the past five years. Almost succeeded in forgetting. I know I still don't deserve it, but God's mercy does hang on."

Alex stood with his back to Gil, the poker shifting the logs on the fire. When Gil spoke again his voice pulled at Alex.

"So what's your story, Alex Donnelly?"

Chapter Twenty-eight

When the taxi pulled up in front of the police station Kenni asked the driver to wait again and, after a deep breath, walked to the door. She stood there for several minutes, then walked in. A female constable nodded to her. "Can I help you?" she asked.

Kenni opened her mouth, then clamped it shut again. She started to turn away. The policewoman flipped part of the counter up, came to Kenni's side, and touched her arm.

"You seem upset. Would you like to sit down?" She led her past the desks to a bench along the wall and sat down beside her.

Kenni took a deep breath. "Sorry," she said. "I just—I'm not sure if this is the right thing to do."

The officer nodded. "Tell me what's happening."

"I think—" Kenni stopped and glanced sideways at the woman.

The woman cocked her head. "You think...?"

"I think the man I'm...a man I know is a... I think he may have done something, something terrible." She turned her head away.

The policewoman waited. It took Kenni a long time to speak again.

○ ○ ○

Alex didn't turn from the fireplace. "That coffee's gotta be ready by now," he said and left the room. When he returned Gil's face was strained.

"You okay?" Alex asked, pulling the blanket back to look at his arm.

"Yeah. Just hurts like...." Gil stopped. "It hurts, that's all." He reached for the coffee.

Alex went back to the chair by the fireplace. Their mugs were almost

185

empty when he started to talk. He told Gil everything, in detail, in a spurt of energy that left him exhausted, his head throbbing. When he was done he stared into his empty cup.

"Guess I've been running from everything, all my life. Everything that's ugly and even the few good things that've come my way." He looked up at Gil. "And you're right—I have been blaming God." He twisted the cup in his hands. "I want to stop running," he said.

Gil shifted to look directly at him. "Facing your demons isn't easy."

"Running from them is no picnic either."

Gil grunted. "You got that right."

"But you've been hiding out for five years too."

Gil's eyes shifted around the room. "Going back means prison." He sighed and rolled onto his back. "I know what God wants, but it's too much."

Alex was quiet for a while. When he spoke it was with conviction. "As soon as this blow passes I'm going to radio for a chopper. You need to see a doctor."

Gil shook his head. "Can't do it, Alex."

"I don't think you've got enough strength to resist."

Gil's bushy eyebrows lowered over his pale eyes. "You might be surprised."

Alex leaned forward. "You're getting on that chopper even if I have to knock you on the head with a two-by-four. So get used to the idea."

A gust of wind rattled the windows, making them both look out at the raging storm.

"Guess we'll cross that bridge when we come to it," Gil said. He leaned into the couch. "Since you're so anxious to get rid of me I wouldn't mind another feed of that grizzly before I go. It gives me particular pleasure to bite into the meat cut from that bear's hide."

Alex grinned. "Just so happens I found a pretty good recipe for bear roast." He got to his feet. "You're not going to try taking off again, are you?"

Gil shook his head. "Don't worry." He pulled a blanket over himself. "Think I'll have another nap."

○ ○ ○

It was late in the afternoon three days later when Alex felt the first pain in his gut. Gil complained just before emptying his stomach all over the floor. Alex was cleaning it up when he had to run for the bathroom. He heard Gil cursing as he wretched again. The nausea lasted through the night. The next day they both had dry heaves and by the morning after that they were too weak to move. Alex was handing Gil a glass of water when the man chuckled. "Guess that bear got the last laugh after all," he said.

Alex nodded. "I've never been this sick."

Gil slumped back into the couch. "Pray it's over," he said.

Alex spent all of that day in the chair while Gil dozed on the couch. The wind still howled outside so he didn't bother dragging himself over to the office to try and call out. He spent most of the time dozing, and most of that dreaming about Kenni.

Five days later the blizzard stopped, leaving a stillness so complete Alex wondered if the rest of the world was still out there. The temperature dropped overnight and thick ice fog settled in. Alex stared out the kitchen window at the gray shroud broken here and there by thin dark green streaks of spruce. He knew a helicopter couldn't fly until it lifted. He let his mind wander, his eyes roaming the fog, seeking some point of reference, something to hang onto.

Suddenly, the mist swirled and Kenni emerged from within it, wrapped in a long parka, her face rimmed with wolf's fur, her eyes gleaming and her cheeks reddened with the cold. Alex lifted his hand and opened his mouth to speak. She turned and slipped back into the fog. He groaned again. "Man, I've got it bad," he mumbled.

"Got what bad?"

Alex turned to see Gil leaning heavily against the doorframe. He was about to answer when the man's knees gave out and Alex had to lunge to catch him. He helped him back onto the couch.

"Stay put," he chided him.

Gil grunted. "What did you see out there?"

"Nothing," he blurted, feeling the redness creeping up his neck. He couldn't believe he was actually blushing.

"Ah," Gil chuckled. "A woman. The one you mentioned? What's her name again?"

"Kenni," Alex answered, then sighed. "I can't stop thinking about her."

"Do you want to?"

"No. But—I'm just torturing myself. I know I'm not...." Alex hesitated.

"What? Not good enough for her?"

Alex shrugged.

Gil shook his head. "Been there, thought that." He pushed himself up on his good elbow. "So you're in love with her. Anything happening from her side?"

Alex nodded. "I think so. That's what makes it hard. If she couldn't care less, it'd be easier."

"Would it?"

Alex slumped into the chair. "No."

"She must be a stunner."

"She's...." Alex's grin was wry. "A saint."

"Ah," Gil said as he lifted his head. "That figures."

"What do you mean?"

"God's after you, Donnelly. Why do you think He's been surrounding you with Christians? Even has-beens like me?"

Alex shook his head. "I was wondering...."

"Has she tried to get you saved?" Gil asked.

"I didn't give her the chance." Alex dropped his eyes. "I ran."

"But she hasn't given up?"

Alex shook his head. "She called just a while ago, said there's a letter from my mother that she wants me to read. Said she wasn't going to stop til she found it and then she was going to come find me."

"Sounds like the girl's a keeper."

Alex's shoulders slumped deeper. "She deserves better."

"How do you know?"

"What?"

"How do you know you aren't exactly what she deserves? How do you know she isn't exactly what you deserve?"

"She's too good. I'd only mess up her life too." Alex's voice was almost a whisper. "But I do wish...." He shook his head.

"You can do more than that," Gil responded. "You can pray."

Alex stared at him for a long time before answering. "God never paid any attention to my prayers until I prayed for you. It was probably a one-shot deal."

"So you think He's holding everything against you?"

Alex turned his head away.

Gil leaned forward. "He used you to heal me, Alex. That's called being blessed."

Alex shook his head again, his eyes cast downward. The words he wanted to say caught in his throat.

Gil stayed silent until Alex looked at him. "There's no sin God won't forgive."

Alex felt something inside him give way. He stood up and paced to the window, keeping his face turned away to keep Gil from seeing how close he was to breaking down completely.

Chapter Twenty-nine

Kenni sat at George's desk and stared out the window at the steady drizzle. It seemed like it had been raining for months. She picked up a pencil and played with the pan of white sand in front of her. The smooth black stone still sat in its center. She picked it up and let it rest in her palm as she prayed. *God, please. I don't know what to do. Should I go after him? Should I try and forget about him?* She took a deep breath. *You'll have to help me out a lot if it's the second option. I won't be able to do it alone.*

"Help me to want only what you want," she whispered. A knock on the door made her head jerk up and she said "Come in" too loudly.

A young face appeared, framed by a set of headphones. The boy lifted one side off his ear as he stepped into the room. "Hey, Miss Adams," he said. "Just collecting the interoffice mail."

Kenni nodded. "Go ahead, Ben," she said and watched him scoop a few envelopes out of a tray on the corner of the desk. The teenager tossed them into a large bag slung over his shoulder. Kenni stared at it as he turned away, then yelled, "Ben, wait!" as the door was about to close behind him.

Ben stepped back into the room, eyebrows raised.

Kenni stood up and moved quickly around the desk. "Dump that bag," she said.

The boy's eyebrows arched even further. "Say what?"

"I said dump the bag. I've been looking for a letter for three months. I think that bag is the only place in this whole building I haven't looked."

Ben pulled the strap off his shoulder and held the bag upside down over the desk. Letters spilled out and they both reached to keep them from falling on the floor.

Kenni started tossing each one back in, glancing quickly at the names. "It will have the name Alex on it," she explained, "No last name and no office number."

"Alex?" The boy mumbled. "Oh yeah, I seem to remember seeing that."

Kenni stopped and stared at him. "You do?"

"Yeah." Ben scratched his head. "Quite a while ago. I sorta remember trying to figure out what to do with it."

Kenni felt like screaming, but she asked calmly, "And what did you do with it?"

The boy tilted his head, then scratched his ear. "Well...I...uh...oh yeah, now I remember." He pulled the bag toward him and fumbled inside. "There's this kinda hidden zippered pocket in here." He withdrew his hand, holding a small yellowed envelope. "I put it in there so it didn't get mixed up with the rest of...."

Kenni snatched it out of his hand, then grabbed him by both ears and kissed him on the cheek. "Benjamin, you're my hero!" she said and ran from the room. She skidded to a stop in front of the receptionist's desk. "Linda, do you know where George is?"

"In the boardroom with...."

Kenni didn't hear the last two words as she whirled around and ran down the corridor. She burst into the room. "George, I found it!" she cried, holding up the letter.

George and his client looked up, startled.

Kenni stopped dead. "Oh, I'm sorry. I didn't know."

Excusing himself to his client George ushered Kenni out of the room by her elbow. "What did you find that's so—"

His eyes widened when Kenni held up the envelope again. "Where?" he asked.

"The mail boy was carrying it around in his bag all this time. It must've gotten dropped into the interoffice mail basket somehow. Ben didn't know what to do with it so he tucked it away for safekeeping!"

George shook his head and chuckled. "Efficient stupidity." He stared at the envelope. "So what now?"

Kenni stared at him. "We have to get it to him."

"But where will you send it? I doubt that he gets his mail delivered."

Kenni sighed. Sometimes men were so dense. "We have to take it to him, George."

George frowned. "But it's December. Do you have any idea what the Yukon is like in December?"

Kenni grinned. "I always wanted to ride on a dogsled."

George groaned. "I have to get back to my client," he said pointing at the boardroom door with his chin. "But don't make any plans without me."

Kenni promised she'd wait, but by the time they met an hour later she'd booked two tickets to Whitehorse. "I hope you have a warm coat, George. The travel agent said it was a balmy forty-eight below there today."

George groaned again. "Can't we just call him?"

"Oh, I'm going to call him to tell him we're on our way. And this time we're not taking no for an answer."

Chapter Thirty

Alex became aware of Gil's hand on his shoulder. He knew the man was too weak to be on his feet. He took a gulp of air and turned to him. "I told you to stay put."

"I have a problem with authority."

Alex's quick grin faded as Gil started to sag. He ducked under the older man's shoulder, wrapped his arm around his back, and helped him return to the couch. As he lowered him down and started to stand straight Gil grabbed his shirt.

"I need to pray for you," he said.

"Thought you said you didn't do that anymore."

Gil shifted and smiled. "Only under special circumstances. It's been a while, but believe it or not, I think God just told me to do it. He hasn't done that for a long time and for a change I'm going to obey, at least this once. On your knees."

Alex drew back. "My knees?"

"I believe in good posture. Besides, as you've noticed I can't stand up. On your knees," he repeated.

Alex took another deep breath and knelt. Gil closed his eyes and put his hand on Alex's shoulder. They remained that way for a minute. Then Gil's eyes popped open again.

"I'm a bit rusty. Why don't you start?"

"This was your idea."

"Humor me."

Alex sighed. Gil closed his eyes. Alex frowned, but did the same and began. "God...." He felt his stomach lurch and sank to his haunches. He clenched his jaw against the sudden surge of emotion

195

that gripped him. *What's wrong with me? Why do I want to blubber like a baby?* Gil's hand gripped his shoulder a bit tighter. He gulped and began again. "God, I don't know how to do this. I don't know why you'd listen to me, even if you're there, but...." He opened his eyes for a moment. Gil's face was still. It reminded Alex of Kenni. "But there's this girl." He sighed and shifted his weight. "But I guess you know all that." A groan escaped him. "I don't deserve to even know her, but...Gil said to pray so I'm doing it." There was so much more he wanted to say, so much more he wanted to pour out, but he was afraid that once he began he'd lose control. He opened his eyes again and said, "Amen."

He was about to stand up when Gil began. "Lord, it seems like you've got a couple of losers on your team here. I know, I'm the one who stomped away and refused to play anymore. I don't understand how you could ask me to do anything, the way I've been trying to ignore you. And this Donnelly, well, it seems we've got a lot in common. But it's obvious you don't give up easily. So here I am, asking for Alex and I guess I'm asking for myself too. Asking for what neither of us deserves—more grace and mercy."

Alex felt the surge of emotion again. He hoped Gil was finished and started to get up. Gil's hand pushed him back down.

"And there's this other thing, Lord. This other thing you're good at. Alex is in love with this girl called Kenni. Sounds like maybe you've got this all under control already, but I'd like to ask that you put these two together somehow. You've shown Alex you're real, but he's still a little skeptical, though you may have noticed he's been talking to you lately. I know you're doing all this for a reason and I think I know what it is. The thing is we're both going to need a strong dose of courage to get us through. We're a couple of mule-headed males. I guess I don't need to tell you that." He was silent for a moment. "Whatever—whatever you have in mind, Lord...." Gil's voice cracked. He cleared his throat and forced the last words out. "Just help us get through it. Amen."

Alex stayed on his knees, but slowly straightened his back.

Gil squeezed his shoulder, then leaned heavily on him as he pushed himself back into the couch. "Don't be ashamed of the tears," he said. "In my experience it's the ones who refuse to cry who are the weakest. They just don't know it."

Alex swiped at his face as he stood. He hadn't realized he'd let them run. "Guess I've held everything in for so long, now that I'm starting to let it out it's like a dam bursting."

"Let it burst." Gil settled himself on the couch. "Keeping it all back does too much damage."

"Speaking from experience again?" Alex asked.

Gil snorted.

"Seems like you know a lot, but don't act on much."

Resting his head on the back of the couch Gil peered up at him. "You do have a way of soft-soaping things, boy. Bet it makes you real popular."

Alex grinned at the sarcasm. "Oh yeah. I've always been Mr. Popularity."

"Uh huh."

Alex returned to his chair.

Gil stared at the fire for a while, then said, "Knowing a thing doesn't give you the strength to do it."

"But you had the strength once. Where did it go?"

"Down the tubes along with my reputation, my friends, my life."

"So you were planning to hide out here forever?"

"Maybe." Gil shifted and winced.

"Now what?"

Gil raised his eyebrows. "I heal. Then I go back to my cabin."

"But you just prayed—"

"Maybe in the spring...."

"You could be dead by spring. If that blood poisoning comes back...."

"It won't."

"You need a doctor."

"And you need a lawyer."

Alex shifted his weight. "I have a job to do here."

Gil smirked. "Uh huh."

"You're going out." Alex said. "As soon as I can get a chopper to fly in."

Gil rolled over, turning his back to Alex. "Nowhere to go," he said.

Chapter Thirty-one

"Listen to this, Gil."

The older man sighed, but couldn't help grinning at the excitement in Alex's voice. He reminded him of himself, long ago, when he could hardly put the Bible down because he was so enthralled. He leaned forward as Alex read the beginning of Matthew, Chapter 21.

"Can you imagine what that must've been like?" Alex asked. "The whole city of Jerusalem welcomed Him."

"And a short time later they cursed Him and cried out for His blood. The wonder is that Jesus walked right into it, knowing what was going to happen. His disciples tried to talk him out of going back to Jerusalem. That was the place of their greatest humiliation, the most dangerous place, because they knew there were men scheming to kill Jesus. But they went back anyway."

"Because it was God's plan."

Gil nodded. "Yeah. It was God's plan and even though it meant his death, Jesus moved steadily forward."

"The place of their greatest humiliation." Alex repeated the words in a soft voice. He closed the Bible on his lap, stood up, and strode to the window. The stillness that had settled in was gone. Another storm was raging. He felt like the swirling winds were inside him, rooting up everything he'd tried to bury for the past five years. "This won't be easy," he mumbled.

"What?"

He'd forgotten Gil was in the room. He turned to him. "I think I know what God wants me to do," he said, "but just like you I'm not sure I can do it. I know I don't want to." He strode back to the chair.

"I guess you and I are a lot alike. We both have a wide yellow streak up our backs."

Gil stared at the floor. "I used to believe I could do anything because God was with me. That was before...."

"Before the accident," Alex finished for him.

"Yeah. Before the accident."

Alex stared into the fire for a long time. When he raised his head he realized he'd slipped into the same pattern of thinking that had kept him from believing God for so long. He knew Gil had too. "I guess we're both still believing we're not good enough." Gil frowned at him as he continued. "Good enough for God to help us do whatever it is He has planned."

Gil grunted. "I never was. Just took me a while to realize it."

Alex sat back down and picked up the Bible again. "But none of these guys were good enough either." He almost shook the book at Gil. "And look what God helped them to do. They started a worldwide movement that still exists. They didn't deserve to have a part in it—they'd abandoned Jesus. But He forgave them, and then He said He'd be there for them, every step of the way." Alex frowned back at the older man. "I haven't been in touch with this God for very long, but He doesn't strike me as someone who'd say that and not do it."

Gil laughed. "Preach it, brother."

Alex stood up and started to pace. "Kenni told me to read David's story, and when I did I didn't really understand. But I think I do now. God forgave David and still let him rule. So that's gotta mean it's not about what you've done. It's about who you believe in, who you hang onto."

Gil shook his head. Alex saw his eyes fill with anguish. "It's not that easy."

"Yes it is!" Alex almost pounced. "It has to be, Gil." He waved the Bible again. "Or most of what's in here is a lie."

Gil grinned. "You going to thump me with it?"

Alex took a step back. "Would it do any good?"

Gil dropped his eyes and shook his head. "I can't, Alex. I just can't. I used to go into the prisons, to preach. Just the idea of being locked up like that...I can't face that."

Alex dropped into the chair. Memories of the last time he'd been in jail surged into his mind. He saw the faces of the young men he'd shared time with—faces with dead eyes. He could smell the place—the antiseptic they used to clean, the greasy food they served at every meal. He could hear the noises—the guttural shouts, the curses, and, what was sometimes worse, the deathly silence.

He gripped the Bible to keep his hands from shaking. *Can I face that again?* He shivered, opened the Bible, and started reading again out loud. Now and then he stopped, but Gil remained silent. When Alex came to the end of Matthew 28 he paused. Then he read verses 19 and 20 again. "Therefore go and make disciples of all nations, baptizing them in the name of the Father and of the Son and of the Holy Spirit, and teaching them to obey everything I have commanded you. And surely I'll be with you always, to the very end of the age."

The strength came back into Alex's voice. "Can't really do that in the middle of the bush, can you?" He gave Gil a sideways grin. "Unless you can make a grizzly into a disciple."

Gil grunted, but said nothing. Alex stared into space for some time, then said quietly, "I've been refusing to trust God all my life. And I've been living scared. But reading these words, it makes me feel like—I feel like maybe I could do it—maybe I could do whatever God tells me to do."

Gil rolled over and pulled the blanket up over himself. "Good for you," he mumbled. "Go for it."

Alex closed the Bible, went to the window again, and stared out at the raging wind. He was suddenly aware that now, for the first time, the storm didn't echo what he felt inside.

○ ○ ○

Two weeks after he and Gil were ill Alex felt a weakness in his legs and arms. That night the fever hit. He thought at first it was nothing, but by mid-morning the next day he was too weak to stand. It was Gil's turn to nurse him. The fever took hold and held on for two days, then began to let go. Just as Alex was feeling like he could move again, it hit Gil.

"Well, at least we weren't both down at the same time." The older man sipped water from the glass Alex held for him.

"You think this is from the bear meat?" Alex asked.

Gil shrugged. "What else?" He laid back on the pillow. "Sure makes you feel like a dishrag, doesn't it?"

When Gil's fever didn't break for the next three days, Alex started to worry. When he felt the weakness creeping into his legs again, he started to pray.

○ ○ ○

When Gil woke his first thought was *This must be how Rip Van Winkle felt.* It seemed like the world had passed him by and he was alone in a foreign place he used to call home. He sat up, winced, and cradled his arm. Alex lay on the floor, a blanket tangled around his legs. Gil's mind cleared enough that he remembered. He stood up. The room swirled and he flopped back down again, clutching his arm as a stab of pain shot through it. He waited for the vertigo to pass, then tried again. He got down on his knees and touched Alex's shoulder. He groaned, but didn't open his eyes. Gil managed to roll him over and put a hand on his forehead. Alex was shivering, but his body was burning. The older man staggered to his feet. He covered Alex with the blanket, then focused on a parka hanging on a hook by the door. He managed to drag himself toward it. Shrugging it on he tugged a scarf from another hook, pulled a glove onto his exposed hand with his teeth, and went outside.

Swaying, he watched his feet push tunnels through the snow. Ice fog hovered about him, its density as oppressive as the solidity of the dread settling in his gut. Tugging on the hood of the parka until the fur shielded his eyes he hunched his body and peered ahead. Engulfed by the white shroud of ice he couldn't see the rest of the camp. An image came to him of a man wrapped in white cloths. Grave cloths. Lazarus. Cerecloths. Jesus. Gil's lips curled into a smirk. The religious imagery wouldn't leave him, no matter how long, how far he ran.

He had to get to the office, had to reach the radio. "Come on, God," he mumbled. "I could use a miracle about now." The edge in his voice was as sharp, as cold, as the crystals hanging in the air. He staggered forward, clenched his jaw. "God." He felt his knees stiffen. "Just"—step—"keep me going"—step—"in a straight"—step—"line." With nothing to guide him, no outline of a path, no indent of footprints, Gil knew he could end up going in circles, or worse, heading away from the camp with nothing between him and Alaska. "God." The word came out in a moan.

A sudden rushing of wind stopped him. His heart skipped a beat, but he let out his breath when he recognized the sound. Ravens—the only creatures that moved in these temperatures. The pulsing sigh of their wings was close, but he couldn't see them, couldn't see anything but the fog. His cerecloth? He shivered and resisted the urge to scream, tried to wipe the ice from his eyelashes, and moved forward.

Staggering now he was halted again by sharp incongruous sounds. The ravens chortled, seemed to mock him. His breathing came hard, erratic puffs of mist escaping his scarf. He wanted to pull it off, rid himself of this heavy coat, but he knew he risked freezing his lungs without the scarf, and freezing to death without the parka. He turned to resume his pace, took one step, and toppled into the snow. Closing his eyes Gil tried to slow the thumping of his heart. "God!" This time the word hung in the fog like an animal's cry. He opened his eyes and looked for some kind of markings on the ground, his sense of direction entirely gone. He visualized the camp in his mind, tried to place the office and bunkhouses in relation to the house. He pushed himself onto his knees, then his feet. *Okay. It has to be this way*. He turned and started off again. His mind wandered, settling around stories he'd heard, stories about ravens. God sent ravens, to feed...who was it? His memory sang with the syrupy voice of an almost forgotten Sunday school teacher, but the name of the one the birds fed wouldn't come to him. The whoosh of wings drew him forward.

Locked in the cold like a shrink-wrapped slab of meat Gil was only aware that he breathed in and out, his legs shuffled, his feet plowed parallel furrows in the snow. He fell twice more. Each time he heard the ravens and forced himself back up. The fourth time he let his head sink deep into the cushion of white, let his breathing slow, his mind stop.

He didn't know how long he'd slept when he felt a sharp jab, something hard digging at him. Then a tug on his hood, another jab to his leg. He forced his eyes open, blinking at a flurry of black wings, then jerked back from an unblinking black eye. The rush of adrenaline roused him. He groaned, stood, moved on. "God." The word had become a prayer. He staggered forward again, the words of Psalm 139:5-10 on his lips. "You hem me in—behind and before; you've laid your hand upon me. Such knowledge is too wonderful for me, too lofty for me to attain. Where can I go from your Spirit?" Gil stopped and screamed the words into the still white air. "Where can I flee from your presence? If I go up to the heavens, you're there; if I make my bed in the depths, you're there. If I rise on the wings of the dawn, if I settle on the far side of the sea, even there...." Gil stopped. A raven hopped a few paces from him. He almost whispered the next words. "...your hand will guide me, your right hand will hold me fast." He took two stumbling steps and fell again, but not onto snow this time. Blinking at the hard surface he reached out and touched it and realized it was the step of a porch. He heaved himself up and staggered through the door. The heat inside was a relief, yet it made him want to return to the cold outside. He lunged for the radiophone, pressed the Call button, and sank to the floor.

Chapter Thirty-two

It disturbed Kenni that she wasn't able to reach Alex on the radiophone. George tried to reason that he wouldn't be sitting by it 24/7, but she shook her head.

"Something's wrong, George. I can feel it."

George shifted in the cramped airline seat beside her. "Well, we'll find out soon enough. We'll be landing in Whitehorse in less than an hour." The frown on her face didn't lift. He reached for her hand. "Want to pray?"

Kenni nodded. They bowed their heads together and George began. "Father, we don't know what's happening with Alex right now, but you do. You've had your eyes on him all along and we pray that you'll keep him safe. We pray that we'll be able to locate him without too much trouble and that everything will soon be resolved."

Kenni squeezed his hand when he was done and gave him a weak smile. "Thanks," she said and turned to peer out the window at the barren white landscape below. She continued to pray silently, for Alex and for herself. *Am I right in running after this man?* Her compulsion to help him had made her nothing but miserable for the past few months. She almost wished she'd never met him. *God, don't let me do anything stupid.*

○ ○ ○

George put his head back on the seat and closed his eyes. He wanted to pray that they wouldn't find Alex Donnelly. He wanted to pray that Kenni would just forget all about him. He rubbed at the

205

frown wrinkles across his forehead. He knew that was a prayer that wasn't likely to be answered. He sighed and tried to relax. But he couldn't get Alex Donnelly out of his mind. He had to admit he kind of liked him, even though Alex definitely had a rough edge to say the least. There was something about him George even admired. But he was bad for Kenni. He wasn't..."good enough" were the words George realized he wanted to use. And that made his head lift off the pillowed seat. *Is that it? Do I think Alex is in some way inferior? God forgive me.* He closed his eyes again and prayed, not that they wouldn't find Alex, but that Alex would find God.

○ ○ ○

December 7, Whitehorse, Yukon

The nurse smiled when she saw Alex watching her.

He frowned. "Where am I? How did I get here?"

"You're in Whitehorse General Hospital. You and your friend were airlifted from the mining camp. The doctor will want to talk to you about him. He has no identification."

"Gil." Alex's frown deepened. "Where is he?"

The nurse tugged a curtain aside and Alex turned his head to the bed beside him. Gil lay there, motionless, his chest rising with the rhythm of shallow breathing. The primitive sling had been replaced with a cast.

"I'll get the doctor," she said and disappeared.

Some time later a doctor arrived with a clipboard in his hand. He took Alex's pulse and temperature again. His voice seemed to come from a long way off. "Hmm...well, that's good," he nodded. "Your fever's down a bit and your pulse is better."

The man smiled. "I'm doctor Carson," he said flipping a page on the chart. "We don't have the results of the blood work yet, but they should be in soon. How are you feeling?"

Alex ignored the question, but roused himself enough to ask, "How's Gil? Is he going to be okay?"

The doctor glanced at the bed beside Alex's. "You both have the same symptoms. His fever is a bit worse than yours—hasn't woken up much. Could be because of the arm. What happened? Dog attack him?"

"Bear," Alex said and closed his eyes. The doctor waited for a few moments, then asked, "Did you eat any of it?"

Alex nodded. "Been sick ever since."

The doctor scribbled on his chart. "I'll order a muscle biopsy immediately. This could clear up the mystery." He glanced at Gil. "Can you tell us his name, his next of kin?"

Alex took a long time to process the words, then he shook his head. "I know him as Gilbert LaPierre, but that's not his real name. I don't know where he's from."

The doctor sighed and scribbled on his clipboard, then moved to Gil's side and checked the chart on the table. He came back to Alex and put his hand on his arm. "Sleep," he said. "I'll be back to check on you later."

Alex closed his eyes and tried to do what the doctor suggested, but Gil's words kept screaming in his head. "They went back to the place of their greatest humiliation."

He squeezed his eyes closed. "That's what I have to do," he whispered. "Kenni...that's what I have to do...what I have to do...."

Chapter Thirty-three

Sal wasted no time getting to the hospital when she learned Alex was there. Visiting hours were almost over, but the nurse said she could see him for a few minutes.

"His fever is still very high," she said.

"What's wrong with him?" Sal asked.

"We don't know yet. The doctor is running tests now." They entered the room quietly. Sal was shocked at how pale Alex looked, his face swathed in perspiration, his black hair clinging to his forehead in tendrils.

The nurse stepped to the bed. "Looks like the fever is peaking again." She took his pulse and tried to put a thermometer in his mouth. Alex groaned and tossed his head. The nurse tried again, without success.

"I'm sorry, you'll have to leave now," she said over her shoulder. "I have to get a reading on his temp and there's only one other way to do it."

Sal turned to go. Alex moaned and tried to sit up. "Kenni," he called out. "Kenni. Don't go. I have to tell you...."

The nurse grasped his shoulders and pushed him gently back onto the bed. "Tell the nurse at the desk I need some help."

Sal did as she was asked, then headed for her truck. She sat behind the wheel for some time staring out the window. Then she smacked the glove box open and rummaged through it until she found what she was looking for. She stared at the small card for a few more minutes, then went back inside to find a phone.

○ ○ ○

George and Kenni were about to check into the Westmark hotel when his cell phone rang.

"This is Sal, from Whitehorse. You remember?"

George frowned. "Of course."

"Alex is sick. He's in the hospital. You and your friend better get here quick. He's—he's asking for her."

"What's wrong with him?"

"I don't know. Just get here."

The phone went dead in George's hand before he could tell her they were already there. It took them less than ten minutes to get to the hospital.

Alex was lying still in the bed when they arrived. Kenni slowly approached him. His face was pale, beads of perspiration standing on his forehead. Deep lines wrinkled his brow and drew her eyes down his face. She took his hand and his head rolled toward her.

"Hey," she said.

He gave a weak smile. "How'd you know?"

"Sal called. We just arrived. I told you I'd find you."

Alex closed his eyes for a moment. "Kenni, I have to tell you...."

Before he could finish his sentence, the door opened and the doctor walked in, clipboard in hand. He seemed surprised to see them and not very pleased.

"I'm sorry, you'll have to leave now. We need to get these patients ready for transport."

"Transport?" George asked.

"Yes. And you are...?"

George introduced himself and Kenni.

"Are you family?"

"They're friends," Alex answered for him. He managed a weak grin as he added, "And my lawyers."

The doctor hesitated for a moment, then said, "Alex is being medivacked to Vancouver along with his friend there." The doctor nodded toward Gil. "A specialist will meet them at the hospital."

Kenni looked from Alex to the doctor and back again. "What is it? What's wrong?"

Alex tried to laugh, but only succeeded in a weak chuckle. "Killed me a bar," he said, "but the old griz has the last laugh."

The doctor opened the door. "They have a severe case of trichinosis. Now I'm sorry, but you'll have to leave."

Kenni started to protest. Alex tried to raise himself. "I want them with me."

The doctor sighed, but nodded. "Alright. I'll arrange it, but please...."

"Okay," George said. "We'll be in the hall." He took Kenni's arm and led her from the room as two aids wheeled in a stretcher. He suggested they retrieve their luggage from the hotel, then meet the ambulance at the airport. Within a short time they were in the air. Alex was in and out of consciousness and seemed too weak to talk when he was awake. All he did was stare at Kenni. Kenni held his hand and stared back.

Chapter Thirty-four

December 8, Whitehorse, Yukon

Constable Ewing stiffened as the plainclothes Vancouver police inspector stepped away from the baggage carousel. He'd heard about "the Swedish Giant," that he was tough on everyone. He'd also heard he was very good at what he did.

"Sorensen." The tall man gave a curt nod. "Anything new?"

Ewing shook his head. "Still waiting for the fog to clear."

Sorensen grunted and shifted his bag. "I'd like to see your report."

"Of course." Ewing turned on his heel and headed for the doors. Sorensen stayed on his tail—so close Ewing thought about pulling a quick stop. They made the short drive in silence.

Sorensen settled himself into the chair behind Ewing's desk. Ewing did his best not to resent it.

"This perp may have committed several more assaults in the past five years," Sorensen said.

Ewing frowned. "I've studied the data. The incident in Whitehorse doesn't match. I don't think it's the same guy."

"The inconsistencies are small."

"But significant. The first assault didn't involve a weapon. The assault here did. And this one involved an older woman. The others were young—just kids."

"His tastes are changing."

Ewing shook his head. "The details are significant."

"You trying to slow this down, Ewing?"

The officer felt the steam rising as his neck went red. "No, Inspector. I'm just trying to determine the truth."

"The truth is this scumbag, Donnelly, is on the loose and needs to be locked up."

"For the crime he committed."

"And maybe a few others. And I want it done before my retirement party."

Ewing didn't respond. But the twist in his gut made him uneasy. Very uneasy.

○ ○ ○

Sorensen tried not to bark the words into the phone. "I can't tell you why we need to get to Beacon Hill." He clenched his teeth, then took a deep breath and tried to control his voice. "Just tell them to get the chopper ready—please!" He hung up before the secretary could give him any more argument. He leaped to his feet and grabbed his coat as Ewing strode into the room. He nodded to him. "Let's go get him."

When they arrived at the hangar Sorensen was more than a little annoyed to see that the helicopter was sitting unattended, its rotors still. He barged into the office. "What's going on?" He growled. "Why isn't the chopper warming up?"

The secretary stared at him with her mouth hanging open. Ewing was about to intervene when one of the pilots stepped between them.

"There's no point in flying all the way out there, Ray."

The inspector turned to him. "We have an arrest to make and if you...."

"There's nobody there."

Ewing clamped his mouth shut. Sorensen growled, "What?"

"We just medivacked two men to the hospital from Beacon Hill. The only one left is the dog."

Sorensen whirled around and headed for the car without another word. Ewing thanked the pilot and barely managed to get into the vehicle before it spun away from the hanger, snow spraying from under its tires. He didn't bother watching their speed as Sorensen drove back, siren blaring all the way into town.

After convincing the woman at the front desk that they had a legitimate reason to know where Alex Donnelly was, Ewing leaned over the nursing station counter and groaned. "You mean we just missed him?"

The nurse nodded. "I'm afraid so."

Sorensen cursed.

The nurse blinked at the two officers. "Alex Donnelly was medi-vacked to Vancouver an hour ago."

"Why?" Sorensen leaned toward her.

The nurse stammered. "I...I'm afraid I can't tell you."

"Right. The flippin' privacy act." Sorensen smacked the side of the partition with the flat of his hand making the nurse jump. Ewing sighed and thanked her, then turned away to follow the inspector.

Sorensen kept his foot on the gas all the way back to the detachment. He wasn't happy to learn the next flight out to Vancouver didn't leave until late the next day.

"I'll need to fax my department," he said. "I want an officer there when that plane lands."

○ ○ ○

The fax machine hadn't quit all day and Officer Stiles wasn't happy about it. She put the pile on her desk and got up for another cup of coffee. As she headed back the staff sergeant called her into his office and handed her a stack of files with directions on what he wanted done with them. She was leaning over her desk with everything still in her arms when another officer brushed by her. It was just enough to throw her off balance. The files started to slip every which way. As she tried to keep them from falling the coffee cup tipped.

Only two faxes were ruined. Stiles studied the small blur at the top of one sheet. *Now did that say Whitehorse or Whiterock?*

Chapter Thirty-five

When they arrived at the hospital the flurry of activity kept Kenni and George out of Alex's room for over an hour. At last the doctor told them they could see him, but just for a few moments.

Alex lay on his back, his swollen eyes closed, his breathing shallow. Kenni took his hand and he opened his eyes, then closed them again in a wince.

"Are you in pain?" she asked.

Alex opened his eyes again and made an effort at a smile. "Only when I breathe," he said. "The doc says that's one of the symptoms. The bugs attack the muscles, including the lungs and heart." He turned his head toward her. "Kenni...I want to tell you everything. About Gil...about...I'm sorry for the way I acted." His eyes moved to George. "I know I've been a jerk."

George grinned. "No argument from me."

Kenni frowned at him. George put his hand on Alex's arm. "But don't sweat it. Just get well, okay?"

Alex slumped deeper into the pillow and closed his eyes. In a few moments he started mumbling something unintelligible. The doctor came into the room and asked them to step into the hall.

"We don't have anyone registered as next of kin for either of these men. Do you know who that would be?"

George shook his head as he answered. "Alex has none. I think we're about the closest thing he's got to family. We don't know anything about the other man."

The doctor nodded. "Well, you have a very sick young friend. I just saw the results of the tests and it's pretty impressive. Worst case of trichinosis I've ever seen and I've seen a few."

"Is it curable?" Kenni asked.

"Ordinarily the medication kills the parasites."

George frowned. "But?"

"As I said I've never seen a case this severe. People have been known to die from trichinosis, but we're using a very aggressive treatment. We'll just have to wait and see how they respond."

○ ○ ○

Two days later three policemen arrived in the hospital room. One of them was very tall with wisps of white hair mingled with blond. Though he was dressed in plainclothes Alex noticed he looked like he'd won his share of wrestling championships.

When they approached Alex's bed Gil distracted them. "I'm the one you're looking for," he said. One of the uniformed cops took the details of his story. The others listened, but the blond didn't take his eyes off Alex.

Alex listened too as Gil told them his real name—Reverend Michael McRae—and that there was a warrant for his arrest on a charge of negligent homicide.

"Reverend?" The officer's eyebrows went up.

Gil closed his eyes. "Bona fide," he mumbled.

The officer told him they'd investigate and get back to him. Gil slumped back onto the bed, the effort of talking exhausting him. Then the moment Alex had been dreading arrived. The tall blond in plainclothes took a step toward him. His eyes narrowed. "Alex Donnelly?" he asked.

Alex swallowed and nodded.

The man's face twitched and Alex thought for a moment he was going to smile. He nodded instead and flipped open a small notepad. "Your date of birth?"

Alex told him.

"Did you once reside at 679 Garth Street, Vancouver?"

Alex nodded again. "Yes."

"Then you're under arrest for the sexual assault of Cindy Vilner." The inspector pocketed his pad and nodded to the younger officer. The constable recited Alex's rights.

"This one likes to run, Constable," Sorensen said. "I think we'd better insure that he doesn't leave his bed." The cold metal of the hand-cuffs he used to shackle Alex's wrist to the bed made him shiver. "Constable Regere will be keeping you company, Mr. Donnelly." Alex didn't like the way he said his name. "And as soon as the doctor gives the okay we'll be finding you other accommodations."

Alex nodded again, but said nothing.

Chapter Thirty-six

Alex explained the presence of the policeman and the handcuffs when Kenni and George came to visit later that day. He was surprised they seemed to expect it.

Kenni dropped her eyes. "I...I'm afraid it's my doing, Alex." She looked into his face. "I went to see Cindy Vilner. Then I went to the police."

Alex felt the color drain from his face as he stared into Kenni's eyes for an agonizing moment, trying to find the words that would make her believe him. "I didn't...." Alex formed the word in his mind, but couldn't say it. He licked his lips. "I didn't do it, Kenni. I didn't touch Cindy Vilner. I came home that day and found Wild Bill on top of her."

Kenni's hand flew to her mouth as Alex continued.

"I tackled him, but he was too big for me. He beat on me til I could hardly move, but I kept screaming that I was going to turn him in. Then he stood back and laughed. He called the cops and told them I'd done it. He threatened to kill Cindy if she didn't go along. Then he told me to run. With my record I knew the cops would never believe me. There was nothing I could do." Alex's voice dropped to almost a whisper. "So I ran. I left her there and ran."

Kenni's eyes remained on his as he spoke and when he was done they didn't waver, didn't blink. Then she took a deep breath. "When I found Cindy, she said...at least I thought...." Her eyes filled and her lips trembled as she reached for him. "I'm sorry, Alex, but I thought...."

Alex grasped her hand. "It's okay."

Kenni wiped at her eyes. "We've been trying to sort it all out. There may be evidence—DNA." Her eyes shone now. "Alex, that will prove you're innocent."

Alex frowned. "After all this time?"

"When a case is unsolved they keep everything," George said. He glanced at Kenni. "Or at least they're supposed to. That means they should still have Cindy's clothing."

Kenni squeezed his hand. "We've also found a good lawyer and he's already looking into it."

Alex let his breath out. "That's the best news I've heard in a while." He sank back onto his pillow, suddenly weak from the exertion. "You don't know...for five years it's been hanging over me." His eyes focused on Kenni again. "Someday I'd like to apologize to Cindy."

He saw George touch Kenni's shoulder. "I think we'd better let you get some rest. You're looking a little pale again."

Alex nodded. "Yeah. I'm feeling pretty wiped."

Kenni smiled. "We'll be back tomorrow."

After they left, Alex heard Gil chuckle. He turned toward him.

"Looks like you may be a free man yet," he said.

"I'm not counting any chickens." Alex tried to shift onto his side, but the handcuffs clanged and kept him from moving. "Maybe they can find you a good lawyer too."

The older man waved his hand and shook his head. "It won't be much of a case. I intend to plead guilty as charged." He grasped the triangle hanging above his head and heaved himself up. "It's weird, you know. Physically I've never felt so weak. But inside...." He smiled. "I guess confession really is good for the soul. I know I'm headed for prison, and I'm still afraid of that, but now I think I can face it. I woke up this morning with that verse from Jeremiah in my head—'I know the plans I have for you....' and I believe it, Alex." Gil's blue eyes sparkled. "God has a plan for both of us. For me it looks like it'll be making disciples in prison." He grinned. "The grizzlies seem to be a lost cause."

Alex chuckled. "You got that right."

"Let's hope you won't end up playing Silas to my Paul."

"Huh?" Alex frowned.

Gil laughed. "Read Acts 16," he said.

Alex got serious again. "I still haven't thanked you for getting that chopper to pick us up."

Gil was still grinning. "Some people will do anything to get a man to do what's right. The two-by-four might've been easier."

"Like you said He does have a sense of irony. I had no intention of getting on that chopper with you."

Gil chuckled. "I know. It's probably a good thing I was so out of it when they got there or I might've tried to resist myself."

Alex let his head drop back onto the pillow. "But here we are."

"Yeah. Til we're well enough for a jail cell."

"There must be something...."

"There is. Pray. You seem to be pretty good in that department."

○ ○ ○

Kenni and George spent every waking hour at Alex's side as the cycle continued and he slipped in and out of fever. Gil's fever was raging again. He opened his eyes a few times, but spoke little. Alex said even less. It was another four days before his fever broke, another two before Gil's temperature started to drop. The police had returned, but the doctor convinced them that Gil was too weak to try and escape so they didn't use the handcuffs.

Alex's head felt like dead weight, his arms like wet noodles, but he rolled over far enough to see his friend. "Hey, old man. How ya doin'?"

Gil gave him a weak grin. "Thought you said you cooked that bear good."

The doctor walked in at that moment and spoke before Alex could reply. "It wouldn't have mattered if you'd incinerated that animal. He'd still have had larvae in him. Worst case I've ever seen, gentlemen, but I think we've got it beat." The doctor tapped the chart in his hand. "That last biopsy was much better."

"So we'll live," Alex said. It was more of a statement than a question.

"Yes, you'll live, but it will take some time to be fully recuperated. Months. Maybe even years."

"How long before we can leave here?" Alex asked.

"It will be at least another week before you feel like going anywhere," the doctor replied. "But with a little luck and the meds you'll be out in time for Christmas."

Out of the fire and into the frying pan. Alex tried not to wonder what it would be like to spend Christmas in jail.

○ ○ ○

A week later Kenni and George convinced the guard to allow Alex to walk with them. Gil was asleep and still seemed too weak to move so the officer handcuffed himself to Alex's wrist and they wandered down the hall to a small atrium full of greenery and natural light. Christmas lights shone all around them as they sat on a small bench and Alex was shackled once again to the furniture. The constable moved a few paces away as Kenni handed Alex the letter. His hand shook as he opened it.

The flowing script blurred when he tried to read it. He handed the pages back to Kenni. "Will you read it to me?" he asked.

Kenni nodded and took the letter.

My dear son: I don't know if you'll ever read this letter. If you do, it will probably mean that I can't be with you when you receive the money we placed in trust for you. I've prayed so fervently that if that happens these meager words will express the inexpressible—my deep, deep love for you.

You may find it hard to believe that I love you, since the money now in your hands came from a lawsuit against a doctor who failed to abort your tiny body from mine. I can only say that the woman who wanted to do that horrific thing no longer exists, and I'm so thankful that the doctor failed. But let me tell you the whole story.

Kenni took a deep breath and continued.

Your dad and I decided when we married that we didn't want children. We were both bent on climbing the ladder of success in our separate careers—Tom in his construction business and me in real estate. We were well on our way and far too busy "enjoying life" to consider having children. I was halfway through the second trimester before I even realized I was pregnant. It was such a shock and I immediately told the doctor I wanted an abortion. She refused to do it because the pregnancy was so far along so a week later I went to an abortion clinic. The procedure was over quickly and I went home thinking everything would be fine. But in the days afterward I struggled with depression. I couldn't seem to shed the idea that I'd done something unnatural and terribly wrong. Guilt overwhelmed me. Then I began feeling ill every morning, but I was gaining weight. I returned to my doctor and was told I was still pregnant.

The conflicting emotions that raged in me then were almost unbearable. On the one hand I was furious that the doctor at the abortion clinic had not done his job properly. On the other, I was secretly relieved that my baby was still alive and terribly fearful that you'd been hurt in some way. I couldn't face the idea of trying another abortion, but I was terrified of having a child that required constant medical care.

Then a friend of your dad's, a law student, told us we should sue and gave us the name of a law firm. Again I struggled with the idea of doing this, but Tom convinced me that we should to make sure we had the money for the medical expenses in case you needed extra care. By this time we had adjusted to the idea that we were going to have a child. Your dad even started bragging about you to the guys he worked with. Before I knew it we were sitting in Max Ferrington's office. He advised us that we had a good case and he thought he could win it for us. But that's not all he did. After all the legal business was taken care of he looked at me and asked how I was handling all of this. I burst into tears. Tom tried to calm me down, but all the pent up emotion just flooded out and I couldn't stop. Mr. Ferrington just sat beside me and patted my hand for a long time. Then I poured out my whole sad story and told him how confused I was.

When I finally got myself under control Max gave me the name of a counselor and suggested I talk with her. I made the appointment right away before I could change my mind. The woman was very skilled. She listened for a long time, then she talked about God's plan and how, when we try to disrupt that, we instinctively know we've done something wrong. She was so gentle, not at all judgmental, but I felt like a terrible person sitting there listening to her.

Then she said something that pierced my heart. She said that the baby growing in me was a gift from God, one of the true signs of His love for us. That made me cry again and I felt so ashamed. I thought God would never forgive me for trying to abort my baby.

The counselor explained that God had already forgiven me and was waiting for me to accept that forgiveness. Suddenly, that's what I wanted more than anything in the world. So I did it, right then in that woman's office. I asked Jesus to come into my life and forgive me.

Kenni's voice trembled for a moment. She cleared her throat and continued.

Oh, my son, I wish I could help you feel what I felt then— the complete peace, the joy, just thinking that God had chosen to bless me even when I was ignoring Him, and worse, cursing Him. I have prayed, ever since, that some day you'll know Him like I do now. He's so good. So entirely good.

When you were born I was the happiest woman on the earth, not just because you were a perfectly healthy baby boy, but because I was a new creation, a woman capable of loving you, because I knew Jesus loved me. I know too that God has a special purpose for your life and I pray that you'll let Him lead you into it.

I have also prayed that this money we've placed in trust won't be a burden to you, but will be used, through you, to expand God's kingdom.

I love you beyond measure.

The letter was signed, simply, "Mom."

Kenni handed it back to Alex. He took it with trembling hands, then wiped the tears coursing down his cheeks. He took a deep breath and sighed as he slipped it back into the small envelope.

"I understand now why this got lost for a while." He turned to Kenni. "I wasn't ready to hear it." He ran his thumb over his name written in flowing script across the envelope. "I've been...." he exhaled and took another deep breath. He shook his head. "I've been so stupid. So blind." He wiped his eyes again. "But now...I want to honor what she said." Alex's eyes flicked from Kenni to George and back again. "About making sure the money is spent on the right things. And I want

226

to find God's purpose for my life." He looked into Kenni's eyes and sighed. "But I think it's going to be a long road."

Kenni smiled. "You've already made a beginning, Alex, and we're here to help, any way we can."

Alex saw the policeman stand up and glance nervously toward his room. He turned toward them, but before he could speak Alex said, "Guess we have to go back."

They were almost there when the policeman whirled around and dragged Alex back toward the nursing station. Kenni peered into the room, then stared at Alex.

"Gil's gone," she said.

Chapter Thirty-seven

There were no Christmas lights adorning the small house. Gil hauled himself out of the taxi and stood staring at it. He took a deep breath as he made his way down the walk toward the front door. Not daring to hesitate when he reached it he rang the bell. His best friend had aged, but apparently not as much as he. Or maybe it was the beard. Steve Gowalchuk didn't recognize him.

Gil cleared his throat. "Hi, Steve."

The man's eyes widened for an instant, then narrowed. "What do you want?"

"I came for two things and you can do them both in a matter of minutes. I need you to forgive me and then I need you to call the police."

Steve's chest expanded as he drew air into his lungs. Gil saw his knuckles go white on the doorknob, then relax. "Come in," he said.

Gil let his breath out when Steve stepped away from the door.

The house was clean and tidy, but Gil sensed that something was missing. Then he felt a sharp stab of guilt as he realized what that something was. He followed Steve into a small living room. They sat opposite one another and for a few moments neither one spoke.

Steve broke the silence first. "I've spent a good part of the last five years trying to forgive you," he said, his eyes on the floor. "It's only been in the last couple of months that I've felt like I could do it." He looked up into Gil's face. "Maybe. I know if you'd come here anytime before now I probably would've pounded my fist into your face. I'm still tempted to do just that."

Gil took a deep breath. It took all his willpower to keep eye contact. "That's pretty much what I expected when I rang your doorbell."

"All that preaching you did on forgiveness, how forgiving sets you free. I guess some of it sank in. Ironic, isn't it?"

"God's word is truth, no matter how flawed the one speaking it."

Steve nodded. "It was hard for a lot of us in the church to believe that. Some still don't."

Gil bowed his head. "You don't know how much I wish I could undo it, Steve. Every day since I've wished I could go back in time."

"But you can't." Steve stood up and went to the window. As he stared outside Gil watched his hands clench into fists, then open again as he turned back to face him. "And neither can I. So...." He took a step forward and Gil stood. "I forgive you," he said and extended his hand to the man who had killed his wife.

Gil fell apart, his face melting into sobs. Steve took a step toward him, then stopped and turned back to the window. Gil sank back into the chair and managed to pull himself together. Steve mopped at his face, then moved toward the kitchen.

"I'll make us some coffee," he said.

He returned with two steaming mugs. "Where have you been all this time?" he asked.

"Holed up in the Yukon." Gil took a sip of his coffee. "I ran as far as I could get, but it wasn't far enough. No place could be far enough."

"So why come back now?"

Gil snorted. "The Lord sent me a pilgrim. A young man who has more courage in his baby finger than I do in my whole body. He made me realize I had to come back and face reality." He shifted the sling on his arm. "The grizzly that did this to me had something to do with it too."

Steve stirred his drink and placed the spoon on the table as he sat down. "You really want me to call the police?"

"No. But there's no alternative. They're probably out looking for me as we speak. It's just a matter of time before they catch up to me."

"I don't imagine they'll think to look here," Steve said.

Silence filled the room until their mugs were empty. There wasn't much more to be said. Gil looked at the man who'd been the best friend he'd ever had. "I'd appreciate it if you'd do it now, Steve, before I lose my nerve."

Steve stood. "I'll drive you to the police station."

"You don't have to...."

"I don't really want the police at my door."

Gil nodded. "Okay, but be warned you may have to drag me into the building."

Steve grunted. "I think I could manage that."

○ ○ ○

December 22, Vancouver Court House

The handcuffs chaffed Alex's wrists as he was led into the court-room. It had been a long time since he'd been before a judge, but he remembered the feelings—guilt, shame, fear, all boiling under the anger. They raged through him now, even though he knew he was innocent, until he wished he could make himself invisible. He stared at the floor and listened as the charge was read and the lawyers went through their motions. He was shocked when he heard the amount set for bail. It was obviously meant to keep him behind bars. He was stunned when George leaned toward him and told him it would be paid. Then he was standing outside, grateful for the feel of a cold rain on his face.

He shook hands with his lawyer as the man assured him he'd keep in touch. The next court date was three months away.

"But you shouldn't ever see it," George said. "Once they find the DNA sample from that clothing and compare it to yours the charge will be dropped."

His lawyer agreed, but cautioned them that it could take a while. "There's a backlog of DNA in the labs," he said. "But I'll keep you posted." He also said he intended to try and convince Cindy Vilner to tell the truth and testify against Bill Mitchell. "Just in case."

As they headed for George's car Alex felt like he was being watched. He glanced over his shoulder more than once, but saw no one. Just as he was climbing into the back seat he saw a shiny black car slide by. And his eyes met those of an inspector who hated loose ends.

○ ○ ○

Alex sat in the airport cafe, a cup of coffee steaming in his hands. "But what if she doesn't? What if Cindy sticks to the original story?"

Kenni reached across the table and touched his hand. "The DNA evidence will make that moot, Alex. The evidence doesn't lie."

Alex frowned. "What if they can't get a DNA sample from the clothes? It seems to be taking them a while."

George flashed a look at Kenni, but his voice sounded confident. "They'll do it. And at just the right time. Just like we found your mother's letter at the right time."

Alex wished he could be that certain. They stood as the loudspeaker announced their flight. As they moved toward the gate Kenni sighed, "I wish we could stay, Alex, but...."

"It's okay," he said. "I'll be fine. I'll call you, okay?"

She nodded, started to turn away, but then spun on her heel and embraced him. Alex wrapped his arms around her and closed his eyes. When she started to pull away he gave her one last squeeze and let go.

George shook his hand, pressing something into it. "You know my cell phone number," he said. "Call anytime, okay?"

As they walked away Alex glanced down at the money in his hand. He didn't stay to watch their plane take off.

Chapter Thirty-eight

Freezing rain fell as Alex made his way toward the downtown church. He hunched his shoulders against the chill and navigated the streets from memory. When he turned the corner and saw the tall stone building he stopped. Gray as slate, with a high black iron fence surrounding it, Grace Church looked impenetrable and reminded him of old fairy tales about castles, dragons and knights in shining armor. But he knew there was a back door where anyone off the street could wander in. The name of the church and the service times were posted on a small sign near the sidewalk, but it didn't list the names of the pastors. *Is Pastor T still there?* He shivered and headed for the door marked "Office."

The secretary smiled when he asked if the youth pastor was in. "No, I'm sorry, Pastor Farley isn't in this afternoon. Is there something I can help you with?"

Alex shook his head. "No. I just wondered...never mind." He turned toward the door. Farley was not Pastor T's last name.

The secretary went back to her typing, then spoke up just as Alex reached the door. "Would you like to talk to Pastor Tilsen?"

Alex froze. "What?"

"Pastor Tilsen. He's our senior pastor. He may have a moment to see you, if you'd like."

"Yeah. Thanks. I'd like to see him."

She smiled as she hit an intercom button. "Just have a seat. He'll be right with you." Alex sat on the edge of the chair and fidgeted with the zipper on his jacket. After a few minutes the pastor appeared in the doorway, then moved toward Alex, hand extended. Alex grasped it.

The pastor pumped his hand. "Good to see you again, Alex."

Alex smiled. "You've come up in the world—senior pastor—and you're what, thirty-five?"

"Thirty-eight. Definitely too over-the-hill for youth ministry." He waved him into his small office. "You've survived. I'm a bit surprised, but pleased."

Alex plopped into a chair. "You're part of the reason."

Pastor T's eyebrows arched. "Really? I didn't think I'd had that much impact. You were a pretty tough case back then."

"It was all an act. I was scared spitless most of the time."

"You had me fooled. Last I heard you were, uh—wanted."

Alex nodded. "That's why I'm here. To clear that up. Or go to jail for something I didn't do."

"You've been to the police?"

"Just had my first court appearance. Next one's in March, unless they put the evidence together and drop the charges before then."

"So where have you been for the past five years?"

Alex ran his hand through his dark hair. "You have time for the long version? Or should I make it quick?"

"Don't tell my secretary, but you caught me on a slow day. Tell me the whole story."

When he was finished Ted leaned forward. "So what's next?"

"I wait. My lawyer says as soon as the DNA is compared, they'll drop the charges. I'm hoping that's soon but...." Alex stared at his shoes. "There's something else I have to do."

Pastor T waited, then asked, "How can I help?"

Alex raised his head. "I need a place to stay, but I don't have much money. I'm willing to work," he added.

Pastor T nodded. "I think we can arrange something. This old building is always in need of repair. I've been thinking of hiring some help for a while. I seem to remember you were pretty good with your hands."

Alex nodded, relief thick in his voice. "That'd be great."

"There's an empty room downstairs that was used for storage. I'll have a bed brought up from our thrift store and you can stay there for the time being. It won't be fancy, but it'll be warm and dry. You can use the kitchen and shower in the gym."

Alex stood and shook the man's hand. "Thanks. This means a lot."

Ted nodded. "Glad to help. If there's anything else...."

Alex dropped his eyes. "There is…." He hesitated. "Just pray for me."

Pastor T smiled. I've been doing that pretty consistently ever since you broke into my house." He leaned forward. "But I can pray more effectively if I have a few clues."

Alex didn't make eye contact. He took a deep breath. "Just pray. I'm going to need all the help I can get."

The pastor came around the desk and put his hand on his shoulder. "Why don't I do that right now?"

Alex felt the tension drain out of him. "Yeah. That would be good," he said. The warmth of the man's hand calmed him even more as he began.

"Lord, I ask for guidance and strength for Alex. I ask for grace above all, Father. I ask that you lead Alex into your will in this situation and that you help him to know you're with him, no matter what the days ahead may hold. I ask that you hold him in the palm of your hand. Amen."

Alex fingered the small smooth stone in his pocket and nodded his Amen.

○ ○ ○

He moved into the church the next day and started to work immediately. It felt good to be doing something with his hands again. Ted— Alex had dropped the "'Pastor'" at his suggestion—worked with him at times, and when he did they talked. They repaired a door that wouldn't close and a window that wouldn't open. They painted a Sunday school room and redid the blackboard in another.

Then Ted took him into the sanctuary. A rectangular table draped with a white cloth stood against one wall near the podium. Ted pulled the cloth off and revealed the scarred surface underneath. Peeling patches of old paint showed layers of different colors. Bare wood showed through here and there.

"I almost tossed this out the other day," Ted said. "Thought it was beyond repair. But then I took a closer look."

Alex bent down and examined the worn surface. "Oak," he said. The table wobbled under his hand. He crouched down and inspected the legs. "Needs a lot of work."

Ted nodded. "It'll take some time, but I think it'd be worth the effort. Don't you?"

Alex stood up and nodded back. "Yeah. It'd be a beauty…eventually."

"Good. It's all yours." He started to turn away, then stopped. "By the way, it's kind of special."

Alex lifted his chin. "I'll keep that in mind."

Ted was almost out the door when Alex called after him. "I'll have to take it completely apart."

The pastor turned. Alex thought he saw a quick smile. "Yes. That's exactly what you'll have to do."

Alex dragged the old table into a back room they used as a workspace. Flipping it over he began by removing the legs. He worked on it until it was almost time for supper. Just as he was becoming aware of his growling stomach Ted walked in. The table was in pieces, the floor covered with a thin layer of dust.

"Looks like this is going to take a lot of elbow grease," he said.

"Yeah." Alex nodded, thinking they'd already covered this ground.

Ted cleared his throat. "I was wondering, Alex—from the conversation we've had, if you'd like to talk more in a more formal way?"

Alex straightened, leaning on one of the legs. "You mean, as in counseling?"

Ted nodded. "There does seem to be something in particular...."

Alex turned, placed the leg on a bench, and began sanding it. "I can handle it on my own," he said.

"Can you?"

Alex looked up. The man's eyes were piercing. He dropped his eyes again and said nothing. Ted turned to go.

"Okay." As soon as the word was out of Alex's mouth his stomach knotted.

Ted nodded. "Good. I have a board meeting at 8:00, but I'm free before then. Why don't you come by my office at 6:30?"

○ ○ ○

"For some reason they didn't do a DNA on the clothes." The rookie fidgeted. "But they shouldn't have any trouble recovering something. It's only been five years."

Inspector Sorensen stared at the file in the rookie's hand. "I'll take care of it," he said reaching for it.

The rookie nodded, handed him the file, and left the office. Sorensen pulled the box out from under his desk and lifted the lid. He fingered one of the baggies of clothing. He'd solved a lot of cases by trusting his gut. His gut told him Alex Donnelly was guilty. The DNA would prove it. He dropped the file into the box and headed for the labs. This one he'd oversee personally.

The man in the white coat sighed when Sorensen walked in. The inspector noticed how he glanced at the evidence box. But at least he tried to appear co-operative as he said, "What can I do for you, Inspector?"

"I need this to be top priority."

The expert smiled. "Uh huh." He pointed with his chin to a shelf full of similar boxes. "Just set it down over there."

Sorensen put it on the table in front of him and leaned forward. "My retirement party is in one week. I want the results before then."

The man in the white coat picked up the box. He sighed again, but nodded. "I'll see what I can do."

○ ○ ○

Ted had cleared his desk except for something wrapped in plastic. When Alex sat down the pastor handed it to him. "Got you something," he said.

Alex unwrapped it and stared. Then he ran his hand over the soft leather cover. "Thanks," he said.

"It's a study Bible," Ted continued. "Has lots of help in it—explanations of hard passages, historical information, that kind of thing." He handed him another book. "You might find this interesting too. It's a pretty good overall view of what the Bible says about forgiveness."

Alex's head snapped up. "Forgiveness?"

"Yes. I think that's a good place to head, don't you?"

Alex took a deep breath and nodded.

Ted put another small book into his hands. "This is another one I'd recommend. This one will tell you who you are."

Alex glanced at the cover, then back at Ted.

"That's something I've wondered all my life. Even finding out the names of my parents didn't help. You're telling me this little book will?"

"The words in there are just that, Alex. Words. They can't do much on their own. But God's spirit will, if you let Him."

Alex sighed again. "Okay. Where do we start?"

"With prayer," Ted said. They both bowed their heads.

By the end of the session Alex felt drained. They'd prayed almost as much as they'd talked, but he couldn't get rid of the churning in his gut. That night he had another nightmare. A bad one. He wondered how long this was going to take. He got his answer the next day.

"The rest of your life," Ted said.

"That's encouraging."

Ted smiled at his sarcasm. "It took twenty-one years to get where you are. Think you can change everything in a few hours?"

"Guess I thought maybe you could."

"Thanks for the vote of confidence, but it doesn't work that way. I'm just here to help you discover what God wants to teach you."

Alex nodded, but made no comment.

Ted leaned forward. "The journey goes on and on. Getting to know the Lord and getting to know yourself as His son will have its ups and downs, times of amazing discovery and times of struggle. But it's the adventure of a lifetime and I can guarantee one thing."

"What's that?"

"He'll never leave you."

Alex nodded again. "I think I believe that. But...I still wonder." He frowned. "Where was He...?"

"When you were a scared little kid?"

Alex squirmed. "Yeah. Where was He then?"

Ted sat back. "Where do you think?"

Alex ran his hand through his hair and shook his head. "I don't know."

Ted wrote down a Scripture verse on a piece of paper and handed it to him. "Homework," he said. "We'll talk about it in our next session."

○ ○ ○

Alex had read the passage a few times by the time they came together again. "I don't get it," he said.

"What did the story tell you?" the pastor asked.

"That Jesus was able to raise people from the dead."

Ted nodded. "Obvious. What else?"

"That the women had a right to dump on Him. He could've kept their brother from dying, but He stalled."

238

"Why do you think He did that?"

"Seems like He wanted to show off."

"Exactly."

Alex's eyebrows shot up. "You're telling me Jesus was an exhibitionist?"

"Read verse forty, out loud."

Alex read, "Then Jesus said, 'Did I not tell you that if you believed, you'd see the glory of God?'"

Ted stretched out his hand. "He's God, Alex. God will glorify himself above all else."

"But—" Alex shook his head, "this doesn't seem like the kind of thing a God who says He loves them would do."

"Read verse thirty-five."

"Jesus wept," Alex read.

"Doesn't that tell you He had compassion for them and loved them? He loved them so much He wanted only the best for them. But what was best? They already knew Jesus could heal Lazarus. He wanted them to know Him more deeply, understand Him more fully. How could He show them that? What would be the best way to show them the depth of His love and His limitless power?"

"Raise their brother from the dead."

"Bingo. Even though it meant they went through a season of pain. It was all meant to glorify Him so they'd see Him. Really see Him. That's the best for all of us."

"So you're saying all the crap in my life...."

"Has opened up opportunities for you to know Him better."

Alex shook his head. "I don't see...."

"Yet."

"I don't think I've got that much faith."

"Yet."

Alex sighed. "You're really a dreamer."

Ted smiled. "Read the book of Job in the Old Testament. Try reading it all in one sitting."

Alex read the book that night and lay awake thinking about it. When he saw Ted the next morning he decided not to wait for the counseling session. "I think I get it," he said. "But I don't like it."

Ted nodded. "I can relate. But we don't have to like it. We just have to get through it until we can get to the same point Job did in Chapter 13, verse 15—"Though he slay me, yet will I hope in Him."

Alex frowned. "Are you trying to prepare me for something?"

The pastor shrugged. "Just don't let your commitment to stay surrendered to God hang on what happens." The pastor was frowning now too. "I'm sure you've seen enough to know life throws people some nasty hooks. But that's when it's really important to hang onto the Lord. He won't desert you, no matter what happens."

Alex nodded. "I think I believe that. Guess I won't know for sure until it happens."

"True, but I kind of get the feeling you're waiting for God to prove Himself. Have you thought about what you'll do if it looks like He's not going to come through?"

"You mean if I end up in prison?"

Ted nodded. Alex shivered. "I've been there. I try not to think about going back."

"It may be the darkest place you've ever been. If you have to go there, you'll need to know who you are in Christ. You'll need to be wholeheartedly His."

Alex knew that what Ted was saying was true. He'd been feeling it for some time. When he found the words to express himself he was surprised that he was willing to say them. "I feel like I'm sort of floating. Like I'm almost watching myself go through all the motions of day to day while another part of me is detached." He fingered the cup in front of him. "It's sort of like there's two of me—one that prays and believes and one that's waiting to see whether or not I end up in a jail cell."

"Kind of like you're not quite sure which one is the real you?"

Alex nodded. "Yeah. And I'm not really sure which one I want to be yet."

Ted leaned forward. "Don't wait too long to choose, Alex." He got up and brought the coffee pot to the table. "That thing you asked me to pray about—has it happened yet?"

Alex shook his head. "No. But I'm still thinking it has to, soon."

Ted eyed him. "Want to talk about it?"

"No." Alex regretted the quickness of his response, but stood up and drained his cup. "I'd better get at that table," he said.

Chapter Thirty-nine

Alex left the church early the next evening. The air was cold, but the rain had stopped. As he wandered the streets memories floated one step ahead of him. The smell coming from a coffee shop reminded him of the day-old donuts he'd sometimes find in the dumpster behind it. Italian music blaring from a pool hall across the street took him back to the drug dealers who used to frequent it. He'd been a mule for them more times than he could count til he'd sold some on the side to try and make a few more bucks. The beating they'd given him almost killed him. Stopping in front of a small bookstore he could see the owner, a tall gangly man who had chased him for three blocks after he'd swiped a book from the outside bin. He moved on, the memories crowding in on him like unwelcome relatives as he continued down alleys and across intersections, not caring where he was going.

A crooked street sign suddenly alerted him to where he was. He peered down the familiar street and headed toward the house. It felt like a magnet was drawing him there.

It hadn't changed at all in five years. The front porch was still sagging, the window boxes full of fake flowers. The facade made Alex clench his jaw. He stood at the end of the walk, staring. When the door suddenly opened he jerked his head to the side in surprise, but didn't move.

A thin boy stepped out onto the sidewalk, his head down, shoulders hunched into himself. He was almost on top of Alex before he noticed and pulled back.

"Hey," Alex said.

The boy didn't respond. His eyes were wary.

"My name's Alex. You live here?" He lifted his chin toward the house.

The boy nodded, but still said nothing.

Alex studied his face. "Bill and Ruby still live here?"

The boy nodded again. "Yeah, they're here." He shifted the pack on his shoulder. "I gotta go."

Alex stared after him. The look in the boy's eyes at the mention of those names told Alex what he wanted—and didn't want—to know. Bill and Ruby Mitchell were still fostering kids. *And still abusing them.* Alex's hands formed into fists and bile rose in his throat as the rage grew in him like a tsunami.

○ ○ ○

Alex paced the streets all night, his mood growing darker as the neon got brighter. He stepped into a bar, but the sound of jumbled voices mixed with grunge music seemed to threaten him and he turned away. He bought a pack of cigarettes and headed for the sea wall. Black water gleamed under the lights from the ships, but it didn't calm him. Images of disturbing nightmares and more disquieting memories filled his mind. Within a few moments he was walking again, a cigarette smoldering to a stub in his hand.

It was almost dawn when he felt weary enough to sleep and returned to his room. But when he lay down on the bed his mind wouldn't stop. *Today. I'll do it today.* Wild Bill's face floated before him. He scrambled off the bed, grabbing the trash can in time to wretch. His throat and stomach burned. His body shook. *Maybe there's only one way to stop this. Maybe forgiveness won't do it.* He sat on the bed and lit a cigarette, watching the slow burn as he drew the smoke into his lungs.

○ ○ ○

He could smell the rain, the fullness of black earth, and his pulse started to slow. *Maybe I could still walk away. Maybe I could fill my mind and soul with what's good and all the rest will fade.* But he stood rooted at the end of the short sidewalk. He drew in a deep breath and a lingering stench almost made him wretch. *No. This is the only way.*

He tugged his baseball cap down until it shadowed his face. Then he shoved his hand into his coat pocket and stepped up to the door. The doorbell still didn't work. He pounded on the door until he heard heavy footsteps. He took two steps down and held his breath as the door swung open. The man loomed over him. He was dressed in dirty jeans and a T-shirt that didn't come anywhere near to covering his beer belly. Alex's eyes were level with the wide black belt around his waist.

Wild Bill scowled. "Yeah? Waddaya want?"

Alex lifted his face, smiled, and drew the gun out of his pocket. "Justice," he said and pulled the trigger.

○ ○ ○

Kenni woke with a start. The room was dark, a faint glow from the moon outlining the furniture in her room. She slipped out of bed and opened the drapes. The sea was in turmoil, the moonlight glinting on the whitecaps. She could hear the pounding surf below the house. *Alex.* She shivered and got back into bed, but lay awake staring at the ceiling. *Alex.* She pulled the covers up to her neck and began to pray.

○ ○ ○

Alex saw the bullet rip into the man's heart, the blood beginning to seep out as he staggered back. It was then he became aware of someone standing behind Bill. He couldn't see him clearly, but Alex could feel his sorrow as though it were his own. And suddenly, regret surged through him. He dropped the gun and lunged toward Bill, slumping to the floor with him. Blood seeped into Alex's shirt as he cradled him. He put a hand over the hole in the man's heart, but couldn't stop the flow.

He started to sob. "Oh God!" he cried, "Oh God." He looked down into the face of the man who had abused him for so long, but his tears blurred the image. He tried to wipe them away and felt hot blood smear across his own face. He looked at the man again and suddenly, the face was his own. He jerked back, gasping, trying to wrestle himself free, but the heavy body pinned him there. Unable to move he stared at the face that was now his own, peering at him with dead eyes. Then Alex heard a sound and the man who had stood in the shadows knelt down and put his arms around them. Alex still couldn't see his face, but he felt the arms, powerful arms, lifting him and the dead body as one and rocking them as though they were children. A low wail full of unbearable sorrow and longing came from the man. The sound mingled with Alex's moans.

Then he saw a hand reaching over Bill's body toward him, a bloodied hand reaching for him. He was at once repelled, yet longed for it to touch him. He drew back, then dropped his head allowing the hand to cradle his cheek. It was then he saw the blood was not from the dead man but was seeping out of a hole in the palm of the hand. Alex couldn't breathe. He gasped for air as a loud sob wrenched out of his mouth.

He woke as the sob filled the room. He lay panting, his body drenched in sweat, his heart racing. His mind filled with the image of that nail-pierced hand reaching for him. He whipped off the covers and got out of bed, the cold floor bringing him totally awake. He stumbled to the kitchen and called Ted. "I need to talk," he said.

Within the hour they were sitting in the church office. Alex told him about the nightmare, the images raw in his mind. "It was so real, but surreal at the same time. Bill's face—at one point it was my face." Alex looked up at the pastor, his eyes wide with realization. "It could've been me. I could've done what he did to me. Maybe still could." He lowered his head into his hands and the tears spilled out freely. "God," he moaned. "I'm capable of worse."

Ted reached out and grasped Alex's shoulder. "We all are, Alex. That's why we all need the righteousness of Jesus so desperately. That's what the Bible means when it says all have sinned and fall short. But there's another verse, 2 Corinthians 5:21, one of my favorites. It says, 'God made him who had no sin to be sin for us so that in him we might become the righteousness of God.' Jesus became sin. Your sin. My sin. Bill Mitchell's sin. He became our sin so that we wouldn't have to face God with the blood still on our hands. That's forgiveness. Complete forgiveness."

Alex took a deep breath, then raised his head and made eye contact with the pastor. "I almost...I was thinking—"

"But you didn't. It was just a dream."

Alex nodded. "I have to face this, Ted. I have to face him. But...I can't confront him on my own. I think...I need someone to go with me."

Ted nodded. "Just say when."

Alex took another deep breath. "Today. Before I lose my nerve."

Ted stood up. "I'll call the police."

Alex shook his head. "No."

Ted hesitated, but then insisted. "We can't do this alone, Alex. The police need to be there."

Alex let out a long sigh and nodded.

○ ○ ○

They arrived at the house just after noon. Ted knocked on the door. Alex stood rigid, using all his willpower to keep from running. Ruby answered the door. She looked older than Alex expected.

She stared at Ted, then at Alex. Her eyes veered away when she saw the police. "He's not here," she said and started to close the door before they could say anything. One of the constables moved forward. A man's voice mumbled from behind her. Bill reached around her and swung the door open. Alex heard Ruby begin to protest, but it was too late. He stood eye to eye with Alex. His eyes widened with recognition, darted to Ted and the policeman, then settled back on Alex. The familiar smirk parted his lips, but Alex saw the fear in his eyes. Fear, and something else.

Ruby tried to push Bill out of the way. "Close the door, Bill. Tell them to go away," she whined. "Close the door."

Bill stood his ground. "No," he said, his eyes never leaving Alex's. "I want to hear what they have to say."

"May we come in, sir?" one of the officers asked.

Bill grunted and turned away, leaving the door wide. They followed him in.

Alex stood in the yellowed kitchen, drawing in breaths that pushed him back ten years into cramped spaces where he could hardly breathe at all. The space of a small chrome chair pushed against the wall, the table touching his chest to allow Ruby's bulk to pass on the other side. The small corner cupboard where a garbage can sometimes yielded a bone with a bit of meat on it, or a dry piece of bread, as good as caviar when he'd gone without for two days or more. The large glass macaroni jar was there, on the scarred counter, half empty and oiled with the fingerprints of dozens of kids. He knew if he opened the old fridge the freezer-burned hot dogs would be there.

So many small things, he thought—small spaces, small words, small actions that ate at a small boy, bite by bite, tearing at who he was until there was nothing left of himself, just a pair of hands always searching, a set of eyes that learned not to focus for long, a pair of ears that heard everything, but a mouth that never spoke. His eyes scanned the room and settled on the door to the cellar, four paces from where he now stood. His hand traced the long scar on his neck. He fought to keep his head from ducking sideways. *That was then. Stay in today. Stay in today. Maybe today will be the first step to putting it all behind me, once and for all.*

Bill pulled one of the chrome chairs out and sat down. Ruby stood behind him. He stared at them, but didn't invite them to sit. "So?" Bill said.

Alex swallowed to try and loosen the dryness in his throat. "I turned myself in. They could be comparing the DNA as we speak," he said. "These cops have some questions to ask you."

Ruby gasped. Bill frowned but nodded. "You came to warn me?"

"I came to tell you...." Alex swallowed again. "I forgive you." He looked at Ruby. "I forgive both of you."

Bill's eyes narrowed. Ruby started to sob. "This some kind of trick?" Bill said.

Alex shook his head. "No. No trick. Just God's grace and mercy." He held Bill's gaze. "I'd like to tell you about a dream I had."

"A dream?"

"Yeah. It'll take less than five minutes, if you'll listen."

Bill flashed a look at the police, then shrugged. "I guess I'm not goin' anywhere."

Alex pulled a chair out and sat down. He described the dream in detail, keeping his eyes glued to Bill's. He saw so many emotions surface in those eyes that when he was finished he wasn't sure what kind of impact the telling had made. They sat in silence for a few moments.

Bill's face remained blank, but when he spoke his voice shook. "So what happens now?" he asked.

The police officer stepped forward. "I suggest you come to the detachment and make a statement, Mr. Mitchell. Admitting your guilt might make things go easier."

Ruby erupted then, screaming, "No! No, you'll go to jail, Bill. You'll go to jail!"

"Shut up, Ruby," Bill screamed back at her. He turned to Alex again. "Always knew it would happen one day." His shoulders slumped, but he smirked. "Knew you'd come back." He nodded to the policeman and dropped his voice. "Let's get it over with."

As the constable took Bill and Ruby away Ted tried to tell them that forgiveness from God was available to them. Bill just stared at him without responding. Ruby cursed at them all. Alex was shocked at how impotent they suddenly seemed.

It took the whole afternoon to give their statements. As soon as he got back to the church Alex called Kenni and told her everything.

"You sound exhausted, Alex."

"Yeah, I am. But I feel...." Alex's eyes filled. "I feel free. Finally free." He paused. "I need to see you. This is going to take a while. Months—maybe more before it gets to court. Then there will be the abuse charges to deal with. But I'd like to come down as soon as I can, as soon as this assault charge is cleared up, just for a few days?"

"I'll arrange some time off. I'll call you tomorrow and let you know, okay?"

"Yeah, okay." He didn't want her to hang up. He needed the comfort of her voice. But his mind had drifted into neutral. He could think of nothing more to say. "Talk to you tomorrow."

"Get some rest, okay?"

"I will."

"Alex?"

"Yeah?"

Her voice suddenly sounded shy. "Maybe you could...stay longer than a few days. If you wanted to."

"I want to," he said.

He'd just hung up the phone when it rang. The lawyer's voice was edged with excitement. "You're free and clear, Alex. Bill Mitchell signed a full confession and Cindy Vilner has agreed to testify. We won't even need the DNA. The charges will be dropped first thing in the morning."

Alex closed his eyes.

"Hello? Are you there?"

"Yeah. I'm here," Alex said. "Thanks. Thanks for letting me know."

"Merry Christmas," the lawyer said.

Alex smiled. "Merry Christmas," he echoed. Exhaustion pulled at him as he stretched out on the bed. He slept that night without getting undressed, without pulling the covers over himself. But it was the best sleep he'd ever had.

○ ○ ○

January 1, The Adams' Beach House

The rain had petered out to a faint drizzle, shrouding the shoreline in mist. The whole world looked gray, but as they walked under the protection of Kenni's bright red umbrella Alex noticed how it cast a warm glow around them. They walked hand in hand, Alex leaning over her slightly to make sure the umbrella sheltered her. When they reached the end of the dock he stepped closer.

Kenni looked up at him. "It's good to have you here," she said.

"I missed you."

"Really? With so much on your mind...."

Alex shook his head. "You're always on my mind."

She smiled, then grew serious. "What will happen next with the court case?"

"It won't take long, but I'll have to be there as a witness."

"How do you feel about that?"

Alex sighed. "Nervous. But it will be good to tell the truth at last, and to ask Cindy to forgive me for bailing on her. Maybe I'll get a chance to ask the others to forgive me too, once the second trial starts."

"Forgive you for what?"

"For not having the guts to stand up to Bill and Ruby. If I'd turned them in a long time ago...."

Kenni turned and faced him. "You were just a little kid, Alex. A kid intimidated and terrorized by adults. You can't blame yourself for everything that Bill and Rudy did."

Alex dropped his eyes. "I know, but...I could've stopped it.

"You have. They can't hurt kids anymore."

Alex nodded and stared into the drifting mist on the water. "The second trial is going to be even harder." He fingered the long white scar on his neck. "Making the statement about...everything. That was bad enough. The trial…I'm hoping he just admits it all so none of us will have to testify."

Kenni put her hand on his arm. "You're not alone anymore."

He reached into his pocket. "I never was." He took out the smooth black stone she'd given him.

Kenni smiled when she saw it. "You kept it."

He nodded. "It's taken me a long time to believe there is a place for me. I still have to find it and I don't know what that will mean." He flipped the stone in his hand. "I'm trying to leave everything up to God, and He hasn't shown me that part yet."

Kenni's smile broadened. "Then I guess we'll just have to be patient." She curled his fingers over the stone and lifted her face to receive his gentle kiss.

○ ○ ○

January 19, 2004, Vancouver, British Columbia

Alex could hardly take his eyes from the table at the front of the church. He could still feel the smoothness of the wood as he'd finished polishing the surface. A long white cloth was draped over it now, the trays of bread and small cups of juice gleaming on its surface. Ted's sermon held his attention, but he was always aware of that table and what was waiting on it.

The congregation rose to its feet for the song that marked the transition from the sermon into the communion time. Then Ted stepped away from the podium and walked to the front of the table. "This isn't just a communion for our church," he said. "It's for all those who have taken Jesus as their Lord. It's one of the most significant metaphors ever instituted." He turned toward the table. "I'd like us to try something a bit different today. I'd like you all to come to the front to receive the bread and wine. It's just a way to break from what's normal for us, to help us focus on what it is we're doing." He took up a small chunk of bread and a cup and held them up for all to see. "The bread and wine. The body and blood of our Lord, Jesus Christ, given for you, to wash away your sins so that you are acceptable and righteous in God's eyes, forgiven, forever."

Two others joined the pastor at the front and people began filing out of the pews toward them. Alex stepped out and back so that Kenni could go ahead of him. He heard Ted say, "The body and blood of Christ, sacrificed for you." He heard her respond with a simple "Amen." Then he was standing there, his eyes focused on the trays in Ted's hands. Alex took a long shaky breath. *Forgiveness. This is what it's all about.* The common noises from the people—the whispers, the sneezes and coughs, the shuffling of feet, the sound of rising and sitting—they all faded away. He heard Ted repeat the words and heard himself say the Amen.

He ripped the bread and the yeasty odor rose up and into him. He held the small piece between his fingers, aware of how stained they were, with dirt he couldn't wash clean. He put the bread into his mouth. It was sweet. He took the small cup, barely able to feel it for the calluses on his hands, and swallowed the juice. He felt it slip down his throat, felt a warmth rise from within him. When he raised his eyes to Ted's they were both weeping. Ted smiled through his tears. Alex nodded and returned to his seat.

He tried to sing the last song, "Faithful one, so unchanging, Ageless one, you're my rock of peace." But he choked on the words. Kenni slipped her soft hand into his. He managed to take a few deep breaths before smiling down at her.

"It's okay," he said. "It's going to be okay now."

Epilogue

Alex flipped the long slim key over in his hand as he waited for a bank teller to record the information he'd given her. When she asked him to follow her he froze. She was halfway across the large lobby before she realized it, stopped, and frowned back at him. He took a long shaking breath and forced his feet to move.

They descended a wide stairway and went through a thick vault door. The teller fingered through a file, pulled out a card, and laid it on a small table. She recorded the time, added her initials, then pointed to a line and asked him to sign his name.

The pen hovered over the spot. Which name should I use? Perrin or Donnelly? He scrawled the former and handed the pen back.

"Your number?" the teller asked.

Alex looked at the small tag attached to the key. "Four four nine," he said.

The woman scanned the high bank of deposit boxes, retrieved a small ladder, stepped up onto it, and reached up to insert her key. Then she stepped down and made way for Alex. He only needed to climb to the second rung. He pushed the key in, opened the small door, and pulled out the long metal box. When he stepped down he felt as though he were on a high wire.

"Do you require some time?"

Alex stared at her.

"Would you like to sit in one of our privacy booths?"

"Yeah, I guess."

He slid the box onto the shiny wooden table and sat down, barely hearing the woman tell him to ring the bell when he was finished. She closed the partition. He sat still, staring at the box. Finally he lifted the small latch and raised the lid. A long brown envelope lay folded in two on top. Alex removed it and opened it, recognizing a copy of the legal document George had read to him months ago. He didn't bother pulling it out. A long white envelope was next. The old glue let go easily as he opened it and reached in. His hand came out holding three photographs. Trembling, he laid them side by side and bent over them.

The first was of a dark-haired woman holding a baby. Her face was dropped and angled toward the child. Alex's heart beat fast. My mother. This woman is my mother. He picked up the photo and flipped it over. "Baby Alex, three months" was penciled on the back. He put it back down and picked up the second photo. A young man in a red checkered shirt smiled back at him. The photographer had caught him in a candid pose. There was a hammer in his hand and the look in his eyes made Alex think of a mischievous kid. He flipped it over. There was no writing on the back, but Alex knew the man in the picture was his father, Tom Perrin.

In the third photo a baby wrapped in a pink blanket was propped beside the little boy on a sofa. He had his arm around her and grinned at the camera. Alex's hand shook as he flipped the photo over. The words were written in the same flowing script. "Alex, age two. Andrea, age six months." He stared at the image again. Andrea.

He stopped breathing.

Andrea—I have a sister!

CASTLE QUAY BOOKS